Herbmaster of Tarodash

Thank you for taking
an interest in my
land of Tarodash

[signature]

A member of HPB

Herbmaster of Tarodash

Colin Hollis

Matador
9 Priory Business Park,
Wistow Road, Kibworth Beauchamp,
Leicestershire. LE8 0RX
Tel: (+44) 116 279 2299
Fax: (+44) 116 279 2277
Email: books@troubador.co.uk
Web: www.troubador.co.uk/matador

ISBN 9781783061396

British Library Cataloguing in Publication Data.
A catalogue record for this book is available from the British Library.

Typeset by Troubador Publishing Ltd, Leicester, UK
Printed and bound in the UK by TJ International, Padstow, Cornwall

Matador is an imprint of Troubador Publishing Ltd

Acknowledgements

For valuable support, encouragement and help, I would like to offer sincere thanks to Dick Pollock, Hannah Pollock, Andrew Wells, Joy Wells, Brian Daly, Dorothy Daly, Ray Sigsworth, Sue Sigsworth, Terry Sigsworth, Terry Moffatt, and Claire Walker.

Particular thanks go to James Hollis, my son. I know of no one with a better understanding of the combination of good writing with good storytelling, and his help has been of enormous importance.

The support and assistance of Valerie, my wife, has been essential.

I have constantly tested my writing against a reading audience, and will continue to do so. If you would like to discuss *Herbmaster of Tarodash,* and wish to share any comments, thoughts, ideas and criticisms, please visit www.tarodash.co.uk. I will be delighted to hear from you.

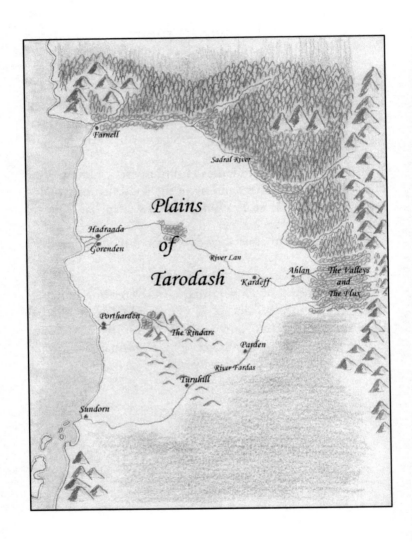

Farnell

Sadral River

Plains

of

Tarodash

Hadraada

Gorenden

River Lan

Ahlan

The Valleys
and
The Flux

Kardeff

Portharden

The Rindars

Parden

River Fardas

Turnhill

Sundorn

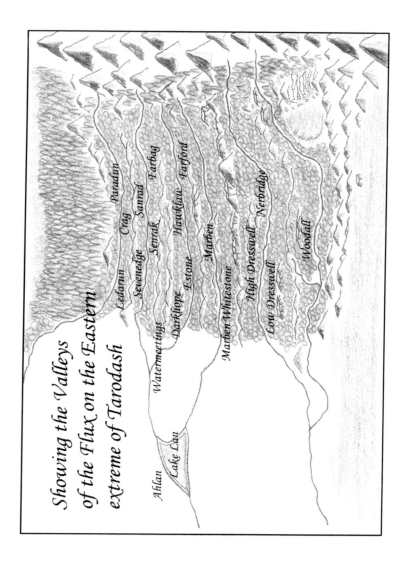

Showing the Valleys
of the Flux on the Eastern
extreme of Tarodash

Ahlan

Lake Lau

Watermeetings

Ledarm
Paradun
Crag
Sevenedge
Sanrad
Senrak
Tarbug
Estone
Darkhope
Hawklaw
Tarford
Marben
Marben Whitestone
High Dresswell
Nerbridge
Low Dresswell
Woodall

vii

Chapter 1

The flux was strong on the day the Gralt came. It had begun the previous evening, built steadily all night, reaching a level rarely encountered, and held most of the day. Every worker in the village, everyone in the Valleys, had toiled from before first light and had stopped only with the sunset and the waning of the flux.

Perad, feeling the glow of a full day's work, had laid out his piles of leaves, grasses, barks, mosses and roots on the long stone flagged counter along the back wall of the inn where he lived with his uncle Tavit, and was contentedly sorting when the Gralt appeared. The first two, large and foreign, pushed the heavy door back and stepped forward into the centre of the room. They had not even drawn their swords. The third one had drawn his sword, and used it as he stepped inside, a fluid backhand stoke upwards through the chest and throat of Kerim, old and blind sitting in his customary place on the bench just inside the door. Perad had half turned at the opening of the door, and saw what was beyond all nightmares, dear old Kerim slumping sideways, blood and ale spraying across the stone floor, wooden flagon clattering, and the doorway and the night outside framing the murderous visitor, a vision of dull steel and hardened leather, helmeted, cloaked to the ground, and with glistening sword.

Rumours of Gralt raids had been worrying the edges of Tarodash for a year and now they were here, in the Valleys. Utter strangers, invaders in a distant land, and they strode to the counter for ale. The killer pushed the door closed, but not before Perad had seen another dark figure outside. The

1

rumours had told of sightings, raids and violent encounters in distant places, not of soldiers entering a village inn to demand ale. Perad, at first shocked beyond movement, forced himself to breathe, and turned back to his herbs. To attract attention now, to be an inconvenience, to be anything other than an insignificant piece of the surroundings, was to die. The three village men playing cards at the table knew it, the two at the chest high counter knew it, and uncle Tavit brewer and aleman knew it.

The Gralt were thought to inhabit a land to the south beyond the desert, but, until a year ago, had not been dealt with for generations. Legend had them as pitiless killers, enemies of all, though the histories showed there had once been trade between Gralt and Tarodash. The ships of Tarodash would not go that far south, and even the pirates from the far islands, wild and fearless, would not attack the Gralt, though they brought back tales of their existence.

Perad fought the dread in his bones and with his back to the room made himself busy moving along the herbs, powders and utensils, shuffling into piles, and scooping handfuls into leather pouches. He tried to breathe normally. From the corner of his eye he saw his uncle, head down avoiding eye contact, place three large flagons on the stone counter. He listened to the foreign talk of the Gralt, short hard words full of consonants.

The card players continued soundlessly, the two villagers at the counter stared into their ale. Uncle Tavit waited. The Gralt talked. There seemed an arrogance to their speech and an appalling haughtiness. They had travelled far into a foreign land, they were surrounded by enemies yet, still felt comfortable, safe, unchallenged.

Perad's fussing took him to the fireplace at the far empty end of the room. This was the first cold night of the autumn and a small pile of logs was burning. He made the brushing of

2

debris from his hands onto the glowing embers in the grate seem like a natural consequence of his work. A single harsh sound, seemingly spat at his back, made him turn. He expected to die at any moment. The nearest of the Gralt had drawn his sword, wide, heavy and deadly, and was pointing it at him. With his chin the Gralt soldier indicated the pile of logs by the side of the fire. There was another harsh sound, more an animal utterance than a word. He wanted wood on the fire!

Perad chose split logs which would catch the flame more quickly, taking care with the arrangement and working on his knees from the side so as to not obstruct the view of the Gralt. He needed to be invisible. Finished, he stood and brushed his hands over the fire once more, pushed the black lever at the side which opened the damper and drew the flames up the chimney, and moved back to the counter and his herbs and mixtures.

The flames roared and the base of the fire intensified. At other times his uncle would have complimented him. A hot flame of hope also rose inside him as he saw his uncle place three more foaming flagons on the counter and the Gralt reach for them. There was still time left! He continued with his work. Each time he neared the fireplace he pushed the lever to close the damper a little. It was a natural part of tending the fire.

The Gralt stopped watching after a while. His uncle didn't. Perad could not delay any longer. Back at the counter, he closed each fist around a handful of powder from two separate piles. The Gralt didn't see. His uncle did. Walking slowly to the fire he dropped the left handful on the hot logs, then the right handful, brushed his hands once more and pushed the damper to fully close the chimney. He had his back to the room and did not know if he was being watched. His hope could vanish in a heartbeat. A thin grey smoke rolled from the fire and began to spread over the floor. He moved back to the scales, emptied the contents of a bowl onto them, bent to eye the balance, tipping his head to view the advance of the fumes. Something in uncle Tavit's posture told him he understood. The two village men at the counter were no longer leaning on their elbows. The manner of the Gralt had not changed. There was, their behaviour suggested, nothing in this room, village or land that could challenge them.

Perad managed a glance at the card players. They were holding their cards in one hand, the other hand below the table top. Two had eased back their chairs and were half facing the door. Somehow uncle Tavit had alerted them. The thin haze spreading through the room was almost invisible, but a hint of sharp odour, something beyond woodsmoke, warned Perad. His hands began to shake, his legs felt weak. He moved as far from the fire as he dared and risked a few deep breaths to clear his lungs, then held his breath.

The men of the Valleys were woodsmen and all carried a knife, sheathed at the belt. These knives were made in the Valleys by craftsmen and brought a good price, but the best, forged when the flux was strongest, were saved for the local men. These were superb knives, one edged and pointed, with a slight curve. Perad himself had a full size one, given by his uncle on his passage a year ago. It was already as much a part of him as his own hands.

He had never seen one used for violence.

A short intake of breath though the nose told Perad that the smoke had filled the room, a small uncontrollable shiver told him that the poison was working. The air seemed suddenly filled with haze, though Perad could not quite trust his eyes now.

Then it was all commotion. The voices of the Gralt suddenly rose in pitch. The centre one dropped his ale and attempted to push back from the counter. The nearest one to the fire swung at the grey smoke with his sword which had lain along the counter, but spun too far and fell to his knee. One of them let out a screech. Perad, nearest to the fumes from the fire missed much of what happened next. He saw the door burst open and a fourth Gralt who had been standing guard outside strode in, sword low. And one blink later all four of the most feared fighters known were toppling, each with a knife in his throat. What signals had arranged the timing Perad did not know, what courage it had taken from these gentle, peaceful men he did not understand, though later, when his head cleared, he was proud beyond measure to be among them.

He was dragged outside to the fresh air and seated on the step at the well in the centre of the village circle. He watched, feeling nothing now, as men from the surrounding houses arrived. There were quiet voices and quickly made arrangements. Men spread purposefully. The fighting unit of the Gralt was five bonded warriors mercilessly trained, it was said, and a lot had been said of the Gralt since the skirmishes had been first reported, though little was truly known. There should be one more on watch somewhere, perhaps on the outskirts of the village. Perad looked dully on while more folk arrived. They were pulling on tunics, tying boots.

The village men split into groups, some to search upstream and downstream on both sides of the river. The remaining men spread in pairs to take up stations around the outer edge of the village circle and to guard the bridge. The weapons were mostly large sticks, farming implements, edged tools. There were few swords in the village. Perad sat on the step of the well and shivered, but not with the cold.

Then the men were arriving back, and the talk on the stone paved area in front of the inn was short and quiet. The fifth Gralt had not been found. Watchers had been placed in the woods for the night. It was guessed that the Gralt were not good enough woodsmen for a single one of them to now be a threat to the village, with the men alert. There were a few lone homesteads dotted mostly downstream and into the woods along the valley which would be checked on at first light. Those men not assigned immediate duty, went off to secure their homes.

Many of the returning men approached Perad and held him by the shoulder with a firm grip, in the quiet gesture used by the men of the Valleys to acknowledge a deed well done. Jevan, the butcher, was the only one who spoke. "What was it you used, lad?" he asked.

"It was a mixture to calm angry goats, before shearing," replied Perad. "They are pushed into a shed filled with the smoke, and it makes them stupid for a little while. I have never seen it done, though I have been taught the mixture. They were fresh powders, flux made."

"Angry goats," said the man with a harsh laugh, then a real laugh, and he hurried off to tell the tale.

And then his uncle was there, with his hand on Perad's shoulder. Uncle Tavit could talk unendingly, but, "Well done, Perad," and a slow nod of the head was all he had now. Perad found it hard to lift his eyes, impossible to speak. His uncle left him alone.

Lenida, wife of Jevan, came and stood in front of him and knelt before him, taking his hands in hers. "You did well, Perad, she said, "Be pleased."

"It is not what I did, but what I saw," said Perad, finding his voice. "They killed Kerim."

"There may be more killed. But there will be less because of you."

But Perad had no more words and Lenida left him there. He stayed there until the cold reached his bones and made him shake violently, and he got up then and made his way around to the back door and up the two flights of stairs to his room in the attic where he lay on his bed and stared at the dark sky through the gaps in the shutters until after midnight when his uncle called him.

Chapter 2

Had the Gralt not arrived that evening, it would still have been the day around which Perad's life turned, for sometime before midnight, grandmother Katada died. She had been in bed in her room above the inn for a week now, with at least one of the village women sitting at her side, but having rallied a little in the past day, she died alone.

She was found by uncle Tavit who came to knock on Perad's door. "Come with me," he said, a tiredness in his voice never before heard by Perad, although he seemed reluctant to go anywhere, and stood with his arms dangling and his chin on his chest and looked down at Perad for a long time. There was dirt on his face and blood on his sleeve and no light in his eyes.

Perad was taken to stand by her bed and place three fingers on her forehead in the manner used throughout the land as a sign of respect for those passed. She was cold and no longer his grandmother.

"Remember her always, but do not be sad for long," he was told by his uncle. "She had seen enough life, and was ready." Perad lifted his head towards the candle flame on the shelf above the bed for somewhere to place his eyes. His uncle stepped towards the table by the shuttered window then turned to Perad. "This will be yours now." Grandmother Katada's book of herbcraft was handed to him.

It was bound in black cracked leather and was said to be the oldest in the Valleys. Unable to hold his grandmother ever again, Perad clutched the book to his chest and watched his tears land on the closed pages and glisten in the candlelight.

"Go on," said uncle Tavit, and Perad hurried back to his own room beneath the rafters where he sat on the floor with his back to the base of his bed, holding his grandmother's book and listening to the quiet footsteps below him of those who came to show their respect.

He dozed a little, and awoke, stiff and cold, still sitting on the floor, to a silent building at first light. He had to pass Grandmother Katada's room on the way downstairs. The door was closed and Perad would not look in.

Uncle Tavit had cleaned the inn room and washed the floor, tasks he would normally have left to the morning. The door to the village circle had been wedged open, and the chill of the air made Perad shiver. He held three fingers to the back of the bench where Kerim would sit, and forced himself not to allow his eyes to search for bloodstains amongst the damp cleaned patches. He cleared the grate and piled logs and lit a fire, for the mornings were cool now, and there were still herbs and leaves to be dried, and it would help with drying the floor.

He heard footsteps outside and a hooded head peered in the door. It would be one of the watchmen guarding the village, but Perad did not recognize him and the man did not see Perad in the shadows, or chose not to see him, for he made no comment and went away.

While the flames grew, Perad sat on the tiny stool by the fire and opened Grandmother Katada's book.

For amusement, those skilled in the gentle craft of herbs had long been referred to as poisoners, and Grandmother Katada had been village poisoner for over two generations.

The materials of the poisoner were made from the plants of the woodlands and there were drawings with names at the beginning of the book. Perad's fingers traced the shapes of roots, leaves, berries and seeds on the first pages, then nuts, barks, mosses and funguses. The poisoner's work was in the collecting of these ingredients, and the preparation, the drying and grinding into powders, which was the way in the Valleys. The craft of the poisoner was in the mixing. Some remedies called for infusions or poultices or dips and the preparation of these was also part of the craft. The important mixes were committed to memory, and Perad had always thought his grandmother's book to be a list of mixes, and instructions for their use. He had seen her consult the book at times, more, it seemed, for effect, for she would open it, touch the page with a fingertip and close it with a flourish.

The pages were yellow with age, but the writing was still clear and strong, ink making being one of the poisoner's arts. The handwriting was upright and tall, much like his own, and Perad felt some link with the ancient writer, though there was no reference to the author anywhere in the book.

He turned the pages to get a feel of the nature of the book. He saw at once it was not what he had thought. The mixes were there, but much that was new to him was also there. He shuffled closer to the fire and turned partially, holding the book up to better illuminate the pages. He understood enough to realize that much study was needed. Now he had the book, he would not be able to consult his grandmother on its use. He closed the book and laid it across his knees and watched the flames twist and flicker in the chimney.

He had thought his uncle to be in bed, but he came in the door with the morning light behind him. He was cloaked and there was mud on his boots. He came over to the fire, picking up a bench on the way, and sat close. "Your grandmother wished me to be a poisoner but I was not suited to it. It always seemed too small for me. I was more comfortable with a sack of grain on my shoulder, or upending a barrel. And I did not have the memory for the mixes. I disappointed her, I think. She did train others as apprentices before you were born, but they gave up or left. She was always pleased with you."

He used his foot to push a wayward log back into place in the fire. The mud from his boot sizzled and spat. "I looked under the bridge for the enemy," he said, tilting his head at the boots. "I found no one, but I did step in the river." They sat still for some time. "There are signs that they were on the bluff above the east bridge."

Perad pictured them on their bellies, watching the village. "But you always enjoyed the collecting, didn't you? Don't you?"

"Yes I did. And we still shall. Is it what you want, Perad, to be a poisoner?"

"Yes, I shall be a poisoner." He stopped then, unsure, but only for a moment. "And I want to journey. And to be an innkeeper."

His uncle smiled at him and placed his hand on Perad's, resting on the edge of the book. "There is room in a lifetime for all of those things, and lots more." He stood to take off his cloak and turned to spread it over the counter. "To journey, yes, there has always been that in you. And where will you journey?"

"All of Tarodash. The ocean. The islands. Lands beyond Tarodash." He could not keep the excitement out of his voice.

Uncle Tavit's smile became a laugh. "Then it had better be a long life. And we must see about some better walking boots." His face kept its smile. "Many who leave the Valleys and return never feel comfortable here again. I think, though, you will."

"Oh, I shall not leave the valley. I shall always live here. I shall travel and return, as we do now. But at times and with luck, my journeys will be longer."

"The appearance of the Gralt may affect the journeys beyond Tarodash, and even in Tarodash, for a while. No more have been seen, and the nearer homesteads have been checked. The valley is well guarded. Two men have ridden to Parden, to see what news there is on the plains, and two have gone to Dresswell. We should know more of the Gralt soon. We shall not worry. A large group could not cross the whole of Tarodash to the Valleys without being seen and challenged." He looked to add more, then stopped and picked up his cloak and turned for the kitchen. "In the meantime, see what the book has for you, and complete becoming a poisoner."

Perad read for a while and thought for a while. When the light was strong enough, he opened the shutters and went to his work counter and laid the book open at one end. His powders were as he had left them, arranged in small heaps in rows along with the bowls and pestles and pouches. There were two scatterings of dried and crushed leaves and moss where he had taken what he had used to make the fumes last night. He used the edge of his hand to push the remains into neat little piles. He stood, unsure, and went back to the book. He was peering into it when Nadira, the valley midwife, came from the kitchen and crossed the inn.

"She enjoyed being the owner of that book, but I do not think she ever understood it. A jumble of jabber she used to call it, when there was only me to hear. We were good friends then. I have just made my respects. Your uncle tells me the book is yours now. Have you made gist of it yet?"

"Not yet. It will take more than a morning." They shared a smile. "But I have made some progress. I did not know there was so much left to learn. If the materials are seen in groups according to their qualities, and not their source, it makes more sense. The way in which one acts on another is described not individually, but as a pattern. I am beginning to learn about the control of potency. And there is much, much else which I did not know existed. Yes, it can improve what I do."

Herbcraft was good amongst the folk of the valley and Nadira, particularly skilled as a healer, nodded her understanding. "Good. I always felt that there was more than just mixes to medicines and healing, as there is more to many crafts, than waiting for the flux and making what has always been made. Knowledge in most crafts may have been lost over the years, and I suspect little has been added. We are too content in our skills. We should be prepared to extend them. Keep studying, Perad.

"And can it help you to help me? The dry weather has ruined the rivercress from which I make my hand wash. Can you make a mix for me?"

Perad lined up his thoughts. "Yes, and what the book is showing me will help. Without rivercress, I shall use bluelily leaves as a cleaner and tarrow root to make it more potent. Then I should add a third ingredient to protect the skin and taroknut will do that." He was reaching for powders as he spoke, tipping from pouches into a bowl. He mixed and ground them with a pestle. "The flux would have been good, but never mind, they are good powders." Nadira watched him work. His hands were sure and his movements were quick and smooth.

"There," said Perad. "A mix I have never made before, or heard of. Do we dare to use it?"

"Let us see it work," she said.

They went to the kitchen and Perad placed the bowl by the sink. He wet a finger in the barrel of clean water and dipped it into the powder. He took a palmful of water and rubbed his hands together. "Let us see how that looks." He held his hands over the sink and Nadira ladled water over them. "That looks clean," he said. "What do you think?"

She took his hands and looked closely, turning them. Her face told Perad she was pleased. "I shall report on its use. Thank you, Perad the poisoner." She took a pouch from her

13

pocket and held it open. She would not touch Perad's bowl and waited for him to dry his hands and pour the mix.

The burial of Grandmother Katada and of Kerim was the accustomed affair, taking place at first light two days after death. The bodies, each wrapped in a rough blanket woven of reeds and carried on a stretcher of woven greenwillow twigs, was taken to the place between the stream and the woods and the curve in the river on the western edge of the village.

Here in the marshy ground a shallow depression was made and the wrapped bodies laid, head towards the village circle, and covered with the stretcher weighted at each end by a small log. At times, the greenwillow from the stretcher would sprout the following spring, so that the burial patch was dotted with the sad untidy shrubs always associated with death.

Barefooted and ankle deep, the villagers stood nearby and watched the dark brown water seep back and cover the disturbed ground, the wrapped body and the stretcher. On those times when the ground was frozen, a bonfire would be built and lit before dawn. This day, the ancient song was sung by a visiting coppersmith from Paradun who was also a chanter and could sing better than anyone in Woodall. His voice rose clear and strong into the lightening sky, and took with it the souls of the two who had passed.

To return immediately to work after the burial was an important mark of respect and as the last words of the chanter rolled across the valley, each of the watchers turned away and went back to the village, or to their homestead. There was no flux today, so no making, but all busied themselves for the morning, a tribute in the Valleys to those who had passed, in the ordinary tasks of maintaining their lives, cleaning, sorting and repairing. Perad chose to reset the great stone flags along the side of the inn which had tripped folk of late. It was good hard work which bruised the shins and grazed the knuckles, and a satisfying task to be done whilst sifting his memories of Grandmother Katada.

By noon most folk had done enough and a long shared lunch of open doors and much walking between homes was followed by a gentle afternoon of talk. Perad had little appetite and few words and no wish for company. He slipped away and took a walk upstream. The river was low, it had been a warm summer with little rain, even up in the mountains, it seemed. Nidal, the young bootmaker was on watch duty, standing on a bend in the river, leaning on a stout stick of almost his own height. "I would not go much further, lad," he said. Perad saw that he was immediately sorry for his choice of words. He was not many years older than Perad. Perad took no offence. If war was coming, he should be thankful to be too young to be part of it.

"What would you do if you saw Gralt?" asked Perad.

"Run," said Nidal. "To give warning. As I have been told to. But I would run quietly. And quickly." He was silent for some time, perhaps thinking of being pursued by Gralt, or perhaps imagining himself a great and courageous warrior driving the Gralt away. "We need soldiers. We are not prepared for this. How can Gralt be here? Where did they come from? They can not have travelled unchallenged from the coast. They cannot have come over the mountains. Did they cross the forest? But their lands are to the south. Were these scouts, or is there an army? Perhaps the desert. Surely nothing can cross the desert? You saw them. What were they like?"

But he did not expect an answer, and Perad did not respond. The two stood and watched the trees and the water for a while, saying nothing, then catching Nidal's eye, Perad gave a nod and turned back to the village.

Part of the way back, he took a route up the slope to just below the ridge where a line of the great tarok trees stood. They seemed to form a broken procession almost from the plain to the mountain, like an ancient wall standing defensively on the northern ridge of the valley, and some believed that they had been planted as such countless generations ago. They were twisted and sparse and Perad found one of the taller ones and climbed to where the trunk broke into a crown, making a seat. He arranged himself looking towards the plain hoping to see distant places, but he had chosen poorly and a turn in the river caused the valley side to obstruct his view. A poisoner he would be, and wished to be, and he would serve his valley all through his life if permitted to do so, but the Gralt had changed the world and no plans now seemed secure. He turned to see the mountain peaks far to the east, but they were hidden by haze as they often were. He let his misery overtake him then, and wept quietly for a good while.

There was more activity than expected as Perad approached the village and he spied a friend, Danat, son of a wheelwright, who came running to his wave to tell him breathlessly that soldiers had come to investigate the appearance of the Gralt. They went together, to see, but found not soldiers but three court officers come to collect the clothes and weapons of the Gralt. They wore new uniforms of blue and black, and had swords, but they were not fighters. They sat on their horses and would not dismount, demanding the items be brought to them in sacks. The folk of Woodall valley were courteous, but clearly disappointed at the arrival of officials and not soldiers, and annoyed at the manner of the visitors.

Perad was more interested in the horses, fine animals the like of which was not seen in the Valleys. The horses stood patiently. The visitors did not. They urged speed from the villagers. Perad saw that they were afraid, and wished to be gone from, what was to them, a remote part of the world.

There was a discussion which almost became an argument when some wanted to keep one of the Gralt swords and some wished other items to stay in the village, but it was settled by Walvin, the most senior of the elder council, who said, "Let all be taken."

Some of the larger children ran to follow the horses as they left, returning to their games when the riders had sufficiently outdistanced them. It was quiet in the circle. Jevan was the one who said what most were thinking. "If the Gralt come again we must be prepared to defend ourselves."

But there was little to do beyond setting sentries and sharpening weapons. Taprad, the rabbit hunter, a homesteader, had skill in bowmaking and suggested he make longbows for the men and give instruction in arrow making. There was more argument as the boys and some of the women demanded bows, to be laughed at by Taprad, which in turn caused voices to be raised even more. Perad had never seen his village quarrelling in this manner and took himself to his book by the fire in the corner of the inn.

Chapter 3

"Enough now," said uncle Tavit. "We deserve a break from such tasks. Get your pack, we are going south for a few days." It was almost a month since the attack of the Gralt and no further sightings had been made. Perad had been working in the warm autumn sun behind the inn, scrubbing with a rough rag and his own mixture of cleaner at the inside of the large wooden barrel used for the first brew. He was thrilled. He loved the long trips away from the valley, and especially enjoyed the desert edge.

He was also surprised. Many folk of Woodall had settled in other parts of the Valleys, and the village and its inn received a steady stream of visitors. And since the incident with the Gralt, there had been more than normal. His uncle must have gone to a lot of trouble to arrange for the inn to be looked after in his absence.

A journey of more than one day required his large pack and few more items than usual, but he was back quickly. And then they were off, crossing the wooden bridge on the eastern edge of the village, into the woods, and out of the valleys.

The wooded and rock filled valleys of Perad's world lay between the great plains of Tarodash and the mountains to the east. Eight days to the west across the plains by cart was the ocean, which Perad had seen the spring before last, though it had taken twice that to walk back, a part of the passage for all those lads in their fifteenth year. Tarodash was bounded on the north by a forest, vast and forbidding, that was said to go on forever, like the mountains, to the end of the world, unchanging but for increasing cold. To the south of Woodall, last of the Valley towns and villages, the woods ran out and Perad's world gave way to the beginnings of a rocky desert, which extended west to the sea and bounded the entire southern border of Tarodash. And beyond that, it was said, were many lands, including the land of the Gralt.

In times long ago, Tarodash had dealings with the southern lands, and even with the Gralt, but this trade, along with the Gralt, had been forgotten for many generations. It was the desert edge that Perad and his uncle Tavit were making for, one day of good striding, directly south.

"The ancient books describe a people who lived in the hills across the river from Sundorn and in much of what is now the desert," uncle Tavit told him. They had picked their way through the treeless hills strewn with splintered rock that fringed the southern edge of the Valleys, and descended towards the desert. Once on flatter ground, they moved east along the desert floor, and the rocky slopes on their left became steeper and developed into cliffs which began the rise of the mountains to the east.

"They were traders between Tarodash and the lands to their south. They knew the routes and had strange beasts which could walk the desert with ease. It was said that they fastened platters to the feet of these beasts to stop them sinking into the deep sand further into the desert. The traders vanished and the trade stopped and Tarodash became isolated. We fell out with the Gralt, the tales do not say why. There were fights and battles then, and we had an army and heroes who you have heard about and read of. Then the Gralt stopped raiding, and the ships stopped going south and Tarodash heard no more of the world since then, but for stories of lands beyond the ocean brought by the pirates of the islands. Our own ships never venture far from the shore.

There never have been reports of peoples to the north."

The cliffs had suddenly become higher and almost vertical and the late afternoon sun was lost behind a wall of rock. The desert to their right had become a vast lake of purple shadow edged with red in the distance.

"I would prefer to camp a little higher," said uncle Tavit, and they scrambled up a gorge until they found flatter ground and could no longer see the desert floor for the shoulders of rock. They continued a little further until they encountered bushes and other plants, sparse, but enough for building a small fire. "Quickly now, a cooking fire and water before the light goes," said uncle Tavit, dropping his pack in a sheltered place where a boulder leaned against a rock face on a wide ledge providing a view of the southern sky. Perad, always pleased to be camping, was eager for this first night out of the woods, and happy with the chores. He built the fire and made supper, a stew of venison and roots, in the small round metal pot which went on all such excursions. He spooned it into bowls and they ate sitting up against their packs watching the sky blacken and the stars come out.

In the morning they moved back down to the desert edge. There were crags and cliffs of bare rock, deep clefts where the sun never reached, and caves that went beyond the limit of vision into the dark. Beyond was the great desert of rocks and sand, and beyond that were lands unknown. In the shadows of the clefts or clinging to cracks in the rocks, scorched by the heat and the wind were plants which had not been named, but there were also plants known by a poisoner to be of real value.

Uncle Tavit could sit for hours in the sun with his back to some high wall of rock, legs dangling over a steep edge, staring to the south, perhaps feeling something of the wanderlust felt by Perad. Perad himself would clamber about, at times collecting, other times simply enjoying the freedom, the new terrain and the enormous sky. He felt at ease amongst the rocks, but the sands of the desert were strange to him, though he did like to walk out until he could look back and look up at his own land as if from outside it.

Each night there was a different place to camp and they would choose sites where the heat of the rocks would warm their backs for hours into the night, then they would wake shivering in the early hours to an open and starlit sky beyond understanding. They would build a fire then, and sit close, knees drawn, wrapped in their blankets until drowsiness overtook them.

Breakfasts, and all meals, were constructed from what they had brought with them, for there was nothing which they could eat here except, perhaps, for the lizards, of startling colours, which they were not willing to try.

They stayed for five days, until on the fifth evening his uncle spied a disturbance of dust and smoke far into the desert which left him uncomfortable. They did not make a fire that night and uncle Tavit was awake before light, sitting on a ledge high on a cliff overlooking the south. Perad awoke and climbed to join him, taking his blanket, and sat huddled and watched the sky lighten in the south and east.

"What do you see, Perad?" asked uncle Tavit.

"There seems to be a camp of some sort, half a day away, perhaps a day. It is difficult to judge. I can see rising smoke and a dark colour that is not rock or sand. It is in a line stretching south to north. Is it the Gralt?"

"It is not a dust storm, and the rising smoke says it is not a herd of animals. It is surely not soldiers or folk of Tarodash. And it surely cannot be the Gralt. My eyes cannot make out the line you see. Is it directed this way?"

"If it is a line, it is aimed further to the east, I think." Perad stared until his eyes hurt, but could make out no more. Slowly the sun rose and the light and shadows changed and it became just one more shimmering mark amongst all the others in the desert. "Perhaps it was simply a trick of the light. There is nothing to be seen, now."

"It is said that desert light can fool the eyes. We shall go back now, but we shall not hurry. Let us try even further east and find a new path north through the hills."

This suited Perad. In his previous expeditions to the desert they had only been to the gentler land to the west.

Fortunately, the cliffs did not go on forever climbing, and though steep, there were numerous places where they had become broken and could be scaled, and they decided to continue. "I have never travelled this far east into the desert before, and have never heard report of anyone doing so, though it must have been explored at some time in the past," uncle Tavit said.

Perad had never imagined such a desolate place. The rock was dark and hard and was well splintered like broken pots, but with shards larger than himself. Nothing grew, although there were tiny black flies which rose in small clouds whenever a small rock was disturbed by their feet. The morning sun had lifted a haze which had turned into a low even cloud, adding to the gloom. They found themselves drifting out into the desert, away from the hills and crags on their left. The walking was easier here on less broken rock, and drifts of shallow sand made a pleasant change.

The line of hills began to turn more to the south taking them further away from their home and they were ready to turn north, spotting ahead of them a lessening in the steepness of the hills which should allow a less challenging climb, when Perad stopped and pointed. "There," he said. "What is that?"

Rising from the desert floor was a curious rock, steep sided and flat topped, perhaps the height of a large building.

It was pale grey, almost the colour of the sky and its smooth sides, from this distance, allowed no shadows. Perad had only seen it as he scanned the horizon for a break in the clouds, or for a sign of the sun to lighten the mood. Now seen, it was a strange entity out in the featureless desert. It was a good distance away, but could not be ignored.

"We must look," said uncle Tavit. "There and back will not delay us for long. We should still have lunch back up in the hills."

The flat grey light of the desert was deceiving, and the structure was a little further than they expected, and somewhat larger. Approaching, they could see that one side to the south was not vertical and featureless, but broken and stepped, and could easily be climbed. They stood a few strides away and surveyed.

The thing rose out of the sand as if it had grown there.

Uncle Tavit slid his pack from his shoulder and stepped towards it. Perad knelt to place his pack on the floor, and was looking up as he rose. Uncle Tavit had reached the base of the rock and placed his hand on the vertical side and a foot on a first rough step. He pulled his hand back and spun around, letting out a curse. "Here! Perad, here! Quick now!"

Perad stumbled forward. His uncle never cursed. He had climbed onto the low ledge that formed the step and was holding his hand out. Perad took it and stepped up and felt what his uncle had felt.

"The flux. The flux, here. It cannot be."

"It is, though."

It was only in the Valleys where the flux was found, and although it was known to extend east beyond the towns and villages towards the mountains it had never been discovered, or even considered, anywhere else. The Valleys were the flux, and the flux was the Valleys.

There were many in Tarodash who would not

acknowledge the flux, claiming it to be an invention of the minds of a folk who lived beyond the edge of the sensible world. Visitors from outside the Valleys found no enhanced skill of their own, and would shake their heads at what seemed a deception. But no one ever denied the supreme craftsmanship to be found in the Valleys.

The best tools, utensils and goods in the land, from axes to carts, from cheeses to tunics, anything which could be crafted from raw materials, were made in the Valleys on the days when the flux was high. The products of this craft were bartered and traded across the Valleys and throughout Tarodash, and valued always. The craftsmanship of the Valleys extended to working with raw materials brought from outside, but the very best goods were made from substances found and prepared at those woodland places where the flux was strong and on the days when the flux was high.

Most of those born in the Valleys felt the flux as a tingling warmth which rose slowly from the ground to cover the feet, then legs, then the whole body. All makers would hurry at these times to their work and find their craftsmanship heightened and the materials of their craft more willing to their hands, their resulting wares of an unequalled standard. And these were already the finest craftsfolk in the whole of Tarodash. Goods from all over the land were sent to the Valleys to be worked on; skins were sent from Kardeff to be returned as boots, wool from the Rindars to be sent back as cloth, and much more, all of exceptional quality.

All of those born out of the Valleys felt nothing of the flux. Folk who left the Valleys for years would return to find diminished their feeling for the flux, and their craftsmanship would never again match that of those who had spent their life forming with the flux.

There was no predicting its appearance, it came and went at its own will, rising and falling at any time, and lasting for anything from moments to a number of days. It varied in strength, and in parts, in location. There were favoured areas where it would almost always reach a good intensity, and places where its emergence was unusual. But it was always found within the slopes and near to the waters and rocks of the river valleys between the great plain of Tarodash and the mountains to the east.

It should not be here, out in the desert.

They climbed to the top, Perad leading. Uncle Tavit spread his feet and stood upright. "It is strong, too. Stronger up here than at the base."

The top had been worked. The rock was formed into grooves and slabs, much worn and rounded by the desert weather, but recognizably shaped. There were places which might once have been usable as table tops and seats. Perad took out his knife and began to sharpen it on a dome of smooth rock. He felt the thrill of the flux through his legs and body and arms and hands, in the contact of his knife blade on the rock, and the effortlessness of the power of the shaping. The rhythm of the movement, the choice of angles, the position of his body, all came without thought. His breathing became slow and steady. He was balanced in mind and muscle and motion. He held the blade up to catch the light on the edge, but there was no need.

"I have often thought that the flux is in the rocks of the Valleys, rather than in the Valleys themselves, even though the rocks may not be visible, hidden under the earth," said uncle Tavit. "Could this somehow be a rock of the valley, or in some way underground connected to the rocks of the valley? Look closely." The pale grey rock, smooth and featureless at arm's length, was flecked with tiny glints of light, evidence of crystal within the structure.

Perad took a small roll of fine leather from his pocket and spread it on the edge of a flat rock. He used his knife to cut a palm size piece in one corner. He cut so deftly that the point of his knife never scraped the rock. His uncle sat to watch. Perad seemed unaware that he was there. He pulled and the piece came free, and he laid it on the rock. He knelt to place his eyes on the same level. Fitting the flat of his spare hand on the leather and tilting his head to see, he inserted his knife point to slit the leather between his hand and the rock, as if splitting a slate along its seam. He worked his blade into the leather, opening and shaping the inside. His movements were sure and certain and quick. He may have closed his eyes and worked by touch. He straightened then and held it for his uncle to see, a pouch like the ones he used to contain his powders. He used his knife point to push holes through the top and handed it to his uncle. Turning back to the spare leather he trimmed a lace from the edge and handed that over. Uncle Tavit threaded the drawstring and pulled it tight and handed it back.

"You could have been a leather worker. I did not know you had such skill."

"I would not attempt that without the flux," said Perad.

His uncle stood and turned a slow circle. "We cannot be the first from the Valleys to find this place. Why did we not know of it?"

"Not many would journey this far east on the desert edge."

"But it only needs one to report a discovery such as this. Then, I have heard that the desert sands shift with the wind over time and collect into hills which can cover a town. Perhaps this happened here."

"And if the wind can bring the sand, the wind can blow it away," said Perad. "This could be newly uncovered."

Uncle Tavit looked north along the line of hills and cliffs that marked the beginnings of the Valleys. "Can you find your way back here?"

26

"Without a doubt. But if we return home directly north, we can mark where we meet the river and we shall have two routes."

"Yes. Through one of those gaps and we should be able to hold a steady line north." He inclined his head towards the cliffs. Climbing what appeared to be a table, the highest point on the entire rock, he stared to the south and east. Perad joined him. There was nothing to be seen, even though the cloud had lifted and the light was better.

"The flux is the flux," said uncle Tavit. He had been silent for a while. "We know nothing of it than that it is, and where it is." They were making their way back to the desert edge, slowly and with many a backward look, as if the rock would vanish if they failed to reaffirm it. "It seems we know even less of it now."

There were fractures where the cliffs could be climbed, and they chose one as near north from the rock as they could. They were ready for their evening meal by the time they were comfortably in the woods. They could feel the valley flux now, but it was weak and diminishing as they walked. It was almost gone by the time the light failed and they stopped to camp.

Next morning they walked until they reached their river and followed it west. They were on the south side, not often used, and Perad would have benefited from a search for herbs, but uncle Tavit was now of a mind to hurry home.

Chapter 4

"You have a visitor, Perad." Uncle Tavit's voice came from inside the inn where he was preparing food for the feast. This was Harvestend, the eve of the middle full moon of autumn, and a holiday throughout Tarodash. The Valleys, where work came and went with the flux as much as with the seasons, did not observe all holidays in the same manner as the rest of the land, but still used this day for entertainments, sports and feasts.

Perad was in the yard behind the inn drying tallrush roots by laying them on the wall to catch the midday sun. They had been split into thin strips and needed turning often to dry evenly. There was a sweetness to them which was used to add to some of the more bitter tasting infusions. They were particularly valuable for children's drinks. He had pulled them from the stream by the burial ground that morning, as a weak flux was waning. There was no flux for the drying, but they were best prepared in the sun. He would wait for a strong flux to grind them into fine powder.

"You have, in fact, two visitors, Perad." This was another voice, and a welcome one, for it was Yafad, a good friend from Nerbridge, apprentice to his father, Farnam, who was poisoner there, and who now came from the back door of the inn.

"Good to see you, Perad," said Farnam from behind his son. He was tall, and had to stoop as he came through the door. Perad was surprised to see how much Yafad had grown since he had last seen him in early spring. He was beginning to approach his father in height, and was heavier, too, than half a year ago.

28

"You now have three visitors, Perad." This was his uncle's voice again. There should have been amusement there, but instead Perad heard a serious tone.

Uncle Tavit came into the yard with Hamana, a young mother from the village, who was carrying a small child. She placed the child at her shoulder and removed a shawl from his legs. "I caught him with a hoe. There was a lot of dirt in the cut. I thought I had cleaned it out." She spoke in a whisper, her voice filled with anxiety. "Should I go to Dresswell?"

The lack of a healer in the village was becoming a worry. Old Hafaf had died a year ago, and his only apprentice, his daughter, had married and left, leaving midwife Nadira and Perad's grandmother, and now Perad, to look after the valley's needs. Anything serious required a journey to one of the healers in the next valley, half a day away.

The child had deep infected cut behind the left knee that was open, and would stay open at any movement of the leg. Much of the leg was red with infection. This was an unpleasant wound. "I have been wrapping it in a bandage soaked in targ root," said the mother. Her sorrow seemed bottomless.

"We shall see you later, Perad," said Farnam, motioning his son towards the door. "You are busy for the moment."

"No wait," said Perad quickly. "Please. I would value your advice."

This was a delicate moment. One poisoner would not wish to interfere with another, especially a young one yet to gain the confidence of his village. Perad's invitation to give an opinion required courage.

"What would you suggest?" Farnam asked quietly.

Perad responded, but he was speaking mostly to himself. "The targ root extract is too strong and is damaging the skin and preventing healing. Tarcup petal is much more gentle but

29

will still remove the infection if used frequently. Bluelily will help the skin heal. I have good powders, flux collected and prepared." He looked up at Farnam then, as if coming out of his spell. "A little dogroot to mix in." The infection was serious and dogroot was a little used, but powerful substance to improve blood flow. He would like Farnam's approval.

Farnam looked at him, considering. "Good," he said. "I shall remember that. Now we will leave you to prepare your mixture, and see you later."

They went, and Perad took Hamana to his work counter to make the mix. The powders were in his two rolls of pouches, quickly found and soon mixed. The child slept at her shoulder. "Come back when the flux is strong and I will make an even better mix. Come back anyway in two days." He poured from his bowl into a pouch, then reached in to take a pinch between thumb and two fingers. "That much in half a cupful of warm water and dab it on." He was reluctant to demonstrate, worried that too much concern would alarm her even more, but she asked to be shown. The leg was hot, and the child whimpered, but did not wake.

"Let it dry before wrapping, and use dry wrappings." He thought for a while. "Five times a day."

He walked with her to the door. "I believe it will work," he said. "If two days do not show an improvement, I shall go to High Dresswell to see Doram." He watched her walk away, and believed her step was lighter.

A little later, Perad sought out Walvin. The senior elder was on the edge of the games field setting out the range for the afternoon's stone throwing competition. Perad told of his concerns regarding the absence of a healer for the village. Walvin nodded.

"Yes, I have left this too long. I shall send word to Dresswell, and Marben, if necessary. There may be a reasonably advanced apprentice, somewhere. And if not, I shall look elsewhere."

He walked out onto the grass. "Now help me with this, Perad. If there are complaints, I can then refer them to you."

The target for the throw was an enormous collection of fat, provided by butcher Jevan, held together by a net of thin rope and hung from a frame. From it, Perad counted twenty two paces, the traditional distance, the size of the pace being a subject of much argument each year. Walvin placed a barrel stave as the toe line, and Perad drove in a peg to hold it in position.

"Let us try this for length," said Walvin, dragging a basket of stones. Perad took one from the top. These were flat river pebbles, selected to fit comfortably between thumb and forefinger, and chipped to a sharp edge on one side. There were three throws, from the shoulder, underarm from the knees, and overarm. Perad placed his feet, steadied himself, and threw from the shoulder. The stone, wide at first, curved nicely in and down to bury itself silently in the target.

"Acceptable," said Walvin. He stepped forward and repeated Perad's throw. The pebble followed the same line, and there was a clink as it found the one already there.

"Also acceptable," said Perad, with a solemn nod, then a grin. Walvin's aim, for many years, had been unsurpassed in the valley.

They tried other throws, and declared the distance and the height of the target to be satisfactory. There were no champions to the throwing, it being a sport of challenges and wagers. It would eventually end when the sharpened stones cut sufficient of the rope for the fat to drop to the floor.

The misses, mostly Perad's, had sailed into the grassy bank behind the target, and they were collecting them when Henata, wife of Walvin arrived with a basket of cakes.

"Freshly baked," she said. "I am unsure of the quality. I would be grateful if someone could try them for me."

31

They pronounced them uncertain at the first trial, acceptable at the second, and quite excellent by the third.

This was a day of fine weather, as the middle of autumn generally was in the Valleys, and the feast was to be taken in the village circle where trestle tables and benches had been set out. Tea was the main feast, with lunch a light meal of nuts, fruit and cold meats, there being a good deal of activity planned for the afternoon. Perad sought out Yafad to sit with and catch up on news, for he had not seen him for a while, but the talk at the table was loud and general and the conversation would have to wait.

A favourite sport of the Valleys was strongarrow. These were short, thick spears only a little longer than a forearm, flighted front and back, with goose feathers at the rear and heavier leather flights behind the tip. They were thrown for distance and accuracy, aiming at a series of target boards shaped, for the feast day, in the manner of hogs seen face on, but comically painted. Perad had always been disappointed with his arm strength and no longer entered the events, although he would still make and throw the spears in play. But he did enjoy the contests and sat amongst the lads and girls on the grassed banking around the games field. He had seen too little of his friends in the last year as more of his time had been devoted to his work as apprentice poisoner, and this time away from his duties had been much anticipated.

Good throws hit the centre of the target with a satisfying sound and brought a roar of approval. There were wagers, applause, jeers, teasing, and a good deal of laughter. It felt good to be surrounded by those he had spent his childhood with.

He watched his uncle, whose thick arms could lift onto the counter all but the largest of barrels, win a contest for the furthest target and then lose a wager to a separate challenge from the runner up.

Then it was the wrestling. This was the preferred sport of all Tarodash, and Perad was quite aware of what would now happen. Yafad, as a young visitor would be asked to challenge a villager to fight for ancient rivalry, in the first bout, and would, of course, choose Perad.

Perad took off his tunic and shirt and stepped onto the ring. It was a circular mat of straw, five strides across and deep enough to cushion a heavy fall. A careless or tired fighter could easily catch his feet in the tangle, and it was important to step high, particularly in the early bouts before the covering was trodden down. Yafad stepped on to face him. He wore a large grin and Perad saw again how much his friend had grown of late, and how he would need to seek every advantage. He pretended to be testing the footing and took a few steps to his right to put the sun in his opponent's eyes. Yafad's grin got bigger. "I think I shall fight you with my eyes closed, today," he said. "I will still beat you, but I would rather not dishonour your village by thrashing you too easily. I have friends here I would not wish to upset."

"There appears to be a lot more of you than there was," countered Perad. "Try not to go down. It will take you a long time to get up again."

"Oh, I do not intend going down."

Walvin, as stickler, positioned himself on the edge of the mat with a belt of cloth in each hand; Yafad took the red one and fastened it around his waist, Perad took the green and was careful with the knot. His waist was narrow and he did not want the trailing ends of his belt to be a nuisance.

"Honour your opponent," Walvin called.

The two fighters moved forward and placed their hands on their opponent's shoulders and touched foreheads, then stepped back. The scorer stood by his frame of beads. The watchers, most of the village and the visitors, sat forward.

"Fight," called Walvin.

There were many varieties of wrestling, but the style in the southern valleys was possibly the fastest, with rules and scoring favouring speed over power to a greater degree than in other regions. There were variations in the north where two giants would grapple for long periods on the floor. Here fighters stayed mostly on their feet.

Perad stepped forward watching Yafad's hands which were hanging by his sides. He made a grab at Yafad's wrist, not a real attack, more an attempt to test his speed.

He did not expect the counter to come so soon. Yafad fell forward and Perad danced away. But the attack was not at his leg, as Perad suspected, and Yafad had his arm, above the elbow, falling and rolling, pulling Perad on top of him and then continuing his roll and bouncing to his feet, leaving Perad on his back. Perad cleared his face of straw and looked up at him. "Fortunate," he said.

"Careless," said Yafad.

"Ten, red," called Walvin.

Perad stood, wincing and holding his left hip. He was unhurt but thought the ruse worth it. Yafad was left handed and Perad wanted him to reach down and across aiming for a weakness.

Being caught had woken him. He moved in fast and made a rapid series of random feints with his hands. Yafad raised his arms, unsure, and Perad found his wrist, a good hold worth a score, and pulled down. Yafad should have gone to his knee, but he fought it and it cost him his balance, and as he stumbled, Perad let go found two more grips on his other arm. He released his hold and stepped back. His villagers applauded.

"Three, green, called Walvin.

Pleased with the effectiveness of the tactic, Perad repeated the attack. Yafad could not prevent his hands coming up and Perad made exactly the same moves.

"Three, green," came the call.

"You never were a good learner," said Perad.

"You seem to lack variety," said Yafad.

Then he simply charged at Perad, pushing his arms away and wrapping his own arms around Perad's waist, lifting him and throwing him on his back. The lift was an illegal move and incurred a penalty, but it brought a roar from the audience and a smile from the fighters.

The talking stopped then, and the contest became serious. Perad scored steadily with good footwork taking him in and out at speed, feinting and grabbing. But on the few times he made a mistake, his larger opponent would catch him and put him on the floor. The red score mounted. Perad did enjoy his finish, though, getting behind his tiring opponent and putting him on his face in the straw by hauling at his ankles, for his only throw of the contest. Yafad pleased the crowd by coming up with a great mouthful of straw. Walvin called time, and the scorer called the count, a comfortable win to red. They finished with hands on each other's shoulders, foreheads touching. They returned to the banking with their arms around each other's shoulders, and sat to much slapping of backs, banter and ruffling of hair.

They watched the next bout and then walked to the river to bathe away the sweat and ease the bruises. Perad had not wrestled since Spring Feast all those months ago. It made him realize how busy he had been of late with his grandmother's failing health.

"Poisoner rather than traveller?" queried Yafad as they sat drying in the sun on the bank. Even living more than half a day apart, they had shared a friendship since their earliest memories and knew each other's hopes and desires.

"Both, but poisoner first."

"And the Gralt," said Yafad. "I was warned not to burden you with it, but I would like to hear you tell the tale if you can stand it. It is becoming a famous tale and must be changing with each telling. I have heard many versions. Can I hear one with some authority to it?"

So Perad told it; the first he had spoken of that night. Yafad heard it through without interruption, and offered no comment. "Let us return," he said. "It will soon be time for the champions' fights."

"Mine was only a small part. I manufactured a distraction." said Perad.

"It is said that poisoners got their name from the court healers who were given the task of removing their king's enemies," said Yafad as they made their way back. "What you did was what you will always do; that is, use your craft for the benefit of your people. Your intentions were right, your skill was excellent. Be comforted by that."

They watched Baran, a bee keeper whose honey was so good, it was sent all the way to the coast, in spite of him farming on the edge of the valley where the flux was weak, become the wrestling champion of the valley for the fourth year in a row, then went to tea.

It was a good day in a good autumn after a good summer.

With a clear sky and a full moon, Yafad and his father intended walking back to Nerbridge through the night. Yafad had hoped to spend some time in the inn, trying the ale, but it was busy and noisy, and he was still young enough to be intimidated by the atmosphere, so they set off quite soon after full dark. Perad would walk with them to the ridge. For a good way they could hear the sounds of laughter and loud chatter, and they could look back and see the strings of lanterns in the village circle. They met folk in the woods, too; couples and groups of friends enjoying a perfect valley evening.

36

Then the trees thickened, and the ground became more broken with gullies and crags and the village was lost behind them. Patches of stingweed and claw bramble covered the better ground, and detours had to be found. There never had been one path between Nerbridge and Woodall, and the narrow and dividing tracks were easily overgrown and lost, so that the journey was an enjoyable one for more adventurous walkers. Those who wished a less challenging journey, or those with ponies or burdens would take the better tracks to High Dresswell and then follow the river eastwards.

They said their goodbyes after sitting under the moon in a clearing for a while, and Perad turned for home.

It was almost midnight when he reached the village. The circle was clear of folk, and most of the lanterns had burned out. He stood outside the inn door thinking of the night a few weeks ago when a Gralt warrior had taken guard there. He could hear singing in the inn, the slow sombre songs of lost love and lost youth, which so often end a day of celebration. Whoever was in there, Blind Kerim would not be among them.

Perad went round to the back of the inn into the kitchen, ate some ham, and went to his bed.

Chapter 5

It was customary amongst poisoners, as it was with some other crafts, for one newly acquiring his or her position to make a journey across the Valleys to visit others more experienced in the craft. This was a casual affair, loosely organized by elder members of the village councils. It was one gladly undertaken by Perad, always eager to travel. He set off in the early evening, seven weeks after attaining his new position, intending to camp on the high ground between the two valleys, looking forward to dropping down into High Dresswell next day. He had spent many nights camping outdoors, rarely refusing an opportunity, but this night he slept alone in the woods for the first time in his life.

His groundsheet, a patchwork of offcuts of tightly woven cloth, oiled and waterproofed on one side, could be slept on, in, or under depending on the weather, and would even become a tent, fastened to a tree, in wind and rain. This night he slept folded in it with his pack for a pillow, and saw the stars through the canopy each time he awoke. He would have preferred to have found a clearing, but the woods, which had held no threats for the folk of the Valleys until the Gralt, had now taken on a different feel, and he was comforted by the nearness of the trees.

It was late when he woke fully, with the sun already above the peaks of the distant mountains. He prepared a fire and put oats on to boil for breakfast. Even though it was still dry these middle days of autumn, it was now cold on a morning, and Perad found a boulder to sit on and let the sun warm his back. He took his time. To arrive early afternoon was his intention, when valley work was mostly finished, unless the flux was up.

He spread his groundsheet on a bush to let the sun take the moisture drawn overnight from the ground, while he washed his pot in a stream. He trod out the fire and used the water in the pot to make a circle around it. He gathered his equipment, swung his pack onto his shoulders and began walking.

Born to navigate these woods, he took a line directly north without thought or effort. He had chosen to ignore the well defined paths. This direction would take him within sight of the river where he could turn west towards High Dresswell. He stepped over many small streams and fallen trees. At one point he heard an axe in the distance, the only sign of other folk he encountered all morning.

The fine early sky had turned dull, but the thick grey cloud was high and held no rain. Autumn was well advanced, and the colours were striking, in the canopy, on the floor and continually falling around him. The trees thinned a little on these north facing slopes, and the walking was good, and before noon Perad was well down into Dresswell river valley.

He found the higher of the two tracks that linked Nerbridge to High Dresswell and recognized where he was. He had walked this track many times. A knee high and flat topped rock by a small stream suggested a good place to eat. Perad filled his leather drinking pouch and sat on the rock with cheese, bread and mutton. A faint tingling in his feet and ankles told him that the flux was up slightly and a close look showed countless fine tool marks covering the surface of the rock. Someone, perhaps a tanner or bootmaker, must come up here from Nerbridge to work, but not today, Perad thought, the flux would not become strong enough.

The man was much closer than Perad would have liked before he noticed him. There was an instant of fear. Perad found his hand on his knife hilt.

"Sorry. Sorry," said the man. "I have a light step. Sorry if I alarmed you. Dran, traveller, of the Valleys." He placed his hand on the trunk of a tree and leaned there to allow an examination.

"Perad, of Woodall. Poisoner." Perad realized he was proud of the title.

"Yes, I know. Or I strongly suspected so. I have been looking out for you since leaving Woodall this morning." Then he added quickly, "Though not hunting you." He appeared eager to avoid alarming Perad. "I was coming this way. Your uncle mentioned that you were about. Tavit, aleman."

"You know uncle Tavit?" Perad asked. He was puzzled, though there was no danger in this man. His speech was northern valley speech, with some of the cities in it. He clearly was a traveller. The long leather hooded coat could be slept in. Perad's belted tunic was more usual wear for the towns and villages of the Valleys. He was heavily laden. "Dran," said Perad, trying the name. "I have never seen you in Woodall."

"Ah, from time to time," said Dran. "Not for a while though. There is little business for me in your village." He had a large canvas pack over his left shoulder and two long leather rolls over his right shoulder. He stepped a little closer, dropped to his knees and unslung one of the leather packs. He moved well, with an easy strength. It was difficult to judge his age. He kept his face up and his hands in sight. Perad's misgivings began to return.

Dran unrolled the bundle with a flourish which was clearly well practiced. "Knives," he said. "I buy them in the Valleys and sell them where I can. They are good, all flux made."

Perad was impressed. There were perhaps two dozen knives of different sizes, arranged for display in two rows, each held in place by a strap. They were not new, but they were good. "Try the feel of that," said Dran. "I could live for half a year when I sell that in one of the plains cities." He held it by the blade for Perad to take the hilt. It was beautifully balanced, straight bladed, worn and many lifetimes old. Perad had never seen its like, but was sure it was valley made and flux made. "Made for a prince, I shouldn't wonder. Found on a battlefield. I had to work for half a year to make the money to buy that." His friendly smile broke into a genuine grin. Perad grinned back. The knife fit his hand perfectly. It would fit any hand perfectly. He passed it back, hilt first. Dran replaced it and pointed to another, thin and dangerous looking, not a workman's knife. "I'll tell you a tale of that one to make you shiver," he said, "in exchange for a small share of your lunch. Also, I've a good meal in my pack that we can share for tea, if you wish."

"There are those in the cities who will not accept the flux, and believe merely in the craftsmanship of the valley folk. I have met people in Sundorn and in the forest villages of Pordenden who would regard you as a black magician and run away for fear of your evil sorcery," Dran said. He had been asking Perad of his craft, making comparisons with the work of poisoners in other parts. He was easy to speak with.

"And you?" asked Perad who had heard the tales before. They were in sight of the valley bottom, the river now visible through the trees. "What is it that you know?"

"I'm flux born, of Ledarun, though I have no craft to make use of the flux, beyond the fashioning of a decent stew, or a batch of oat cakes."

High Dresswell was a town built around four bridges over a narrow river. They agreed to meet on the lowest of the bridges in the middle of the afternoon, or a little before sunset if either was detained.

Perad had been told to find the poisoner, whose name was Farrod, and introduce himself. His call was expected. Farrod had visited Woodall and grandmother Katada, some years ago, and Perad had seen him, but, only as a small child, and he had not spoken with him. There were streets here where houses leaned against each other in long crooked rows and finding anyone looked difficult, but the first person he asked, a young mother with a baby in a sling and two bags of fruits, changed directions to lead him to a narrow doorway in a large courtyard off what appeared to be the main street of the town. The door was open and Perad took a step in to knock. There was a curtain of beads a little way along a narrow passageway. The curtain was parted and Perad looked up into a long narrow face, pale in the gloom of the interior.

"Perad, of Woodall," he said to the tall, gaunt, cheerless Farrod.

The man looked down at him for a while before speaking. "Piren nuts, two sacks, for pony transport to the plains, winter, damper than usual. A rare and valuable cargo. How would you prepare them?"

Surprised at the man's abrupt manner, but immediately interested in the test, Perad made a quick review, took a deep breathe and formed his reply. This was indeed a valuable cargo, a pocketful of piren nuts was a treasure, two sackfuls would be a royal cargo. More thinking aloud than reciting, Perad gave his answer. "Damp when collected so no gain in drying them first. Sorrow weed and grey willow moss, sun dried but as fresh as possible, a palmful of each in a small tub, a sprinkle of reedginger stirred in, dip the nuts, then dry them on racks, but well away from smoke. That should keep the mould away and keep them fresh for weeks. Dusted with powdered flyfern root to keep the weevils off. Pack them in woollen bags."

Farrod hadn't moved, but continued to look down on him

and slowly nodded his head. "Yes," he said. And then after a while, "Yes," again. Perad thought he heard respect in the voice, though none was to be seen in the face. "But light with the reedginger, piran nuts will pick up any taste." Almost without pause, Farrod continued, "We in the southern valleys don't appreciate enough the value of tree funguses. Learn what you can. I may come and see you in a year's time."

Then Perad was back on the street with an afternoon to spare. He decided on a walk around the outer edge of the town. He crossed three of the bridges, and discovered three inns.

The town straddled the fast narrow river, though with most of the buildings on the south side. Perad spied upstream the remains of a fourth bridge where the river came shooting out of a gorge. He had been here a number of times, passing through or playing with other children in the streets while his uncle conducted business, but he saw it differently now. Woodall was large for a village, as large as some towns, but was called such because of its shape around a circle, and its use of a council of elders. But High Dresswell was much larger.

There were many dogs, mostly a stout untidy breed, always within a stride of their master, good with wild hogs, it was said. There were pigs with brown bristly fur tethered behind buildings. High Dresswell was noted for its skill with pigskin, producing a soft leather valued for gloves and inner boots. Indeed, there was a sharp smell in the air which must have been due to the tanning. His walk attracted glances rather than stares. In Woodall a stranger would be a stranger for only a short time, greeted and accompanied on arrival.

He saw Dran from a distance at one point, his knife packs open on the floor and a group of men looking down, but chose not to join him, and continued his exploration.

He found the courage to try the inn near the town centre.

Youths of his age would not often be found in uncle Tavit's inn, but there were a number here among the older men. Food was being served, never seen in the inn at Woodall, stews and pies, good ones by the smell of them. There was the quiet clatter of pebbles from turnaturn boards. There was even a game of four sided turnaturn, and after buying a half flagon of ale, nervously, for he had never done this before, Perad seated himself at a table within sight of the rack of pebbles of one of the players. He had only ever heard of this form of the game, never seen it played. He considered the complexities of playing three opponents, and decided it was something to explore. There were spectators of the game standing behind the player whose go it was, silently shuffling around the table as the turns progressed.

The inn was large enough for a pot boy, a tiny man with face and hands like bark, old but with a back and stance as straight as a post. He unloaded his collection of platters and pots, and came and sat beside Perad.

"A young traveller," he said, placing his fist on the table between them, a rather formal greeting more used in meetings and to seal deals. "From where and to where?"

Perad copied the gesture, not to have done so would have been rude. "From Woodall, visiting the valleys." He did not offer his name, not having been given one.

"Woodall, eh. We've been hearing a lot of Woodall of late. Did you see the Gralt?"

Perad was aware the room had quietened. Ears, if not heads were turned his way. Their curiosity was natural, but Perad would have preferred to be less visible. "Yes, I did see them. And I hope I never see them again."

"The bodies are hung from trees to rot in the sun and rain, I hear," said the old man.

"No, buried face down in the bog, without wrappings," said Perad, amazed how rumour could be so wrong. "Their

44

clothes and weapons have been taken to the garrison at Parden." Perad, having then been asked to describe the appearance and visit of the warriors, did so, though he offered no mention of his part in the events. After a while, heads began to turn away, the chatter began again and the old pot boy went about his work. Perad finished his ale and left.

As he approached the bridge where he was to meet Dran, a squealing caused him to turn. A pig, large, golden in colour, and wearing a harness, was scrambling by him, sliding down the banking trailing a rope. An old man was sprawling by the track.

"Catch him, catch him," the man shouted to Perad, who leaped forward and stamped on the rope. The pig did not falter and the rope pulled from under his boot and Perad found himself on his back, the rope slithering away among the grasses. He sat up to see the pig splash into the water.

"Pig in the river. Pig in the river," called the man above him.

By the time Perad had made his way to the edge of the water, the pig was rolling on a mud bank well into the river. The flow around the mud bank was strong, and the rope whipped in the current. The length of the rope puzzled Perad. Surely a pig, valuable or otherwise, should be held close. He conceded to himself that he knew nothing of the craft of keeping pigs. Still, the length of the rope helped as its movements brought it close to the bank, affording an opportunity to catch it. His first attempts found him short, unwilling to lean too far over the water. The promise of a soaking did not unduly worry Perad, but having his pack in the river did. He shrugged the pack from his back and heeled it away from the water. Holding onto a clump of grass, he stretched out and caught a loop of the rope. He looked back up the bank. The man was sitting back, watching. He had

45

taken out a knife and appeared to be whittling at a stick. Perad wondered if he was constructing some sort of device required for the rescue of a pig from a river. A group of folk had collected on the far bank. No one was hurrying to assist. Perad stood, holding the rope. The pig rooted in the mud of the bank. Advice was called across the water. The gist of it seemed to be that Perad should pull on the rope. He did so. The pig instantly took to the water in the opposite direction. Off the ridge of mud, it rolled in the current and was taken towards the bridge, and Perad was able to heave and follow until he had the thrashing animal close to the bank. Near the massive wooden support post of the bridge, the river edge was shallow. The pig's feet found the river bed and it fought its way from the water.

Covered in dripping mud, with its colour spoiled, it did not look the magnificent animal it had a few moments ago.

It did look angry. It squinted at Perad. Behind its long lashes, were the meanest eyes Perad had ever seen. And when the beast opened its mouth, Perad was astonished at the size of the teeth. He conceded once again that his knowledge of pigs was lacking somewhat. He placed himself behind the bridge support, and looked towards the owner. He was still sitting, and still with knife and stick in his hands. He was not looking this way. He may have been calling a conversation with someone in the crowd opposite.

Perad gave a pull on the rope and the soft soil under his feet gave way and he slipped and sat heavily. His head came up, and his eyes caught a glint of something in the distance. To the east, where the steep sided valley was lost around a bend, a high shoulder of hillside, dark and tree covered, reached from the ridge to overlook the river. In the shadows amongst the trunks were two figures, tall and cloaked in black, looking down, it seemed, on the town. One appeared, from the angle of its stance, to be leaning on a stick, or a sword perhaps, which reflected a narrow sliver of light. An icy fear filled Perad and froze him. He was unable to move, unable to call out.

The townsfolk lining the bank were all looking his way. No one would have any reason to follow his gaze. No one called an alarm.

His efforts had blurred his vision, and he shook his head and blinked, and when he looked back, the figures were not there.

He did not dare to let go of the rope, and he twisted his head to attempt to wipe his eyes on his shoulders, and when he searched again, there was nothing to be seen but for the trees and the dark spaces between them.

He checked the skyline in case he had the wrong place, and checked again, but still saw nothing.

A little further from the river than he first thought, and a little higher, a gap between the trunks let through a vertical slit of light from the sky behind. Was that all he had seen, shadows and a piece of the sky? The trees there leaned a little. They could have made the darkness between into the shapes of figures. And it was a long way away. He should not have seen faces at that distance.

The pig took a step forward and the rope slackened and Perad clambered to his feet. The slight change in height altered the whole perspective, and when he moved his eyes along the hilltop, he could neither see figures, nor locate the place where they had appeared to be.

The pig pulled backwards again. Enough, thought Perad, weary of the contest. He reached the rope around the bridge support, and quickly fastened it. He thought a while, considered what he did not know of a pig's ability with rope, and added another knot. He placed his foot on the support and leaned back and pulled the knots tight with his full weight. The pig showed more teeth and Perad backed away.

He collected his pack and made his way up the banking. The old man was now nowhere to be seen, and the crowd was dispersing.

Dran was leaning with his elbows on the parapet of the bridge, watching the water flow down towards the plains when Perad approached him.

"I believe you have given rise to a new valley sport," he said, without turning his head. He was working hard to keep the humour out of his voice.

"Is there a curse on the bridge?" Perad asked, examining the rope burns on his palms. "Why did no one cross to help?"

"We decided the pig needed no help. It was doing fine by itself."

Perad made no reply. He decided to not speak of what he may have seen, though he turned to examine the woods once more.

They crossed back to the north side and sat on a log looking back over the river towards the main part of the town. The man was gone. The pig was sleeping. To the east there was nothing to be seen in the woods which should not be there. Dran unwrapped two pies from a cloth and Perad scrambled once more down the steep bank to fill his water bag. He kept a good distance from the pig.

"Well," said Dran, with his mouth full, "could you stand a travelling companion for a while? We are going the same way, and seem to have the same appetites. I can tell stories of far lands and you can tell tales to remind me of youth. And entertain me with heroic animal rescues."

Perad was glad of the offer of company, and said so.

Chapter 6

Perad and Dran travelled north through the Valleys, Perad choosing the route, Dran content to follow. "I have known the entire journey from Woodall to Crag to be covered in three and a half days," said Dran. "I prefer your manner. It is a while since I enjoyed time in the woods."

That morning they had met a family travelling to Farford and had sat to share a meal at the roadside. As they were opening their packs, a line of goats passed them, rich brown and cream in colour, walking primly, the dust of the road clinging to their legs. A young woman with a stick followed. She accepted the offer of food, and retrieved the goats with a short series of whistles which brought them trotting to her, pushing against her legs until she spoke to them and released them to spread into the forest a little way and find their own lunch. They shared talk and news, as well as food, and the gathering grew when a woodcutter and his son came along dragging a sled of logs. Perad enjoyed the company and the conversation.

Back on their journey, they had climbed an outcrop of rock, scrambling on hands and knees at the end, to put themselves above the treetops. Perad had stood for a long time staring at the view.

Although the plains and mountains, west and east, were lost in haze, the north was clear, and the great northern forest could be seen, a dark and unbroken tract rising all the way to the horizon, but for occasional peaks of protruding mountain, and those only visible in the nearer part. Even the ocean, on his one visit to the coast, had not looked so endless.

A good part of his own land could be seen around him, gentler than the forest, patched and more broken, with the lines of at least two rivers visible. Dran stood with him to identify what landmarks they could.

The six valleys in the eastern corner of the land of Tarodash contained seventeen named towns and villages, a number of tiny hamlets and many scattered homesteads. Travel between the valleys was common for many reasons and no town was more than an easy day's walk from a neighbour.

The main paths were well worn and straightforward to follow. Roads and tracks along the rivers to the plains would suit a cart, but to travel between the valleys required walking, or a very good pony. Away from the paths, particularly on the south facing slopes, the woodland could become dense, almost impenetrable. There were areas where the trees fought with rocks and boulders and the slopes became small broken cliffs. Some of the ridges were chains of ragged hill where passes had to be found.

There were also very many small streams which could be taken in a stride, or at times jumped, but crossing the main rivers which shaped the valleys required bridges and even an occasional ferry where the rivers widened near to the plains.

Perad had visited all but the two northernmost valleys accompanying his uncle, or anyone who would endure the presence of an obedient and inquisitive child on their journey. During his years, to his knowledge, grandmother Katada had never left the Woodall valley on poisoner business, and uncle Tavit had been happy to undertake the errands she required, in addition to his own.

Not all towns and villages had a poisoner, some of the smaller ones sharing with a neighbouring town. Even then, a poisoner in the Valleys, as with similar crafts of service such as healer or midwife, was not often a full time livelihood. There was no payment for the work, other than that of returned favours and the support of the council when needed. These folk of the woods normally relied on their own fine herbcraft, and a poisoner would only be referred to when problems occurred or an unusual circumstance was encountered. Perad himself would in all likelihood become a brewer and innkeeper, and poisoner for Woodall valley, serving the homesteads as well as his village.

In all, Perad had been given a list of ten poisoners he was expected to visit, and two whom he should not visit, although he had not been told why. He had a letter of introduction which he should not need initially, for the first two encounters had been arranged by a member of the village council during an outing on the previous week.

Most craftsfolk would train an apprentice or two, young family members or those who showed an interest or aptitude. Some would leave to take work in the cities, or to live a life outside the Valleys. "I have seen poisoners in a city," Dran told him as they descended into Marben valley, "who earn a living by selling mixes. They would sell from a room, or a stall run by an assistant. They would buy materials from traders and mix them and sell them in glass bottles and leather pouches. A poisoner in a city would sell anything a customer asked for. A poisoner in a city would sell poison. You have made the passing journey to the ocean?"

"Yes," said Perad. "The spring before last. A score of us from the three valleys, and some fathers and some council members. Uncle Tavit came. We took the southern route and passed through Kardeff, and Portharden where we saw the ships which sail the ocean. I shall journey on one of those ships one day."

"I do not doubt it," said Dran. "At my passing we took the northern route to Hadraada, but I have been to Portharden at times."

"And have you sailed?"

"Once, to the islands. I had business there, once." But Dran offered no more and Perad would not ask.

Marben, noted for its paper making was upriver from Marben Whitestone. The two towns shared a rivalry which some other towns of the Valleys envied, competing in the skills of pastimes and sports, as well as in crafts. Each town would claim to provide the best of its products and would compete for prices in the cities. The games, races and throwing contests where the two towns fought for honour each summer solstice week attracted visitors from the other valleys.

It was said that on the plains and in the cities the folk there would work at their chosen or given living from dawn to dusk. Perad did not know if this was true. He had certainly seen enormous amounts of inactivity and even idleness, on his journey to the ocean and his few visits to the farming towns to the west of the Valleys. In the Valleys, work was done when required, and not working was enjoyed when the chosen tasks completed. At the times when the flux was high, and at seasonal times when work was necessary, there could be long days of toil. But in the Valleys, the days were to be lived in, not worked through.

Marben valley river was fast and constant, and the two towns had developed, more than anywhere else in the Valleys, the use of machinery. Perad had been here before and was much anticipating the view as they made the last steep descent. It seemed from the path above that parts of the river had been trapped into many pools, dark and still, from which, on the lower side the water would shoot out of a stone gully to turn a waterwheel, or to vanish into a stone building which appeared to have been fashioned out of the steep rock of the river's edge. This was a great contrast to Woodall valley, much of which was flat and often marshy, and a wonder to Perad.

There were two poisoners attending to the needs of the town, and Perad had been told that he must not leave the town without visiting both. His instruction was to visit the man called Gartan first. Perad had a memory of seeing Gartan before, on an errand of his grandmother, with uncle Tavit.

He was a kind and gentle old man, who remembered Perad as a young child, knew of the passing of his grandmother and asked of the welfare of a number of folk of Woodall. Gartan, it turned out, had travelled much in his time, and knew a great deal of the happenings in the Valleys. He knew of the attack of the Gralt on Woodall and speculated on the precautions of the rulers of Tarodash to protect its boundaries. He offered no advice on the craft of the poisoner, beyond an invitation. "When you have completed your tour I would be pleased if you could return here. You could accompany me back to Woodall. There are folk in your village I have not seen for some time. I would enjoy the journey, and we could share talk of our craft. Then you could show me how you work, and I could offer suggestions." Perad was delighted and humbled by the offer.

The other poisoner of Marben was Farana, an extraordinarily beautiful young woman with a pale face and long pale hair in braids, and wide dreamy eyes and a dreamy manner. Perad found her sitting beside a pool in a garden of herbs and flowers, having been led to her through a large stone house on the south western edge of the village, by what appeared to be an ancient servant. She was trailing her hand in the water and had a collection of flowers in her lap. She seemed to Perad a princess from the ancient stories and he could not, at first, take his eyes from her face, until he realized she was as empty as the bowls which she had left unused on the wall of the pond. She gazed into the water and clearly lacked any interest in Perad and his visit. She was polite enough, though, to tell him of the properties of the herbs and blooms in her garden which she believed to be specific to Marben valley, and she knew her craft well. But she soon tired of the conversation and indicated so by simply ceasing to speak. Perad stood and the old man appeared from the shadows of a porch to lead him away. He stopped Perad by his arm at the door to the road and spoke. "I wished to see my daughter a poisoner before I died, and so passed the position to her. Did I do well?" His voice was strained.

"If she works at her craft, you will be proud of her," was the best that Perad could manage.

Dran had not arrived when Perad reached the agreed meeting place, the lowest of the three bridges of the town. Perad leaned on the parapet in the centre of the bridge and watched the water hurry down stream. The river, having left the Valleys, flowed to lake Lan on the plains, and by the farming and trading city of Ahlan, which Perad had never visited, and then to the ocean. Perad let his thoughts flow with the current.

Dran had a companion with him, a cousin, he was told. They had approached striding along the bridge. It was the first time Perad had seen Dran without his packs. "Supper provided for us tonight," said Dran. "And a bed." This news suited Perad, although the evening did not. Supper was platters of cold meats and roasted roots and lots of ale in the inn of Dran's cousin. It became busy and noisy and any conversation was soon lost in the din. Perad left early. Bed was a reed filled pallet in an attic above the inn with the sound of the customers below. He had spent his life in circumstances much like these, but this night it felt bleak and wrong. He would have preferred to be in the woods beneath the stars.

He had expected Dran to take the other pallet in the attic, but when he awoke Dran was not there and the blanket was still folded.

There was no one about when he went down. He supposed that he should earn his supper and bed, and set about clearing the remains of the night's happenings. Uncle Tavit would not have gone to bed leaving his inn in this state, but then uncle Tavit would never have had the trade that this inn had. The drinking vessels here were pot, as they were in almost all of Tarodash, Perad believed. He was used to wooden flagons, and was fearful of breaking the pots, and carried then carefully, two at a time. He could not see where they were to be washed, so contented himself with lining them on the counter top. He found a mop and swabbed the floor. There were no cloths about so he lifted the mop to wipe the table tops, realized that he was doing no more than spreading the spilled ale in a thin layer over every surface, so decided on a better look.

He found a kitchen behind the counter where the ends of a fire smoldered deep red in a large fireplace. It was cozy and pleasant in the kitchen, there was a lamp hung from the wall, and a smell of fried food. There was an arrangement whereby steaming water dripped from an iron pipe above the fire into a waist high stone trough at the side. The water in there was hot. Perad filled the mop bucket, found cloths folded by the sink and went to work properly. He cleaned the tables and floor, and arranged the tables, seats and benches.

On one of his returns to the kitchen, he found he was being watched. In the shadowed corner opposite the door was an enormous seat, padded and with high sides. Perad had barely noticed the seat, and had certainly missed the tiny figure huddled in a blanket deep in the chair. It was the eyes, open and catching the yellow glint of a lamp which made Perad stop and let go of the mop. He grabbed at it and caught it before it could clatter to the floor. The steps he took in doing so took him nearer to the figure. It was an old lady. She reached out a hand and touched Perad's sleeve. "Too young to be working for your ale," she said. Her voice was high and cracked, but held friendship. "So who are you?"

"Perad, of Woodall. Travelling the Valleys. I had a bed for the night and I was up early. I am doing what I can to repay your hospitality."

"Not my hospitality, although I would have extended it, had I the opportunity. Have you a craft?"

"Poisoner." He felt bound to add, "Although I am new to the position."

"If you are new you may not yet have been taught the cure for old age." She smiled then, and her eyes danced among the deep wrinkles. "Still, I should not complain. To fall asleep in the evening and wake in the morning in the same chair is better than to not wake at all, is it not?"

"I shall let you know when I am old enough for it to happen to me," replied Perad, liking this old woman who could find the enthusiasm to joke with a young stranger.

"Yes, poisoner, I will await your report. You have your powders?"

"I have."

"Then a hot drink of herbs to improve my mood. I have been lost in gloom, of late."

So she sipped at a simple mixture of thornpepper and blueberry in a flagon of hot water while Perad washed pots and told her of his home and his travels, and she interrupted him with comments and questions. She had a remarkable knowledge of the Valleys and its people.

At some point Dran arrived. Perad looked up to see him leaning in the doorway. He could have been there some time.

"So you are with this rascal, then. Why did you not tell me?" she asked Perad when he greeted Dran by name.

"He has been in sounder company with me than his present company," said Dran before Perad could answer.

56

He could only stand and grin as the two exchanged insults for a good while.

"Help me to my feet, new poisoner, and I shall make you a breakfast. I must provide my share of the welcome." She gripped his wrist and pulled herself up. Perad kept hold of her arm as she directed him to the oven between the fire and the counter top. He was told to sit at the table while she cooked. Perad, brought up by his uncle, had never seen anything to match her kitchen skill. In a very short time Perad and Dran were feasting on slices of pork and liver, giant mushrooms and eggs fried in fat so hot they still sizzled on the platter. There were oatcakes browned in the fire and buttered to accompany the meal, and a warmed loaf.

"Will that persuade you to stay another meal?" she said, when Perad sat back. Dran was still eating and Perad waited for him to look up to catch his eye.

"Yours to decide," said Dran. "It is your journey."

"Thank you, then. But I shall continue. Farford is my next destination."

"Then I shall not delay you," said Dran, folding the last of his breakfast into a piece of loaf to eat as he stood and reached for his packs.

"And I shall see you to the bridge. Pass my shawl, Dran."

Concern showed in Dran's face. "There is no need for that, Herana."

"The need is mine, young man. Take my arm, Perad."

Still early, the town was busy when they stepped out, busier than Woodall would have been on a day with no flux. "Do not wait, I shall only be a moment," said Dran, turning and going back into the inn.

"You shall need the east bridge to Farford. This way." The old lady nodded to the right and they moved slowly along. Dran joined them and they reached the bridge which was a stone one, arched and strong. The river was narrow here and churned beneath it.

The old lady held Perad by his arm and squeezed, and reached towards Dran. He had to bend so that she could touch his cheek. "Travel well," she said. "Come back to see me soon. And you, young poisoner."

She turned and called, "Come on, then, whoever you are. No need to hide behind a wall. You may as well walk back with me." She faced Dran with a smile. "Who did you fetch to watch over me? Is it Badat? Yes here he is." A young man came from behind the corner of a building to take her arm. He had a wide grin for all three, and love in his eyes for the old lady.

It was a steep climb out of the valley, which took their breath, and they rested near the end. Perad looked back through the trees and thought how much he liked Marben and how he would look forward to going back.

Chapter 7

Sadral valley and Crag valley, where Dran counted his home of Ledarun, were the two most northerly of the Valleys, particularly noted for their metal working. Perad had never been this far north and was much looking forward to it. Crag, in particular excited him, bordering the great northern forest, mysterious and vast, perhaps endless, carrying on to the limit of the world. He would take a walk into it, and camp for a night there.

This was close to Dran's world, and Perad let him choose the course now, though Dran claimed no worthwhile memory of the paths they were using. Still, his aim was good, and as they descended a steep slope they saw below them their path widen and join a road from the west which curved down into the large sprawling town of Sadral. Indeed Sadral and its neighbour to the west, Senrak, had so many buildings along the road between them that they looked from the path above to be one long untidy place.

Some of the steeper track had been fashioned into steps, and as Dran neared the bottom of one series, he stumbled and reached for a sapling to steady himself. Perad, a stride behind, sprung to his assistance. It was a ruse. With their heads close, Dran spoke in an urgent whisper. "We are being watched. Low to your right, the patch of stoneroot bush."

"Yes I have seen them. Two. They hid as we rounded the last bend."

"Let me sit," Dran said aloud.

"Who are they?" said Perad. He kept his voice low.

"I cannot see. Sit with me. Do not release your pack. Be ready to act."

Perad made a pretence of refastening his boot, placing his head in a good position to watch.

Dran took out his knife and picked up a stick and began to whittle. Perad began a proper refastening of his boots. The two figures in the bushes did not move.

A good while passed. Dran's stick was almost gone. Perad tired of his uncomfortable position and leaned back.

"Whatever they are, they are not the Gralt," Perad said quietly.

"No, they are not."

"Whoever you are, there in the trees, you are not enemies," said Dran out loud. "Nor are we. Come out."

There was some movement and whispers.

"State your name and business," came a voice. The speech was of the northern valleys. Perad relaxed. Dran became angry.

"Do not skulk in the bushes. We are of the Valleys. Come out and greet weary travellers."

"State your name and business." This time the voice was less certain.

"Dran, Perad, travelling north. And hoping for customary hospitality." Dran was on his feet.

"And your business?"

"Enough!" Dran strode towards the bushes. "We are of the Valleys and are visiting Sadral. The last time I was here, that would have brought a warmer greeting."

A young man stepped from the shadows. He wore a black tunic and a round leather helmet. He carried a spear of newly cut wood and with a new forged tip. His face was red.

"We were sent to watch the fork in the paths. You were the first to come along." He called over his shoulder. "Quarl, come out."

When Quarl appeared, he held his spear in front of him until he saw Dran's face.

"And what were you sent to watch for?" asked Dran, his manner softening.

"The governors have become worried by rumours, of late, and wish to keep a watch on our borders. We have been told to report movements."

"Sadral does not have borders," said Dran. "And were you told to point spears at these movements?

"Ah, no matter. My apologies. I am Dran, trader, of Ledarun. Perad here, is of Woodall, and is visiting your poisoner. If I come upon your governors, I will tell them you are doing well what was asked of you."

Perad expected the air to be filled with smoke from the furnaces and the sound of hammers on anvils, but on entering Sadral, it seemed no different in manner from the other larger towns he had seen.

By asking passing locals, they found the poisoner, Fardrel by name, in a hut on the eastern edge of the town, more in the woods than among the streets. Dran turned and left, and Perad walked clear of the trees and stood quietly. It seemed a strange habitation for the poisoner of such a large place, a ramshackle and disorderly looking construction in amongst the trees. In front of the house was an old man with grey hair and a brown wrinkled face sitting on a log trimming the bark from one of a pile of small branches of a tree which Perad did not recognize. The man held up each strip to the sky and peered at it. Perad was reluctant to disturb his concentration, unsure whether to move forward or wait until he stopped work. He was saved a decision when the man noticed him and motioned him forward with a movement of his head.

"Perad, new poisoner, of Woodall."

The man looked up sharply and held Perad's eyes. An instant of sadness crossed the old face. "Woodall. Then Katada is gone."

"She was my grandmother."

"I knew her. It is a long time since I last saw her. And you are the new poisoner. You have the old book?"

"Yes, but not with me," Perad said.

"The oldest of them all. I would have liked to see that. Katada would allow no one near it. She was a strong one." He smiled broadly then. "Stronger than I was. And the book passed directly to you?"

Perad nodded. He had never asked of his mother and father, and it struck him that this old acquaintance of his grandmother may possess some knowledge. That it had never been spoken of at home, had led him to believe that his uncle and his grandmother would have been uncomfortable with the discussion.

But this place and this time were not the ones for discussing it. The old poisoner must have sensed this. "Plant a twig for me when you return," he said, closing the subject.

"Sit and tell me what you have seen. I travel little these days." So Perad told him of the journey across the Valleys and of life in the southernmost valley, and the edge of the desert and his passing journey to the ocean. Each time Perad stopped to ask the old poisoner of his experiences, he would receive the reply, "Travel there yourself young Perad. You can only see through your own eyes." He would sit and smile gently then, and listen, as he revisited places he had known in his life, now to be seen only through Perad's eyes. The afternoon passed and Perad's mouth became dry with the talking and a time came when he had no more to say.

The old poisoner reached down and picked a strip of the bark he had been working on from the pile at his feet. "This is a forest tree we call Drappa. Based on old rumour, I have discovered that soaked in nothing more than salt, it is a fine remedy for burns of the skin. It lets the light through, see, which helps with the healing." He handed it to Perad. "I have three apprentices, one of them is good. I hope he will continue my researches."

Was the old man telling him that research should be part of the work of a poisoner? Until this trip, he had never considered that. Grandmother Katada would never have considered it. Or perhaps she would have when she was younger.

They said their goodbyes. The old poisoner bent back to his work and Perad turned to make his way down the track. He realised then that he and Dran had not arranged a meeting place.

He need not have worried. Dran was sitting with his knees up and his back to a tree at the bottom of the track. He seemed asleep and had, in all probability, been there a long time. But he rose quickly as Perad approached. "I would like you to return home, back to Woodall," he said. There was concern in his voice. It was not a request, Perad realized. "If you permit it, I would like to accompany you. There is talk of the Gralt. In the forest. It is almost beyond belief that the Gralt should be in the forest. I would like to get you home."

"What of Ledarun?" Perad asked. "Do you not wish to see your home?"

"It would be better if we went south," said Dran. He waited then, looking intently at Perad. There would be no arguing with him.

"What have you found out?" he asked.

"Fur trappers from Ledarun not far into the forest encountered three armed warriors. The trappers hid and heard foreign speech. The description they gave leaves no question. That was two days ago, and news has just reached here. The trappers are to be trusted. Two loggers are missing, also, but that is less reliable. I have little doubt. I believe the Gralt are in the forest, at the least. We should go back now. The world is less safe."

"What can the Gralt want? Is there an army to invade us?"

"My best guess is that the Gralt nation is awakening and requires new lands. If they were exploring, they would not send warriors. Or perhaps they would. According to some old stories, they know only conflict. They could only know of life as warriors."

Perad was remembering their manner, their arrogance. "They are not explorers," he said.

"They behave as if they do not know resistance," said Dran. "We must oppose them. And that will happen. Soldiers are being recruited and trained. Still, we are some way away from an army, and the world is less safe until we know the purpose of the Gralt and how to deal with them. You should go home."

It required no more than shouldering their packs and setting off. They took a track on the hill above the towns to avoid any delay. Dran asked if they could go by Darkhope and skirt the edge of the plain. It would take a day longer, but should be safer, he said. Perad had no objection.

They camped that night below the ridge looking back down on Sevenedge valley having walked until well after dark. Perad's spirits lifted when Dran lit a fire. The danger could not be so bad if they could risk being seen from a distance, and it was now late in autumn and the nights were cold.

It rained in the night and they set off next morning wearing their groundsheets as cloaks to dry them. They went without breakfast, hoping to find a meal at an inn before mid morning.

Dran had miscalculated, though. The ridge where they had camped was only the first of a number of ridges, and not the high point between the valleys. It was late in the morning when they dropped into Darkhope and the inns were filling for lunch. Dran found them a platter of hot meats and warm bread which they ate standing at a stone counter. The inn was noisier and busier than any place he had ever seen, and talk was impossible. They ate quickly, and drank water at a stone trough by a well in the market square.

Much of the traffic from the north western parts of the Valleys used the bridge at Darkhope. It was the largest in the Valleys, a great wooden structure that creaked and groaned and swayed as laden carts crossed. It had been washed away many times and rebuilt. The folk of Darkhope boasted of their ability to keep the roads open and to cope with a temperamental and dangerous river.

Dran sought news from the bridgemaster, a barrel of a man who controlled access to the crossing on the northern side and who greeted Dran by name. Yes, he had heard the story of the Gralt in the forest and knew of the attack on Woodall, that was all. "If they come, they will not cross my bridge," he said, at which Dran laughed. Perad did not.

They bought food at a stall to last them at least to Dresswell, and by mid afternoon were looking down on the plains. Here the Valleys and the flux ended and the great plains of Tarodash began. They could see, looking west, a patchwork of fields, walled and fenced and ploughed and sown, all the way to the curve of the river just below the horizon.

The rugged and untidy hills of the Valleys gave way to rounded and smoother uplands where the trees were thinner and the bushy undergrowth replaced by rough grasses, ferns and gorses, before finally falling to the plain. They camped a little below the trees on a shoulder of hill overlooking the plain with a view of the river. Dran pointed out lake Lan where two rivers met, and the nearer towns of Ardford and Watermeetings. The setting sun reflected off the lake and reddened the narrow lines of smoke rising from farms dotted about the plain. They lit a fire and watched the sun down as their stew boiled. As the darkness grew, red and yellow sparks of autumn fires filled the pool of darkness in the plain and white points of stars filled the sky to the distant wide horizon. It seemed to Perad the most gentle and agreeable place in the world.

When he woke he was chilled to the bone. The blades of grass near his face were edged with frost. When he sat up it was to see a sparkling whiteness cover over all the land. His breath was white smoke against the startling blue sky. Dran was reheating the stew on a small fire and watching three figures approach up the hill. "There is no alarm. It is merely a farmer and his dogs. I have watched them leave yonder farmyard. He must have seen our fire and wondered about us."

They stood to greet him. The sun was just risen behind them, and their shadows stretched impossibly long and thin down the hill and onto the plain, blue against the frost. The farmer stopped some distance away and leaned on his stick, stout and steady, and his dogs which had followed at his heels scampered away to sniff the ground. Their feet left a tangle of bruised frosted grass about the hillside.

"With tales of the Gralt about, I thought to check on you. You, I take it, are not the Gralt?"

"Nor are you," replied Dran. "So sit with us and share our breakfast. We have a fine stew no more than a week old."

"It is long past my breakfast, but it does smell good. If you load your bowls, I can take from the pot." He came forward and sat by the fire looking back over his land.

Dran placed the pot by the farmer and spooned stew into two bowls and Perad took out his knife to cut a strip of bark from a small log rescued from the edge of the fire. He trimmed the corners and fashioned a serviceable spoon to hand to the farmer.

"Valley folk," he said, nodding his approval at Perad's skill. "You have chosen a cold place to spend a night."

Dran had a full mouth, so Perad answered. "We love our woods, but we can also enjoy an open sky."

"And make sure no one can sneak up on you." The farmer tipped the pot to get his spoon in and began eating. "These are worrying times."

"The Gralt, then," said Dran, "what have you heard of them?"

"I have heard that they are marching across Tarodash as an army, five abreast. The centre one of each row is a fearsome warrior, and he is flanked by spirit warriors of his ancestors. They carry mighty swords, but no shields, for arrows pass though them without causing harm. I have heard that they cross rivers by walking, even though the waters cover their heads. I have heard that they can appear at will out of shadows, murder in less than a blink of the eye, and return to the shadows. I have heard that their only vulnerability is that they are consumed by smoke from a fire, that smoke will seek them out and wrap around them and they become smoke themselves and are dispersed. I have heard that their cloaks take the colour of their surroundings so that they can approach unseen. I have heard that they wear black boots."

"And how much of what you hear do you believe to be the truth?" asked Dran, unable to hold back a grin.

"The farmer matched his grin. "I doubt their boots are black," he said.

He ate the remains of the pot without speaking. When he had finished, he folded the spoon and placed it in his pocket. "I shall show my wife that," he said. "We know of the Gralt attack on Woodall, which by your voice, young man, is near to your home." He looked at Perad. "And we have just heard of sightings in the forest. We believe there are Gralt warships near to the southern coast and we know of attacks near Parden."

Dran sat up. "Attacks at Parden. What is this? What have you heard?" All trace of good humour had vanished.

The farmer spoke slowly now, choosing his words carefully. Dran was clearly alarmed. "There are reports from farms to the west of folk from near Parden and the Rindar hills fleeing to their kin in the north. I have heard this passed through a number of tellers and not directly. The reports seemed clear, though."

Dran was already on his knees fastening his packs. Perad spread the fire with his boot and eased up sods of grass and earth to cover the sparks. The farmer, caught up with the haste, pulled up grass to wipe out the cooking pot. He stood and passed it to Perad. "My thanks for the breakfast. Travel with care. There will be fog here soon, with sun on the frost and cold air pushing down the hills. I do not know if it will help or hinder you." He was right. The floor of the plain had vanished beneath a flat topped cloud of mist, climbing the hillside and thickening as they watched.

"You have a wagon?" asked Dran. "It would do no hurt to prepare it for travel. Look to the river if matters go badly. Take care." He spun around to check the campsite, faced south and strode down the slope. Perad watched the farmer take his own route down to his farm. With no command that Perad could see, the dogs raced to the heels of their master. Within strides, the fog closed about them and they disappeared, and moments later Perad, following Dran, felt himself wrapped by the fog, not safe in its blanket, but trapped in a small space with peril all around.

Chapter 8

"Careful now." Dran put out an arm to stop Perad. "The river must be close by." They had descended the hill and drifted out into the plain for better walking, but the fog was even thicker here, and there had been the walls and fences of farmland to hinder them. Now, more open land scattered with reeds and rushes announced the nearness of water. "A more pleasant day and we may have forded the river. Not in this, though."

It was cold and damp and Perad watched the ground with care. This was not his woodland and he was ill at ease. He did not want to stumble into water and soak his boots or his clothes. Dran changed direction, turning a little to their right, moving further into the plain. He hoped to find a farmer to take them across the river, rather than make the trek eastwards to the bridge at Marben Whitestone. "Many farmers have accumulated lands on both sides of this river. Crossing it is a part of their daily work," he had explained. "Here, we may already be in luck."

A long, low stone building thatched with reeds loomed in front of them. The ground to their left fell quickly and Perad thought he could see a glint of water. Dran knocked on the door and stepped back. It was answered by an old woman holding a dog in one arm and a roll of cloth in the other. Her eyes were friendly but she did not speak.

"We are looking to cross the river," said Dran. "Do you have a vessel and someone to take us, or should we try elsewhere?"

"Aljed will assist you," she said, inclining her head to

indicate where they should go. She stood beaming and said no more.

Dran gave his thanks and they walked to the corner of the building. There was a large door, partly open. Dran pushed at it and called, "Aljed," into the gloom broken only by the yellow light of a candle in a lantern. Perad peered around Dran's shoulder to see the old farmer kneeling by a beast of a species of horned cattle which he did not recognize. He was finishing a cast of mud and straw on the beast's front leg. He smoothed down the last handful and wiped his hands on the floor. The cast would not take, though. The beast did no more than adjust its weight and the mud split and fell away, taking two wooden splints with it. The old man rose slowly and stood back shaking his head, and as he did so, he caught sight of his visitors and turned to face them. The beast, unwilling to put weight on the injured leg, stood with its head down. "I can fix that," said Perad.

Aljed did not respond. Perad had unbelted his tunic and dropped his pack to the floor, but the farmer remained in the way. He cupped his hands behind his ears and looked at Dran, then at Perad. "He is deaf," said Dran, at the same moment that Perad understood. Dran picked up the lantern and held it at face height. Aljed turned to watch his mouth. "He is a poisoner from the Valleys," Dran said, loudly and carefully. "He can fix the cast."

Perad held open his tunic to show the rows of pouches, unsure if they would indicate a poisoner in these parts. The farmer nodded once and moved back. Dran placed the lantern on the floor close to the beast's leg. Perad knelt and pulled the pail of mud towards him. He picked up the spoiled cast and wiped the mud from the splints, flat wooden sticks, and found the cloth used as bandage within the mud. Dran and Aljed found and upturned pails to sit on, placing them to watch the work.

"Bloodroot and freeherb," said Perad, speaking to himself as he often did when working with his powders. "That will help the mud stick, and fairygrass root will speed its setting." He reached into pouches with fingers and thumb to draw out amounts to be sprinkled into the mud. He used one of the splints to stir it. In the poor light, it did not look any different. He pulled fresh straw from the pile and used his knife to cut it into pieces the width of his hand and stirred these into the mud. He cut more straw, half the length, and more, half that length, to be added to the mixture. He nodded slowly at the result.

The skin of the animal leg was not broken, but a spongy swelling below the knee showed where the damage was. He did not know what the injury was and could only apply the splint as the old farmer had intended. He dipped the strip of cloth in the pail and began to wrap it around the leg, fastening the splints at either side of the swelling. He worked as tightly as he dared and covered the whole of the lower leg. Even without the flux, his hands were quick and accurate.

He spoke to Dran over his shoulder. "My uncle says of me that if a task needs doing, I will do it. He also says of me that if a task does not need doing, I will do it. I know we are in a hurry, but here is something I can help with. I would feel bad if I did not try."

"We are not in too much of a hurry that we can not stop to help someone in need. Particularly someone of whom we are going to ask for help ourselves." Dran watched in silence for a while. "How often are you required to do this?"

"Oh, I have never done this before. But I have been taught enough to know what can be done with what is available. And all the powders I carry are flux collected and flux made." He scooped handfuls from the pail and let much of the mud drain from the straw. The mixture was already sticky and stayed where he applied it. When the cast was shaped he covered and

71

smoothed it with the remaining mud. He wiped his hands on the pile of straw as the old farmer had done.

"It will …" Perad began, then remembered. He stood back from the lantern and lifted his head and faced the farmer. "The cast will fall away in ten or twelve days of damp weather. You may have to unwind the bandage yourself." He could not stop himself using his hands to make the motions of his described actions. The farmer never looked at his hands, but watched his mouth, and nodded.

Dran took the lantern and held to his own face. "Can you take us across the river?" he asked. Aljed nodded again. The beast had a loose collar of thick rope around its neck, and the old farmer took that in one hand and the beast's ear in the other, and led it towards the door. He used his chin to indicate the lantern and the place on the floor away from the straw where Dran was to place it. Perad hurried to open the door. He had to lift it to clear an obstruction.

In the light outside he turned to watch the beast walk, assessing his work. He wondered if he should have extended the cast further above the knee. "It has a peculiar gait," he said, "but that may be its manner. I do not know this breed." The farmer appeared unconcerned.

They were led down a slope and stopped at the river where a rope was looped over a stout post. It hung down into the river and a few strides downstream from the post came up out of the water and was fastened to an iron hoop secured to a construction of boards. This river craft was about the size of, and similar in appearance, Perad realized, to the floor of his attic bedroom. The whole thing dipped as the farmer led the beast onto it and showed with his eyes that they were to follow. Dran stepped on and turned to laugh out loud at Perad's hesitation. "The young explorer who will one day sail the ocean should not be afraid of a raft on the Marben river."

"Wary, rather than afraid," Perad answered. His attempted

smile still faltered a little as he mounted the craft and felt it move. "Ships are built for the ocean. This, I suspect, was built to be a barn door."

Even with the thick fog, he could see the far bank no more than a dozen strides away. He did not see what action the farmer took, but the craft moved slowly out into the river. The rope lifted from the surface in a dark, dripping, shallow curve. The water was smooth and the current gentle and they swung gradually towards the southern bank.

The water lapped. For a few heartbeats it was companion to them on its journey from the mountains to the ocean. The mist swirled and both banks were lost to view, and Perad felt the uniqueness of the situation, the two of them with the old man and his injured animal in the middle of Marben river, on a boat of boards, in the fog and the peace, and he felt the sheer wonder of it all.

Dran caught his eye and knew his thoughts completely. "All of life is full of simple moments of wonder and delight. It is not even necessary to travel to find them; merely to have your mind open to them," he said quietly.

Aljed seemed to be nodding in agreement, perhaps hearing the thoughts, for he could not have caught the words, or perhaps merely with the movement of the raft.

They bumped softly into the southern bank and the old farmer dropped a loop of rope over a stake and pulled the beast by its ear onto the land. Dran handed him a coin as they stepped off. Each of them raised a hand as a gesture of parting and disappeared into the fog.

Chapter 9

A gentle breeze from the south west worked with the sun to thin the fog to a mist and promised to remove it altogether. A high rounded hill, outlined against the brilliant blue sky, faced them, and rather than go round it Dran considered the view to be worth the climb. He had spoken little since crossing the river.

"You are more than a trader in old knives," Perad said as he sat on bare rock high above the great plains of Tarodash. The air was clearing quickly, but for ribbons and pools of mist along the line of the rivers and in the lowest ground. The Marben river was to their right, carrying water from the mountains and the valleys behind them, to meet the far curve of the Darkhope river at lake Lan, a day and a half distance to the northwest. There was the city of Ahlan beyond the lake, but Perad could not make it out. He wondered how high he would have to be to see the ocean. He looked to identify the place where they had crossed the river, but could not do so.

He had been cleaning the rust from one of Dran's knives, and handed it back. It was a beautiful thing; handle made from some dark root wood, worn smooth from many generations of use, the metal of the blade a dull red colour, a material Perad had never seen before. He had tried a number of mixes before he found an effective one, and he had both of his rolls and his vest of pouches spread on the ground. He put on his vest and tunic and knelt to pack his rolls.

Dran had scanned the plain endlessly since they had emerged from the mist, and even more intently as they had gained height. Now he stood on the tallest of the rocks on the summit of the hill, pointing out the places he knew. He made Perad stand beside him to see far in the north a faint line of darkness which was Porenden, an inhabited strip north of the Sadral river which set the boundary of the great forest.

Perad sat again and looked up. "What are you looking for? What are you?"

Dran made one more slow turn before sitting beside Perad. "In truth, only a little more than a trader in old knives. Do not be disturbed when I tell you that I work for the court of the brother princes. You could call me a spy, some do. But it is much less than that. A spy watches the enemy, and we have no enemy to watch. Or had not. I travel a lot as I trade. I have been asked to report on what I see. I get paid a little in expenses. Until a year ago, until sightings of the Gralt, it was no more than that. Whenever I returned to Gorenden, I made a report to ministers. Now I report at any garrison I encounter, and my reports are added to others and passed on to those charged with organising the defence of Tarodash."

"A watcher, then. You do not spy on the people of Tarodash?" asked Perad.

"I do not," said Dran. "The brother princes are good rulers, the best for many generations. They never make a decision without advice, lots of advice. And they do not surround themselves with followers. They send for and ask those who know and see. Knowing their kingdom and its people is important to them. They wish to be guardians and governors of Tarodash, not overlords. It is important to them to find out what is happening in their kingdom. Communication has suffered in past years. They wish to improve matters. Believe me, if they wanted to know of the properties of woodland mosses in one of the smaller southern valleys, they may even send for you.

"I make a report to one who collects and makes reports to the princes. It is less even than it sounds. It is only that I travel this way a lot, and not many do, except for busy traders. At times I have been sent on missions. That is how I have been to the islands. All I do is look and report on the welfare of good folk."

"And what have you seen on this journey?" asked Perad. "What will you report back?"

"That the good people of the Valleys may be among the first to face the threat of the Gralt. My task, of late, has been to sift rumour. Though events seem to have overtaken me. If the Gralt are in numbers at Parden, we can be a little clearer of their intent. I do not think they are here for trade. They had been seen in many places on the edges of Tarodash, but no one knew where they were coming from. An invasion is suspected, and our preparations are urgent. We need to construct an army in order to defend ourselves. But first we need to know the nature of the threat." He was silent for a while. Perad considered what had been told.

"How did you become this watcher?"

"I had no particular craft as a youth, and worked as a carter between the valley and Ahlan, yonder. Then I would join the expeditions along the great road through Kardeff to the coast. At times I would stay at the coast, until I was no longer one of the Valleys. I became a traveller."

"Where do you call your home?"

"Ledarun was always my home. But I have friends in Gorenden and would live there if I had to choose."

"And your journey with me, is that part of your watching?"

"It is. And it is part of my trading. It is a while since I have crossed the Valleys, and in such good company. I have acquired three new knives. Look."

Perad leaned forward as he unrolled his pack. "And have you been watching me?"

"No. I had been asked at Parden to look in on Woodall,

and talked with your uncle about the fight with the Gralt. You had just left in the direction I was heading, and I kept a look out for you. You were not hard to find. Your uncle said of you that you travel in straight lines. It was a compliment with a wide meaning. I simply headed north. I may have scouted further east had I been alone, but this has been a preferable trip.

"Now what do you think of that?" He held up a closed fist which he opened to show a tiny knife. "Made for peeling roots, I should think. I can sell it as an assassin's weapon on the coast." He stood again and stretched, taking the opportunity to inspect the tree line behind. He took a narrow scroll from the corner of his pack, unrolled it and passed it to Perad. It was a map of Tarodash, a good one, on fine bleached leather. "I understand a little the sightings to the south, but what are the Gralt doing in the Valleys and the northern forest?"

The lettering of the map was strange to Perad, and difficult to read. He found lake Lan, followed the rivers and placed a finger above their present position. He thought, as he always did when looking at maps, how small a part of the world the Valleys were.

"Your uncle told me of the disturbance you saw in the desert. I am beginning to suspect they may have crossed the desert, and it is even possible that they have followed the line of the eastern mountains. If so, I fear for the Valleys."

Perad scrutinized the map, weighing the possibilities. "Could they have approached by the coast and marched this way south of the Fardas river?"

"We have scouts watching as far south as the coast mountains and the Gralt have been seen in numbers around Sundorn bay, so you are correct, that is still the most likely course. That would leave the Valleys a little safer. It would also cause Parden to become more important to them and to us. They will struggle to cross the river west of Parden.

"The wind has dropped. I think the fog will be back before tea. We should cover more distance while we can still see."

From the next rise, they watched the mist thicken in the woods, and fog reclaim the plains. "A cold breeze from the mountains is meeting damp air from the ocean," said Dran. "I am afraid it will put an end to our progress for the day, even before dark. Let us increase the pace a little while we can." He lengthened his stride and Perad had to concentrate to match him.

But the forced speed did not last long and Dran had to ease off after a while, which allowed Perad to talk. "You have lived by the ocean. When we reached the end of the land at my Passing, I had no words. My uncle said that he also was left speechless at his passing. If so, it must be the only time Uncle Tavit had nothing to say."

"Gorenden is half a day's journey from the sea, but when I visit Portharden, I make sure I watch the ocean for a while every day. It is unendingly changing, and the sun setting over it still brings out gatherings, even of those who have lived there and seen for a lifetime. Make a promise to yourself, Perad, to spend enough of one winter there to see the storms which send white waves higher than the tallest trees crashing over the cliffs and onto the land.

"Let us make for the trees now. We can follow their line for a while, and we can camp among them when we have to stop." He seemed anxious and had taken to looking behind at times. They did, though, find a track going south on the edge of the woods which allowed them to continue past dusk and into the first of the night.

There was a little of the flux here, on the very edge of its region. A few hundred paces down the slope to their right onto the plain and it would be gone. Perad asked Dran of his awareness of it.

"Yes, I feel it as I have always felt it. I think it is improving my vision, even. I draw a little energy from it. When I return to the Valleys I greet it as a friend. Or it greets me."

The mist lifted from the ground, but no more than knee high, and for a while they could see stars through the thin canopy. It was not very long after dark, though, when the fog thickened and they moved a few paces into the wood to camp. Perad began to build a fire and Dran asked that he keep it small. Perad made them a hot drink of peppernut which they had with cold salted pork and dried nuts as a meal to be both tea and supper.

The fire had died and the fog must have become dense with cloud above it, for there was a blackness so absolute that when Perad woke he could see nothing. Dran was by him with his hands cupped by Perad's ear. "Make no sound. Put your boots on. Stand up." The words were whispered and urgent. Perad pushed his blanket to one side, sat and reached for his boots. He was quick, but habit made him arrange his bindings and take care with his laces. When he stood, Dran's voice was there. "Listen."

He could not determine the direction, but there were voices, muffled by the fog and unrecognizable, harsh and abrupt. He heard the crack of small twigs and the soft crunch of leaves being trod on. And they were close. No more than the distance across a room, if the sound through fog was to be trusted. He caught the rustle of clothing and strained to hear the clink of metal. There were faint flashes which he took to be tricks of his eyes straining in the total dark. His breathing sounded deafening in his nose. He breathed through his mouth. He dared not move his feet to adjust his balance.

It was impossible to make out words. Just one fragment

of his own language was all he needed to feel safe. Dran's voice came again. "There is a tree to your left. Five paces. It will give protection. Then wait." How could he know? Nothing could be seen. But then, how could anyone move through the wood, or even on the path, in this blackness? And the voices were moving, coming closer. Perad side stepped until he felt the trunk of the tree. He held the tree with one hand and the hilt of his knife with the other.

The voices and disturbance passed, then receded. Silence returned. Perad grew stiff waiting. He would not move. He counted one thousand, and still would not move. Then Dran was back. Perad did not hear his movements; only his voice, a stride away. "They are gone. To the south, I think. Back to your bed."

"Were they the Gralt?"

"I do not know. Perhaps. Folk who belong in the wood should not bump into trees so readily as they did. They may have been our own soldiers, or scouts. I have been expecting to see our scouts. Whoever they were, I doubt they will retrace their steps. Let us try and get some rest."

They kept their boots on and dozed sitting up, backs to a tree, resting on their packs. At one point, Perad asked Dran how he could move so readily in the complete dark. "I lived as a child and a young man on the edge of the great forest. It was first an adventure, and then a challenge, to camp deep into the forest, choosing the darkest of nights and the worst of the weather."

The remains of the night were uncomfortable, but undisturbed.

Chapter 10

The fog dropped out in the cold of the end of the night, and at first light Dran circled the camp looking for signs of the night's visitors. "Someone passed. I know no more than that. I am no tracker."

They set off early and strode well, and by the time the sun had cleared the mountains, they had met the road from Kardeff to Low Dresswell. This was a good road, made and maintained for carts, and it was fortunate, for the fog soon returned and thickened. Progress without the road would have been more difficult.

They were approaching the town when they heard hooves behind them. The visibility here near the river was so poor that they could see little beyond their feet. They stood still and Perad turned his head to catch the sound. It was of a single animal, moving at walking pace. Dran was at the road edge examining the undergrowth for possible cover. "Should we hide," Perad whispered.

Dran turned back. "I shall not skulk in bushes on a road in my own land." He was angry.

But it was only a traveller on a pony. He appeared out of the fog.

"Gredet, from Kardeff, with information for the Valleys," he said, dismounting and facing them. Strain showed in his face.

"And is your information anything for travellers in the Valleys?" asked Dran. "We are Dran and Perad, of the Valleys."

"Yes, it is for all. It is not good news though. The Gralt have crossed the river Fardas and set up a base in the Rindar hills. At the moment, we are cut off from our forces in the west. The news is no more than to prepare and hope. Riders have gone to the northern valleys. I am bound for Dresswell and Woodall. That is all I have. I wish I had better to offer."

"That is what we had feared," said Dran. "And what damage have the Gralt done? Is Parden taken?"

"They crossed south of Parden. The river is low, with the dry weather. Our forces there have not engaged them yet. Their march to the hills was slow and most of our folk escaped. There was some slaughter near the river. You may get some refugees in the Valleys, though most escaped north, or to the coast. My news may be out of date before I give it." He looked bewildered and exhausted.

"I do not know this road. Do I have far to go? I have taken the wrong turning twice. I am late in my errand. I hope no harm comes of it. I will be expected back, soon."

"You have almost reached Low Dresswell," said Perad. "Once over the bridge seek the hostelry on the left. You will find warmth and a meal, even this early. Are you to leave your news there?"

"My instructions are to ride on to High Dresswell and then to Woodall. I have been told to ask for a communication to be sent to Nerbridge. I believe it is remote."

"You will be looked after in the Valleys. If your pony can manage the woodland path over the ridge to Woodall, you should be on your way back well before nightfall."

"Thank you for that." His misery, for a moment, overtook him, and he slumped against his pony. But he quickly straightened his back and remounted.

"You can help us a little," said Dran, placing a hand on the pony's neck. "At Woodall, ask for Tavit, the innkeeper, and tell him you have seen Perad with Dran, here at Low Dresswell, and that they will be home before dark. It will be one less worry for him."

"That I shall do. It will be the only good news I bring." He nudged his pony forward. "Travel well," he said as he disappeared into the fog.

"Travel quickly," said Dran, perhaps to himself. "Events are moving, now."

There was no one about when they crossed the lower bridge at Low Dresswell, choosing to leave the road and head more directly to Woodall, although they could hear the clamour of excited voices nearby in the village. "I think it will be a good while now before anyone crosses any bridge in the whole of Tarodash without being noticed," said Dran.

They met again with the main track from Low Dresswell to Woodall soon after the river crossing. It climbed steadily towards the ridge and was good to travel on. Around was some of the most difficult ground in the whole of the Valleys, thick with trees and undergrowth, disrupted with steps and patches of crags and broken rocky outcrops. The road cut comfortably through, though, and was as ancient as the knowledge of the Valleys. Once away from the river, the fog began to disappear, and in the occasional exposed places, a southerly breeze could be felt.

At one point, Dran spied a rising line of smoke in the woods to their left, and drew Perad's attention to it. "That is the place of Getar and his family," Perad told him. "It is a hamlet, really, rather than a homestead, and a calling point for travellers on this road. Should we make a stop? I have friends here."

"We can spare a little time. It is good to know there are corners of the Valleys I have not encountered before, even though I have travelled this road a number of times. And we all may benefit from an exchange of information. We shall not stay long, though."

"And here is the path in," said Perad. It was well maintained, but fully wooded at the sides, and dark with the trees overhanging and meeting above, giving the entrance the appearance of a tunnel leading to a cave. There were shallow ruts showing the tracks of cart wheels.

Dran stood back from the track and examined it. "I shall suggest that they make some attempt to conceal it. It is an invitation to enemies at the moment."

The path sloped down and turned to reveal an almost circular clearing, partly surrounded by walls of low cliffs, with steep wooded slopes at irregular intervals between, and containing over a dozen buildings and much activity. The flux was up and strong, and the autumn weather fair and everyone was at work. Perad felt a little guilty.

A young man came to greet them. Perad had spoken with him on other meetings, but could not recall his name. He wore no shirt and rested a long handled axe across his shoulders. There were chippings of pale yellow wood stuck to the sweat on his skin. "Welcome, Perad of Woodall. Newly appointed poisoner, I have heard. And possessor of other interesting stories, I believe. You are to be congratulated. And welcome, friend. I do not think you have called here before. Can we offer you food or drink?" He left no room in his speech for Dran to introduce himself.

"A hot drink would be much appreciated," said Dran, "and I would like to speak to your council elders."

"We have no council here," said the youth. "But my grandmother will be pleased to talk to a new visitor. And provide you with an invigorating brew. This way."

Perad remembered his name. "We shall not be staying long, Denrap," he called to his back. "I shall see a few friends while I have the time."

Although Low Dresswell was much nearer, and their main place of trade, the folk from here were also frequent

84

visitors to Woodall and Perad knew some of them well. He had already sighted Kedan, a long time friend and wrestling opponent, who had called to him across the clearing, but could not leave the task he was doing. Perad hurried to him.

"Take hold of that corner and pull," Kedan instructed, nodding towards the corner opposite to the one he was holding. It was a large sheet of bark which was being stretched over a frame on a rough table. Kedan pulled hard and hooked his corner on a peg and came round to take Perad's corner and fasten it likewise. He turned and placed his hand on Perad's shoulder. "I have been hearing tales of you. Well done, friend." He walked around the table making adjustments to the fastenings. When there was no reply, he must have grasped Perad's discomfort, for he did not press any further. He made another round of his fastenings.

The settlement was here because the flux was reliable here. Getar's family and group produced some of the finest items in the land made from wood. Their wheels and axles were sought after throughout the Valleys and beyond, and their bark was used for important documents in the royal court. Perad saw both being worked, and much more.

"Come on. There are others who will wish to see you." Kedan crouched to sight along the table top, nodded his approval, tweaked one of the fastenings, and set off.

The eastern edge of the clearing was bordered by an arc of rockface a little higher than the rest. Centuries of wear and shaping had produced recesses and flattened areas, like table tops, at its base where much of the work was being done. The pale grey surface, the colour of heavy cloud, reminded Perad of the rock he had seen with his uncle in the desert. He stood still to look more carefully. It really was very similar, hard and smooth with no graininess and little cracking. He reached to touch it and felt the flux within it, stronger than that which came from the ground. He resolved to look more carefully for this rock in other places.

He stopped at each work area and exchanged greetings from acquaintances, and from others he had not spoken to before. They had some knowledge of his deeds of the night the Gralt came to Woodall. He received their approval with a smile and a nod. These were a people who appreciated any undertaking done well.

His circuit became slower. He delighted in watching these folk at work, craftsmen all, amongst the most skilful in Tarodash, and perhaps the whole world, using a strong flux and the abilities they had been born with, and had learned.

He stood in awe to observe a shawl being woven. It was patterned with a design of leaves and buds, and in the most vibrant of yellows, golds and browns. It grew before his eyes as the young woman added line after line, intertwining the threads from the bundles of goatswool on her knees, her hands moving with a dexterity and sureness which seemed barely believable. These shawls, using dyes made in the hamlet from treebark, were used in wedding ceremonies throughout the Valleys and much of eastern Tarodash, and were valued as keepsakes and tokens of good fortune. "And she redesigned and constructed the loom herself when the previous one wore out," Kedan told him from behind his shoulder.

The flux weakened, quite suddenly as it did at times, and around the hamlet workers were moving away from their tasks, stretching legs and shoulders, easing muscles. This sudden fading could be frustrating to those with unfinished tasks. Here all seemed content to rest. They would be back at work when the flux returned.

Dran tapped him on the shoulder. So engrossed in the weaving, Perad had not noticed his approach. "We have been offered lunch," he said. "Do you think we can afford the time here?"

"They enjoy visitors as much as visitors enjoy calling. Yes, I would like to stay."

A woman, plump, jolly and beautiful was with Dran. Perad remembered her as the older sister of Denrap. She led them to a place on the northern edge of the clearing where the rock was stepped in wide, shallow shelves, south facing and warm from the morning sun. She bounded onto the first level and offered her hand to help Dran up. He accepted graciously then laughed hugely when she jumped down and waited for Dran to offer his hand to her.

The entire hamlet assembled, the food brought in cloths and the drink, watered fruit juices, in wooden jugs.

The old lady, who Perad knew only by the name of Grandmother, joined them. She sat with Dran and as she did so, there was a shuffling by many of the youngsters who moved to sit close to her. The children, with sideways glances, watched her eat, working hard to remain patient.

She swallowed her last bite, dabbed her mouth with a cloth, and sat still.

"What do you remember, Grandmother?" asked one child. The words were softly intoned and were clearly part of a ritual.

Another child of five or six years leaned his head on her shoulder, and she scooped him up with surprisingly strong arms and placed him in her lap. He settled in and put his thumb in his mouth. She removed it gently, and put her arms around him, and spoke to him, but her story was for all.

"I remember when the snow hawks came. I remember the worst ever winter when storm winds brought ice and snow beyond anything known before, and the snow hawks came. The hunters said that they were from mountains beyond the great forest, and that the winter there would be even worse, and that the snow hawks had been forced south in order to seek food and shelter. They would fly low over the trees with great slow beats of the wings and their shadows would take longer than a heartbeat to pass. They would fly south as far as the desert, and return, the hunters said, because there was nothing to eat there, either. Some tried to find a haven in our Valleys. Their voices were like the cries of a child. They would perch on the high rocks and lean forward and glide down among the trees. I do not know what they ate. Snow covered everything, but for the very tops of trees and the steepest slopes. And it was so cold. We rarely left our homes, and wrapped ourselves in blankets, whole families, and goats and fowl, sharing our warmth. When the snow rested and the storm winds eased, we would hurry to the woods to seek fallen branches under the snow for the fires. The rivers and streams were ice, and we had to melt snow for our water. For weeks we ate only stews and boiled oats. And at times we would find a snow hawk dead and frozen on the ground. They were larger than a man, white all over, but for a yellow edge to the wings and tail, and talons and beak as black as night. It was terrible to see them on the ground. They would spread their wings and lay their head on one side, to die. We would not touch them.

"Near the end, when spring was close, you could feel the weather begin to change, until one morning I was first awake and I went out to look around outside the clearing, a small girl who should have done as she was told, and stay in the cabin. The cloud was breaking and the sun came out and lit a tiny rainbow in each of the thousand thousand drops of water melting on the trees. And there before me on the path was a live snow hawk. It was standing, wings folded, before a dead companion, a mate perhaps. Its eyes were the strongest yellow, almost level with mine, and it looked at me for a long time. Three times it lowered its head and nuzzled its friend, spoke one word of its strange speech, and flew away. And in all my years since and all I have seen, there has never been a more wonderful sight than that great white bird opening its vast wings and rising up through the trees with their rainbowed drops, into the bright blue morning sky, and turning to seek its home in the north."

She was still and silent for a while, as was everyone, then she lifted her hand, and let her sleeve fall. It revealed a bracelet high on her forearm, a wide band of white metal, and curved and embedded in the full circle of it was a faded white feather with a yellow edge.

Dran aimed a wave into the dark entrance. "There is a place I did not know of, and am pleased to have found. I have already arranged to return for a longer visit sometime. My thanks, Perad for leading me here.

"They had already decided that they would conceal their entrance and make some attempts to reduce their smoke. They seem well informed."

"This is a busy place and they travel and trade all the time," Perad said. "Some of the homesteaders do not and they will not be so well informed. I hope they are being looked after."

Chapter 11

From the ridge they could see mist on the plain that the sun would not penetrate or lift, but up here a warm breeze had cleared the air. The road to Woodall went south east and could often be a busy route. Today it remained stubbornly empty. They began the descent, and on the first distant sighting of the river, turned directly south, towards it, on paths less used, but still not difficult. Woodall had the widest of the valley bottoms and its slopes were not severe, particularly towards the plain.

Dran was careful about his course, wishing to keep in view the track, the river and as much as possible of the region across the river, while remaining partly hidden. They stayed well above the track, keeping its line, and moving quietly in the trees. The track was the most direct route to Parden and good enough for ponies and even small carts except during floods, but little used. Most traffic between Woodall and the Plains would use the crossing at Low Dresswell.

They walked and spoke softly, and watched everywhere. They had become very cautious.

This was Perad's valley. It was strange to him to be wary here. Its slopes and vegetation were his home. He knew of a patch of garrey bushes nearby which would yield a good crop of its small berries, used for cleansing stomachs. Garrey berries were at their most effective when sun ripened on the bush, and the warm summer should have produced excellent fruit. If he could pick them on the move it should not delay them much. He wondered if he dare ask Dran. They had walked steadily since the hamlet, and lunch had been taken sitting on a fallen trunk for no longer than the time it took to chew two oatcakes.

By mid afternoon, they were no more then five thousand paces from Woodall and Perad was looking forward to telling uncle Tavit of his experiences over a tea in his own home. A little ahead was the bridge crossing the stream which fed the marshy ground west of the village. They were angling down the gentle slope to take the river path when Dran gripped him by the arm. Perad had heard sounds which did not belong, and had already stopped and was searching the wood ahead of them with alert eyes. They moved silently on using trees as cover. They heard the snort of a horse, and the voices of men. A few more steps and they spied a group of soldiers.

They were soldiers of Tarodash. They were clustered in a clearing by the track, three horses, two of them laden with packs, and a number of men. One of the men was kneeling by something on the floor. One, holding the reins of a horse, turned fully towards them. He wore a uniform of darker green than the others, and his bearing and age marked him out as being senior. A captain, thought Perad.

"Dran and Perad, of the Valleys, travelling to Woodall," called Dran, stepping forward.

The captain responded instantly. "Perad, Poisoner of Woodall. Yes it must be. We know of you. This is fortunate!" His manner of speech made him a man of the northern plains. He strode to meet them. Although he had released his hold on the horse, it stepped with him. The rest of the group remained where they were.

"You know me?" said Perad, looking not at the soldier, but at Dran. He was suddenly afraid.

"We know of you," was the reply. "Come with me. A healer would have been better, but a poisoner can do some good. We have an injured man. I rode to your village for assistance. I spoke to your uncle." He turned and strode down the hill, lifting a finger at the horse which followed at his shoulder.

Perad hurried after him; Dran trailed a little behind. "Why do you know me?" asked Perad. "Are you looking for me?" Perad saw the injured soldier had been laid on a roughly made drag sled, amongst the waiting horses and soldiers.

The one kneeling looked up and nodded. "Greetings, Perad." It was Jevan, the butcher from his own village. "Midwife Nadira is not well, so I am the best we have," he said. "He has a deep wound, a sword wound. I am going to fasten it with thread, but you can clean it better than I can."

The wound was terrible, a ragged gash from hip to knee on the outside of the right leg which had severed muscle and exposed the bone. The injured man's face was white, and his eyes were closed, but he must have been conscious, because he was mumbling.

Jevan had pulled back the leather and cloth of the tunic to make room for his hands. "I have brought needle and thread," he said, "The muscle is separated and I need to rejoin it, so I will use large single loops to pull the muscle and skin together at the same time. Do what you can while I work." His voice was taut, but his words and hands were steady.

Perad was already kneeling and had unfastened his pack. Opening the strings of an empty mixing bag, he added two powders from the pouches on his tunic. "Water," he said, and a soldier was there with his flask, a corked flask of hard leather, from his saddle. "Half fill it," said Perad, holding out his bag. The mixture foamed slightly and Perad nodded to himself. He rested the bag between his knees, thought for a while, nodded at a decision made, and added another powder, this one from his pack. He pulled the strings to close the top and mixed the contents with a swirling motion. A pale yellow liquid oozed from the draw holes and spread over his fingers. He would have preferred warm water, but there was no time. Steady now, he leaned forward and dribbled the liquid into the wound as Jevan worked. He had started at the hip and had made eight or ten loops of thread. It looked impossible to make good this damage, but the butcher's hands were good and he worked methodically, sewing with a long curved needle and tying off each loop in the way he would present a roll of meat. There was a faint flux and Perad began to feel more hopeful as the wound closed.

The captain watched for a while, left to speak to one of the men, and came back to look down on his fallen soldier.

The soldier's eyes shut as he passed into unconsciousness. His breathing seemed more regular.

The sound from the hillside of a sword being drawn lifted Perad's eyes from his work. "Gralt! Prepare!" came the cry, and a soldier was backing towards them, sword high, and then he was turned and running as three Gralt warriors came through the trees. There was a call from one of them, a sound or word Perad may have heard before, and a fourth Gralt appeared on the hillside some distance away to their left. It could not have been a planned encounter, they were not abreast, but straggling. They must have been passing, travelling south, and had come upon the Tarodash soldiers.

"This is a new group," hissed a nearby soldier. "How many are there in these woods?"

The Gralt were outnumbered and simply charged through. But they did have drawn swords. One came straight at Perad and for an instant he saw the glint of metal and heard the sound of air being cut apart. He was frozen on his knees by the injured soldier. Jevan had leaped to his feet. One of the Tarodash soldiers stepped in front to protect his injured comrade and the two unarmed villagers. He was shouldered aside and fell across Perad. It was a moment of fear and limbs and glimpses of the floor and the sky. Perad could smell sweat, dirt and leather. And then the Gralt were gone, running through the waist deep river and south into the woods.

The Tarodash soldier was up quickly. Perad, breathless on the floor, saw him look to where the Gralt had gone, then look towards his captain.

"Stay. We do not give chase," called the captain.

The soldier reached towards Perad and pulled him by his shoulder to his feet. It seemed that everyone was standing, eyes probing the woods, but Jevan let out a small gasp and dropped to his knees. When Perad looked he wished he had not. The soldier on whom he and Jevan had been working had taken a slash from the Gralt sword across his stomach and chest, and was dead.

Two of the soldiers had fresh blood on their swords. One had run a few strides in the direction of the fleeing Gralt warriors. He called back over his shoulder. "I got a good blow, captain. At his sword arm. Are we to follow them?" Perad saw his face and saw that the soldier was only a little older than he himself.

"No, lad, but scout that hill there. Go no further. Stay in sight."

Perad looked at the dead soldier again. He felt sick, and may have toppled if Dran had not held his shoulder. "This, I believe, is war. Do not look for a reason," said Dran quietly.

One of the defenders had a gashed hand and allowed Perad to pour the remains of his mixture over it. The wound did not need stitching, Jevan announced, a dressing would do the job. "The gauntlet will not mend," he said and Perad thought he had attempted a jest, until he saw his face.

The young soldier came hurrying back. He was excited. "A Gralt sword," he said. "He dropped his sword." He was holding it by the blade and had wrapped a cloth around it as if its touch were poison. There was blood on the handle. His voice was high. "We have captured a Gralt sword."

"Steady, lad," said the captain. "Report."

"I did not see a fifth. They are across the river and hurrying south. I lost sight of them in the trees. I do not think they will be back."

"We do not know what they will do. Terrab, walk that ridge south of the river. Stay in view. We shall go back to the village." A soldier, small and stout dropped the reins of a packhorse and moved down the slope and waded the river, chest deep here, but slow after the dry summer. He moved well, like a woodsman, but his dark beard and broad face said he was not of the Valleys. A recruit from Porenden, perhaps, thought Perad.

"A Gralt sword," said the captain, holding out his hand. The young soldier offered it by the blade, realized and changed his grip. He was shaking and white faced.

All closed in to see the enemy weapon. The captain stood it on its point next to his own sword. It was shorter, but broader and clearly heavier. The ones Perad had seen two months ago had been longer. The captain held the Gralt sword up before his eyes, its weight causing him to twist his wrist to lift it. "Inferior steel," he said. "And a poor edge. I see now how they can wear them unsheathed. This is a weapon for blows as much as cuts. Good technique can beat this. We are beginning to train with a two edged weapon. It should be a good move. I shall get this back to the garrison, although I hope we have captured others by now. Take care of it, Fedab." He handed it back to the young soldier.

"We shall accompany you to your village," he said to Jevan. "We should like to use your burial place for our comrade. How to deal with the fallen, I fear, is going to become an issue."

Without further instruction, the men spread. The captain mounted his horse, a fluid movement of a lifetime riding. Perad wondered at the functioning of a captain on horseback and his troops on foot.

"The Gralt are invading," The captain said. "They are coming from the south across the edges of the desert, we think. Mostly by the coast. But they are being seen in the Valleys all the way up to the northern forest, so they could have an eastern route by the mountains. The bridge at Parden holds, but they have found other crossings and caused trouble on the southern plains. The enemy in these parts are only small groups and they are hiding, mostly. There are many more of them by the coast mountains. We have seen large encampments beyond Tarod Bay, a growing army. They are supported by ships. They are not good sailors and keep out of the way of our ships. Then, our ships are not fighting vessels, and the islanders have not always been best of friends with the rest of Tarodash. A few attacks by the Gralt and they will side with us. The Gralt do not use bows, and do not carry shields, so our archers are preparing. But we are not warriors, we have not been warriors for many generations. Only in the old tales has Tarodash been a warrior land. If we do not prepare quickly, I fear for our land in battles on the plain."

There was silence for a while, then Perad spoke. "So there is to be war. And the Valleys, what of our place in this?"

"This is strange," said the captain. "Why they are sneaking around the east of our land when they appear to be preparing for attack in the west is a mystery. Perhaps they wish to divide our defence. Perhaps they see some strategic value in this area. Or they may simply be exploring. However, your distant corner of Tarodash seems to have significance."

Perad had never felt that Woodall valley was a distant corner. "And is there to be an army to protect us?" he asked.

"The whole of Tarodash does not have an army yet, and the threat seems greatest at the coast, there is little to spare for here. We shall do what we can." The captain's voice had tightened, his words clipped as if presenting a report to senior officers. "I am here to find information. We need to know more of what the Gralt intend. We have lost Koret; he was a ferryman and a volunteer for this patrol."

He paused for a while and turned in his saddle to examine the woods.

"There is one other item, you, Perad the Poisoner, must hear. I have informed your uncle of it. I would prefer that you receive this news from him."

Without command, it seemed to Perad, the captain's horse stepped ahead. Behind Perad, a soldier had taken the other two horses, one in each hand, and was following. Perad slowed to let them draw level. He walked with his hand on the great beast's neck. Its warmth surprised him and comforted him.

Someone must have seen them coming, for a group of men were striding to meet them on the edge of the village. Perad could see they were armed, and there were swords as well as sticks. Uncle Tavit was there, but a catch of the eyes and a slight nod was his only greeting. Perad had not wanted his return home to be like this. He stood alone, in a grey daze while the two groups joined.

The talks went on for some time and others had drifted out from the village. Perad remained standing, head down. Dresana, daughter of an orchard keeper, of his age, came hesitantly to him. He hardly saw her. There were tears in his eyes and no colour in the world. He had seen too much of late.

She took his arm. "They are to bury the soldier," she said softly. "You should be there." She said other things to him and she held him firm when he stumbled, but he did not hear her.

He watched as the dead soldier sank into the marshes, then turned to walk back to the village. Dresana had stood with him all through the rite. She squeezed his arm and touched the back of her fingers to his cheek. "Take care," she said. She left him then. They set off back to the village and Perad walked alone. Dran passed him, striding away from the village and spoke as he passed, but Perad did not hear his words. He looked back once to the burial place and saw the captain on his horse leading his band of soldiers west.

He sat once more on the stone step at the base of the well in the village circle. He sat there a while and tried to clear his mind of unpleasant thoughts. His uncle arrived.

"Why were the soldiers here, and why did they know me? What did they tell you?" Perad asked. He felt a mounting dread as he waited for an answer.

Uncle Tavit sat on the wall of the well above Perad and rested his arm on his shoulder. "I think it will become less than it sounds," he said. He struggled to form what he needed to say into the right words. "In the west, stories have been heard of a Gralt fighting unit being defeated by a magic spell from the book of a poisoner. There are those who wonder if it will help with the war." He paused then, and tightened his grip. "They cannot understand why Gralt should be in these parts. If they wish war with Tarodash, there can be no value in using their forces in the Valleys." He stopped again, and Perad's dread deepened for he knew what was left to be said.

"What they suggest is that there have been captures by the Gralt, and no doubt questioning and torture. The pirates have been used, who know both our speech and Gralt speech. Some in the west think that the Gralt may have heard of a magical book in this part." Uncle Tavit forced a laugh. "Some wonder if the Gralt wish to capture this book."

"And the one who uses it," continued Perad. The world spun and he felt numb.

Uncle Tavit moved off the wall and sat beside Perad, never lifting his hand from Perad's shoulder. "This is no more than the words of desperate folk searching for answers. We do not know why the Gralt are interested in the Valleys, any more than we know why they have come to Tarodash, but they are not coming for Perad of Woodall. Remember, they were here already, before you or anyone else played a part. Whatever their reason, they knew nothing of us. I suspect they were doing no more than explore the boundaries of our land.

"Actually, I think it makes us safer, because the Valleys may now get more support and increased vigilance from the soldiers."

He stood purposefully. "Come now, Perad, tea and then archery practice. We have been working hard while you were away and you have some catching up to do." He pulled gently and Perad stood with him. His uncle realized that more was needed. "Let tea wait for a while. You can choose your bow first. In fact, your poisoner skill may be required. We are having trouble with the arrow flights. We have been using crow feathers, and Taprad believes they need stiffening."

Perad did not respond, but did allowed himself to be led to the room behind the meeting hall where the newly made bows had been stored. Uncle Tavit managed a smile when Perad went not to find a bow, but to the racks of arrows and picked one and tested its flight between his finger and thumb. "Yes, I can prepare a simple dip that will improve these. I shall treat a few and see what Taprad thinks.

"Now where are the bows?"

Chapter 12

Each time the inn door opened after dark, Perad would look up and remember that night at the beginning of autumn.

This night, there was no flux and he was not making or mixing, but reading by the fire when Dran returned. He had left with the soldiers ten days ago to deliver his reports, with a promise to be back soon. He entered slowly with his hands empty and in front of him, perhaps anticipating unease from those inside. The wind gusted and brought dry brown leaves in with him. Winter was near, the air colder and more often from the mountains, although the weather remained, as the whole year had been, much drier than was normal.

Dran's brows were low and his eyes dark and he had no more than a nod for Perad, who had stood at his entering. His shoulders were drooped. He may have been limping. Perad took the tall stool from his work area and placed it by the counter.

"Perad, greetings and thank you," he said, before turning towards uncle Tavit. "I have a little news to add to what you already have. This is a good place to tell it. The village can be informed by you." There were a dozen customers, standing and seated; all now turned to face him. Dran kept his eyes on the counter before him. "We knew, or suspected, much of this. It is confirmed that the Gralt have crossed the Fardas river. Perhaps not a large army, but an army still. They forded it both sides of Parden. We have patrols from Parden to the coast, but not to the east. We do not know how they crossed. Perhaps they had boats. The river is very low now, they could have waded. One sizeable group has made for the Rindar hills. Another is camped by the river. They have constant marches between these two groups and that enemy line is difficult to cross. Some farms have been destroyed and villages routed, but many folk made for Parden and are safe, for now. The Gralt have sent warriors this way along the river and are near. I have seen them. I have had to avoid them. A company of our own soldiers is marching to challenge them, but it is difficult and Parden is stretched. We have looked to Kardeff for help, but they have their own defence to worry about." He stopped then and looked around. Someone slid his tankard of ale in front of him and he took a sip and then a long swallow.

A voice, deep and grave, so changed with anxiety that Perad did not know who had spoken, asked, "How did they get to our lands? Did they cross the desert?"

"Perhaps. Perhaps they marched from the coast. Their main force is on the coast near Sundorn. There is much we do not know. They have horses. Could horses cross the desert?"

"Have you come from Parden?" uncle Tavit asked.

"No. I was at Parden, but I have come from Kardeff. News had to be sent to the Valleys. We have assigned messengers, now, on good mounts. I offered to come to Woodall and was delivered on horseback to the crossing at Low Dresswell. I have walked from there."

There was a long silence. Dran picked up the ale, looked at it, and put it down again. They could hear the wind in the chimney. Leaves rattled against the door. "What is to be done?" Perad was surprised to find he had given voice to his thoughts.

"I do not know," said Dran. "It must be difficult to defend against an enemy whose purpose is not known and movements not understood. We must put some faith in our own soldiers, we are building an army."

"And in the time we are waiting for the army to build, we must do no more than hope the Gralt do not find us?" This was from Faren, the young woodcutter with newly born twins.

Dran looked towards him for a while, then looked over to the fire and watched the flames dance. "Yes, do not be found. That seems good counsel."

He held the counter and pulled himself wearily to his feet. He went to sit on the stool by the fire with his elbows on his knees and his chin in his hands. A short discussion ended with uncle Tavit leaving to gather the village elders. Most of the other men went with him. Perad took Dran's ale and placed it on the hearth by his feet. No one spoke. Gradually the few remaining villagers rose and left. Perad took himself to the kitchen to find chores to keep him busy.

The men of the village would gather at the meeting hall. The news would not take long in the telling; the talk would last far into the evening. He heard the inn door and when he looked from the kitchen he saw that Dran had gone. He hurried across the inn and looked out. Dran was crossing the edge of the village circle towards the meeting hall where lanterns had been lit. The men were gathering outside. Perad resisted the urge to join them, knowing that although he would not be sent away, it was not his place.

He went back to his chores. When he collected the flagons, there was a good deal of unfinished ale. He poured it into a bucket. It would go to Walvin's pregnant sow and be much appreciated. He washed the flagons and swept the leaves which had blown in and threw them on the fire and watched them burn. He found other tasks, mostly unnecessary, until he was tired.

Dran slept at the inn that night and Perad found him at first light in the kitchen cleaning the grate. No one had put logs on the fire the night before and it had died out. Uncle Tavit, in his hooded winter tunic, was fastening his boots. Perad had heard their voices in whispered argument as he opened the door at the bottom of the stairs. The whispers were not secrets, but to avoid waking anyone, and continued as Perad entered. "...my village and my people," uncle Tavit was saying. "If the Gralt are to come, then I will be watching their coming. Lives can be saved."

"And if you are at the bottom of the valley and the enemy come over the hill from the side, then what good will that do?" said Dran.

"If they come from the plains to Woodall, they will come up the river. I cannot wait here to see if the swords that arrive are ours or theirs. I shall go and watch the plains from the edge of the woods."

Dran sighed. "Someone should be watching, I suppose. You cannot object if I come with you."

"I shall go, also," said Perad from the bottom stair.

Uncle Tavit stood and stamped his boots into place. "Yes," he said. "While you collect your pack, I shall boil some oats. We will have breakfast before we leave. And pack for overnight. We do not know when we can return."

The valley narrowed for a while to the west beyond the burial place and they walked close to the ridge, keeping the river and path in sight. There was no conversation. Uncle Tavit strode grimly ahead, Dran a little behind and higher up the slope, with Perad trailing.

It had rained in the night, the first heavy fall for some time. There were even muddy pools in the dips where the dust of the dry summer had collected. The canopy was thin, now, and much of the colour had faded from the woods. There was a hint of winter about.

Perad wore his hat, wide brimmed and pulled low. He

would stop at times, and lift his head. There was no bird song, and he listened to the fat, irregular sound of the drips, or the rapid patter as some small breeze disturbed the treetops. Leaves fell at times, wet and heavy. But before long, the cloud thinned and blue sky showed. Dappled sunlight warmed him and autumn returned and he removed his hat.

There would be funguses out within a day, and he wondered if he would now find the opportunity to collect them. Such an outing, in more comfortable times, would have him searching endlessly for the materials of his craft.

To make up the lost distance, he would trot then, striding the knee high drifts of leaves which had collected by rocky outcrops or fallen trunks.

After a while, he put his head down and walked hard and saw little. It was normally a half day of good walking to Last Hill, even on the track, but they were there before midday, having stopped for neither rest nor drink.

Out of the woods they could feel a breeze from the north east, and it was chill on top of Last Hill, but the air was clear. Even so, there was little to be seen. The soil was thin here near the desert edge and out of the Valleys, and there were few farmsteads. Once off the hills, there was no flux. This was a poor area, difficult to farm and sparsely populated. The two rivers, their own Woodall river and the one from Dresswell valley, wound into the plain, flowing close together then parting for a while, before joining to become the Fardas river which marked the boundary between Tarodash and the desert, then west towards the ocean. To the south was the desert, the horizon lost in its distant shimmering. It was as empty as ever. It was said that on the very best days, Lake Lan, north from here, could be seen, but Perad never had. The Rindar hills were a smudge on the horizon west and south towards Parden.

They ate lunch up there standing in the cold wind and stared into the distance. Marks in the landscape were examined but none resolved into anything which would provide information. Uncle Tavit would not hide his nervousness, constantly referring features on the horizon for the inspection of the other two. He pointed to the meeting of the rivers and the place of the little used wooden bridge allowing access to the west. To leave Woodall valley, most travellers would turn northwards before Last Hill and take the bridge across the Dresswell river east of Low Dresswell. From there, roads could be taken to Parden, Kardeff or Lan. He spoke mostly to Dran, but Perad thought he was speaking to himself also. "Anyone following the river from the west is more likely to enter Dresswell valley than Woodall valley. Horses can cross the bridge at Riversmeet, but wagons cannot. The council discussed burning that bridge and the one below Low Dresswell, but the river is wide and shallow at both places and can easily be forded. We have left them intact. They may be of more use to us than the enemy."

He nodded towards a group of untidy farm buildings down on the plain. "That is Jarak and his two sons. I shall go speak with them."

Dran went with him. Perad chose to remain standing on the hill top. He looked north along the line of the Valleys and supposed that every valley had a Last Hill. After a while he placed his pack on a low rock and sat on it facing west. The wind dropped a little and the sun warmed him. He could see the two figures working their way onto the plain. He thought how rarely he had been down onto this place between the two rivers so close to his own home. He again thought of how much of Tarodash he did not know, and then of how much of the world he did not know, and of how the coming of the Gralt would change his dreams.

In a while, he saw the two men leave the farm taking a

more northerly route and selected a path down the hill to intercept them.

Nothing had been seen down on the plain, but the journey seemed to have satisfied uncle Tavit who was now willing to return home. "We shall organize a daily patrol. Along the river, Last Hill, and Riversmeet, and round to the Dresswell bridge. That should keep us informed. I shall put it to the elders. They will agree."

They had climbed up off the plain and had reached the edge of the woodland when uncle Tavit took a long look back. "Wait," he said. A horseman had appeared in view, following the curve of Last Hill, out on the plain. He was moving fast. They watched as he swung around in a large arc, changing his course from north east to east, until he was heading directly towards them.

"Behind the trees," said uncle Tavit. "Out of sight."

"Stay," said Dran. "He is a soldier of Tarodash. A captain by his tunic." Perad saw nothing which would distinguish him as such.

The rider had reached the slope and was beginning the gentle climb towards the valley woods. His pace had slowed. Dran stepped forward and raised a hand and the rider saw him and stood in his stirrups and shouted up at them.

"There are Gralt approaching. Remove yourselves." His voice came to them on the breeze, the words clear, even at such a distance.

Perad lifted his eyes and saw more riders rounding the hill in the path of the first. They were close together and it was a few beats before they were close enough for Perad to count. There were five of them, moving fast, and their cloaks spread behind them.

Perad watched them swing around to face this way, dropping to a canter. They would have seen the captain on the grassy slope, but not the valley folk backed by trees, Perad thought. He took a step back into the shadows. The Gralt were still almost four thousand paces away, and showed no urgency.

The captain changed course towards the south, where the slope dropped steeply towards the distant river.

"He is leading them away from us," said Dran. "But the ground that way is broken and will favour the enemy. They will close the distance on him." He put his hands around his mouth and shouted. "This way. We can help."

Perad watched the captain hesitate, stop, turn his horse, and start again, south.

Uncle Tavit added his support. "We know the woods. We can assist you." His voice boomed and Perad wondered if the Gralt would hear. They were now at a trot and had spread a little.

The captain turned again and galloped towards the trees.

The horse was covered in foamy sweat, its great chest heaving, and there was blood on its flanks, but it still had the bearing of a warrior. The rider, to Perad's eyes, was magnificent. His uniform was a dark green tunic over a grey shirt and pants. Pale grey pads were sewn onto the shoulders of his tunic. His boots were black, worn and ancient, and looked flux made. His right hand, his sword hand, was wrapped in a bloodied rag. His scabbard on his left belt was empty.

"We need to hide, but take me away from your homes. I am sorry for this, for bringing them to you. East was my only escape. I did not think they would follow me so far. I did not see you until it was too late. Had I done so, I would have guided them elsewhere." His voice was of the cities and of wealth, and of command.

"Still, I do not think they will bring their horses into the woods. Which way?"

"North," said uncle Tavit, "The wood is thicker there. We

can seek some way to hide tracks." A few dozen strides into the wood the trees were much closer together, the shadows deeper, the banks rockier.

"Keep me a view of the plain and the enemy. I would rather know their movements."

Staying close to the edge of the trees, uncle Tavit led them towards a rocky outcrop of low broken cliffs, thick with evergreen Firepine trees, the captain still mounted, ducking below the low branches. They had good glimpses of the plain, and an occasional view of the enemy. The soft ground gave way to a gently sloping floor of smooth rock, rimmed with drifts of pine needles. They trod carefully across leaving no marks. The horse followed, seemingly choosing the placing of its feet with the same precision. Once behind the higher rocks, uncle Tavit looked back. "Only a good woodsman would spot our passing. I doubt they are that."

A little higher up the slope, they stopped. The soldier dismounted, took a long look at the Gralt out to the west, and sat on a boulder in the lee of the low cliff.

"We should be safe here. They are not wizards, they are not giants, they are only men," he said. "They are experienced fighters which we are not. But we are becoming more so. Our equipment matches theirs, as does our resolve. Perhaps our resolve exceeds theirs. We are defending our land and our homes. They can return to theirs. We must make them wish to return to theirs. Their organisation is superior to ours, but we are learning. We encountered some of their scouts, three groups of five, on the pain east of Dunfield and matched them but for numbers. There was a stand off. I dispatched my men back to garrison. I made for here. It was a mistake. I did not think they would bother to follow a lone rider, seemingly escaping a battlefield. I outrode them. They are inferior horsemen, which has surprised us."

He pulled at the rag on his hand and folded the loose end

under the bindings. Beneath the blood, Perad could see that his fingers were long and slender. He stood to scan the plain. The Gralt were only a little closer, moving slowly. It was difficult to judge their line. He sat again.

"We do not know how they exist, the shape of their lives in their own lands which are to the south of the desert, but we are learning. We have made captures and we can make them talk. We have sailors from Brig who know a little of their language, from trade with the islands. We do not know why they are here, why they have chosen our time to invade our lands." He began to slump, exhaustion overtaking him, then righted himself, and stood. "We will defeat them. We will send them home."

His eyes searched through the trees to the west, as they had done ceaselessly as he spoke. "My sword was knocked from my grasp. I would rather face them with a weapon."

"We will find you a sword back at our village," said uncle Tavit, "Though it may be rusty."

The edge of the rocky bank was out in the open where the ground dropped away steeply and offered an uninterrupted view of the plain. The captain went to it and leaned on a chest high shelf of rock. The others followed.

The captain suddenly straightened and reached around for his missing sword.

"Quick youth, your young eyes. What do you see?" He pulled Perad by the shoulder and spun him to look over the shelf towards the plain.

Perad squinted, then blinked to clear his vision and focus on the distance. The haze and the soft light made it difficult. "Horsemen, seven, perhaps eight, coming this way. Galloping fast." Even as distant specks, their movement across the ground was impressive.

"Colours. What colours do you see?"

"I cannot see colours yet."

"Strain, youth. What can you tell me?"

Perad steadied his chin on the rock and narrowed his eyes. The specks had become shapes and resolved a little more as they changed angle for some obstacle Perad could not see. "They are wearing tunics, not cloaks. One of the horses is a grey, the others dark. No, two greys."

"They are ours. The Gralt have only blacks and bays. They are my men. I must ride to them. We can trap the enemy." He pulled his horse around and leaped to the saddle.

"You have no sword," said uncle Tavit.

"A stick, then, woodman, cut me a stick. A stout one." He was urging his horse through the tangle of trees and bushes, ducking to avoid branches.

"A few moments, I shall have you a weapon." Uncle Tavit was leaning on a small branch and taking out his knife. The branch snapped, and with a few deft movements, he sliced away the twigs and fashioned a point at the narrow end.

The captain was clear of the trees. Uncle Tavit ran to him and handed him the branch, the length almost equal to his own height. The captain swung it, testing its balance. "A fine weapon," he said, and was off, galloping on ground not suitable for such a gait, then onto the slope and down towards the enemy.

Chapter 13

The Gralt must have seen the captain immediately, for they slowed to a walk, turned, and stopped. They were a thousand paces away. Perad watched them draw their swords. One adjusted his helmet. They seemed in no hurry. Behind them, the captain's men, seven of them, were another thousand and half paces further and had lessened their pace to a trot.

The captain had also reduced pace, to a slow walk, or his horse had chosen to on the steep rock strewn slope.

"He may be judging the distances to meet them as his men arrive. The Gralt do not appear to have seen them yet," said Dran.

"Then should we make sure that they do not turn around?" said uncle Tavit. He began to climb the rocky shelf.

"It may be wiser to stay hidden," Dran said, reaching out his hand to stop him. Then immediately, "No you are correct. We must do what we can to help."

They were quickly onto the narrow shelf. Perad was the last to scramble up and there was little room for him. His uncle took a handful of the shoulder of his tunic to keep him in place.

Dran held his cloak out to the side, and high. "The more they see, the more they may consider us a threat, and the more we will keep their attention."

Perad studied the situation, the arrangement of the combatants, attempting to work out where an attack could be made, how the Gralt position could be defended. The Gralt riders were moving forward again. They spread out into a line.

The captain must have been making similar evaluations. He stopped moving forward, still a good way up the slope, and turned the horse to its left. It cantered a few paces and stopped.

The Gralt horsemen sidestepped their line to their right to match the captain's movement. They increased their spacing a little.

Behind them, still unseen by the Gralt, the captain's men were within a thousand paces, and closing steadily.

The captain turned his horse and returned to his original heading, a little further down the slope.

The Gralt matched him with a movement to their left. They were at a good walk and the adjustment was smooth.

The captain suddenly swung his horse to the left and made a short gallop down and across the slope to a small hillock. Perad could see no particular advantage to the position, other than to make his opponents wonder at his actions. Perhaps that was enough.

This time, though, rather than shuffle across the greater distance, the Gralt farthest away from the captain's turned his horse to ride behind the line to extend it at the other end. A sensible move, thought Perad, one adjustment to leave the others in position. They were a little over five hundred paces beyond the captain.

But on turning, the Gralt could not fail to see the approaching horsemen of Tarodash.

The Tarodash soldiers were in a tight group with one rider a little ahead of the others. Perad watched them sit more upright in their saddles and the trot became a canter.

The Gralt came to a halt, uncertain, with opponents in front and behind, and a new assessment needed.

And the captain chose this moment to attack. He leaned over, appearing to speak in the horse's ear, then sat tall and held his weapon high. There must have been sap on the cut end, for it caught the sun and glinted for a moment like polished metal. The horse sprung forward, at a full gallop within ten strides, aimed for the centre of the Gralt line.

The captain's riders had also reached a gallop. Perad had expected them to spread into a line to match the Gralt, but they held their tight formation and aimed also for the centre of the enemy line. The speed increased. It looked like a race, the captain one contender, his men the other, hurtling towards each other, the prize in the centre. Perad realized he was speaking out loud, calling the moves, evaluating the tactics. He glanced sideways. Dran was also mouthing words. His uncle was silent.

Until the last few months, Tarodash had been without serious conflict for generations, with court officials rather than soldiers, and sport in the place of battle, and yet to Perad it seemed the manoeuvres were planned and practised, the results of training and experience. But how could they be? He marvelled at them.

"Eight against five, with the slope in the captain's favour," he heard Dran say.

The captain's men would beat him to the contact by a heartbeat or two. The Gralt closed together holding a line. There was some turning as they jostled, deciding which way to face. Why did they not escape the trap, Perad thought, ridden to the side and reformed? Were they confident of their ability, in spite of the numbers? They made more adjustments which disturbed their formation.

Then it was too late.

The captain's men hit the ragged line of Gralt at a full gallop, with the captain a few horse lengths away. Perad was astonished. He had expected the horsemen to meet and stop and exchange blows. The riders of Tarodash simply went through the Gralt line without any slowing, with the captain passing through his own men and on through the Gralt at the same speed.

But not the first of the captain's men; he had hit the central Gralt rider with a sideways swing of his sword and the force of the blow took himself and his target off their horses and onto the floor. The Gralt horse fell and rolled, crushing its rider. The exchange was so rapid, Perad missed much of it. He saw the captain's horse leap the fallen beast. There was another Gralt down; Perad had not seen what action had caused it. The riders of Tarodash pulled on their reins, the heads of their mounts came up they skidded to a halt. Dusty turfs flew around their hooves. The speed and weight of their charge had taken them over a hundred paces beyond the Gralt, but they were round quickly and coming back, the riderless horse still with them.

"Seven against three. It is ours," muttered Dran, loud enough again for Perad to hear.

The fallen horse was thrashing its legs and rolling and it separated one of the Gralt from the other two. It was here at the single enemy where the second charge was aimed. The captain had turned faster than his men and was closer, and the isolated Gralt spun his mount to face downhill and take the captain's charge. He stood in his stirrups and held his sword high, and shouted a single word. But the captain's men had the slope and were there half a beat before the captain and one of them took the Gralt from behind with a short precise blow across his shoulder and back which took the Gralt from his horse. Even at this distance, and among the snorts of the horses and the thuds of their hooves, Perad could hear the sound of the sword's impact and the crack of smashed bone. Uncle Tavit raised his arm in front of his face at the moment of contact, releasing his grip on Perad's shoulder. Perad, not able to adjust, lost his balance and began to fall. He had to jump from the ledge, and landed hard, determined to stay on his feet, for he could not take his eyes from the battle.

There were two Gralt left mounted and they still would

not escape. They stayed near their fallen comrades, and prepared for the attack, side by side, one facing down, one up the slope.

The Tarodash riders had lined up the next charge and were on their way. There was no need to change the tactics.

One of the Gralt must have taken an injury for, even as the men of Tarodash closed, he toppled from his horse. He was sitting on the ground when the attackers reached him, then he was no longer sitting. Two swords took him, matched slicing blows, one from each side, as the riders galloped past.

The last of the Gralt dismounted and stood astride his fallen comrade and waited for his end. He gripped his sword in both hands, shortening his reach and reducing his opportunity for a telling blow, a stance of defiance rather than defence, Perad thought.

This time the captain was the first there, slightly wide and leaning far out of his saddle to swing his weapon in an enormous arc. The Gralt ducked and the weapon passed over his head. But the charges were well timed, and as he rose and turned to face the other direction, he was overtaken. The first of the horses swerved to avoid the bodies on the floor and the rider must have not trusted his sword blow, for he simply stuck out his foot and his boot hit the Gralt in the side of the head at a terrible speed. The invader went down and was still.

The Tarodash riders pulled up and swung around to view the battlefield. Six men were on the ground, and two Gralt horses. One of the horses was on its side thrashing its legs. A rider of Tarodash was slumped over his horse's neck, and his mount had walked off down the slope. One of his comrades rode to him. The others moved slowly forward and gathered by the side of the small battlefield. All but the captain dismounted.

One of the Gralt on the floor rolled and let out a sound, a long low unknown word, more a cry of anger, it seemed, than pain. The men standing walked forward to the fallen. They had a task to do, and Perad did not wish to witness it. He sank to the floor and lowered his eyes. Uncle Tavit climbed down and placed his hand on Perad's head. It was not long before he said, "It is done. You can stand now Perad."

They set off down the slope and the captain rode to meet them.

He began speaking as he approached. "It does not always go so well. We were fortunate to catch them between us on open ground." He seemed to be apologising.

"Have you any injured?" asked uncle Tavit. "We have Perad here who is a poisoner and who may be able to help."

"Danal is unconscious and cannot be roused, and Bord has a broken knee, but we have Faral who has trained as a healer and will do what he can. You do not want to go down there." He was looking at Perad.

The captain dismounted when he reached them. "We have a little less urgency now, and can speak. You may be able to advise me. We have much to do. The Gralt are coming. They are coming this way. We can save lives by clearing this area. We must spread the warning."

"How many Gralt? And how near?" asked Dran.

"They have arranged themselves with a few score on each side of the river, half the distance from Parden, and a they have a number of groups of scouts like the ones we have just fought. Perhaps two hundred in total. Why they should arrange themselves so, we do not know. They are marching this way. It is not a large force, but it is one we cannot stop. We cannot spare the men from their other tasks. And the farmers here and the craftsfolk of the Valleys do not have the arms to resist them. I have never been to this part of Tarodash before. There are few folk here, it should not be difficult to send them off, north to Kardeff, or Lan. Both are well defended, now. The Valleys, I do not know. Can the valley folk hide in the woods?"

116

He followed the lines of the two rivers, east to the woodland, with his eyes. "The maps tell me that the towns of Dresswell and Woodall are closest and may face the greatest danger. I am also told that there are many families scattered in the woods away from the towns. They will need warning."

"We are valley folk," said uncle Tavit. "From Woodall."

The captain's head spun to face the three, his eyes settling on Perad. "From Woodall. And you are a young poisoner. So there may be something in the tales."

Dran reached a hand to hold Perad's shoulder. "We know the tales," he said.

The captain read something in Perad's face. "My belief is that the Gralt have another force which has made an easterly crossing of the desert by the mountains, and the groups along the river are attempting to meet them. Stories of vengeance against sorcerers are nonsense. The Gralt are moving according to tactics of invasion, known to themselves." He stopped then and surveyed the landscape, allowing his eyes to rest on Last Hill. "That would be valuable ground should armies met in this area."

He looked back at their faces. "It will not happen. If only a little of what I have heard of the courage of the men of Woodall is true, then I am pleased to encounter you. No, I do not know why the Gralt are here, but they are not moving armies to bring doom onto a small village in a remote corner of Tarodash. Still, your village may be along their route, and you must be prepared."

The captain reached inside his tunic and brought out a folded piece of fabric which he opened to reveal a map. They moved close to view it. It was roughly drawn and showed little more than rivers and towns, the lines of the rivers drawn much straighter than Perad knew them to be. "Which is the best way to give warning to all those who need it? We have two or three days."

"That is more time than I expected," said Dran.

"Yes, they move camp slowly. They display no haste. They may be timing a meeting. I would give a great deal to know their purpose."

He looked up from the map into the face of uncle Tavit. "This is your land. What would you advise?"

Uncle Tavit moved his finger over the map. "Your horsemen could inform these folk on the plain. It would not take long. Can you spare the horsemen, Captain?" He waved to the west to indicate the area bound by the two rivers.

"We are at the disposal of these folk," said the captain.

Uncle Tavit tapped at a place on the map. "Two thousand paces west of the hill you will find Farak and his sons. If you begin with them, they know all in this area and can help arrange for everyone between the rivers to be warned. They will be reluctant to leave their farms, but the appearance of soldiers will convince them."

The captain studied the map. "If the Gralt continue their march along the river, they will have a decision to make. My guess is that they will stay south. But a wrong guess will cost lives." He looked again at Last Hill and turned the map. "That meeting of rivers is where I crossed this morning fleeing from the Gralt. A small wooden bridge. Can it be seen from the top of this hill?"

"Yes, with ease."

"Good. If the enemy follow the Dresswell river, it will be monitored, and swift riders can warn Low Dresswell in enough time.

"So, my men will clear this area between the rivers, with the help of friend Farak. We can then warn those a little north of this river to make ready to flee. I shall have two men ride to Low Dresswell to alert them and have them make preparations. And what of your village?"

118

"We shall attend to that, if you have no more need of us here."

"Then go break the news. If you can stay out of harm's way, things may improve. Remember, we were fortunate today. The Gralt are a terrible and destructive enemy. Be vigilant and avoid them at all costs.

"We have not given up on you. Men throughout Tarodash are becoming soldiers. Our army is growing quickly. We shall drive the enemy from our lands." He pulled himself into his saddle. "Do what you can to keep your people safe for a while. Fortunes will change.

"We will keep you well informed. We shall follow the river to your village within two days to see if we can be of help in your arrangements.

"And thank you for your weapon. I never blooded it, but it played its part." As he rode away, his men came to meet him.

"The situation is much clearer," said uncle Tavit. "We shall carry this new information back. And quickly. There are preparations to be made."

Chapter 14

The afternoon darkened early, with thick cloud over the plain to the west. A strengthening wind brought dry heat from the south. Although it was not yet sunset, Perad saw the yellow glow of lamps and candles through the thinning trees as he approached the village. It looked secure and welcoming and Perad felt an uncomfortable guilt at the news they were about to bring, and the turmoil that would result.

He had fallen behind at the end. Most of the afternoon he had led the walk back, containing his impatience as uncle Tavit left the riverside track to call at nearby homesteads along the way. These ranged from shacks, to solid homes of logs and stones, and clusters of farm buildings, where he had waited silently with Dran each time, while uncle Tavit had explained that the Gralt were coming and were only a few days away. At one point, the three of them had rested on a fallen tree near Foral's dwelling, a cave with a front of boards and logs, while the old homesteader who lived alone there, split a sack of grain for his hogs, threw a long cape over his tunic, and left his home to walk with them. There were other homesteaders, further from the river, who would need to be informed soon.

Doors were opening and shadowed folk spilling out into the village circle as he left the last of the trees. Perad went to the well and scooped a mugful of water from the trough and drank it, watching more folk pour between the buildings, from the homes further out. The trough was almost empty and he lowered and raised a bucket to replenish it.

The meeting hall would not be large enough for so many, and someone had hung lanterns on the outside. They swung in the wind spraying light on the nearby features of the council elders gathered there to listen to his uncle, and to Dran, while the space around filled with faces unlit.

A whispered conversation between Walvin and uncle Tavit ended in Perad's uncle turning to face the crowd. He was clearly uncomfortable. He would not choose to impart bad news, or to speak to such a large group, but he would do what needed doing. Someone placed a wooden box by his feet and Walvin motioned for him to stand on it, but he shook his head. Perad knew his uncle and knew he would struggle for the first few words. He watched him take a deep breath, look over the heads of the gathering, then back to the faces of those nearest.

"The Gralt are coming." He had to raise his voice over the wind and the shuffling of folk and the rattle of dry leaves on the floor and in the trees. "The Gralt are coming. They are not coming for us, but they are coming this way towards our village. We must leave." Some heads turned to the spaces, now filled with night, between the buildings to the west and south, towards the river, then turned back. Uncle Tavit had stopped. He took another careful breath.

"We may have to leave." His voice was stronger now, stronger than the wind, and Perad knew he would finish his account. "We know the Gralt are marching along both sides of the River Fardas and will soon reach Riversmeet. There are perhaps two hundred of them. If they carry on along Woodall river, they will reach here two days after that. Our soldiers are watching them but are not enough to stop them. Nor are we. We cannot defend our village against such numbers without slaughter. Our options are to abandon the village as a whole, or to scatter into the woods. Do not be too alarmed. The enemy are a few days away. There are soldiers of Tarodash between us and them. We are safe for tonight." He stopped then and Walvin pulled at his shoulder and spoke into his ear.

When he continued, his voice was quieter. A lull in the wind assisted him. "We shall know more in the morning. Use the night to consider how you may arrange to leave your homes."

The gathering broke up into groups. Those nearest put their comments and questions to uncle Tavit and the elders. Replies were passed on. Discussions and arguments developed. Perad used the time to refill the ring of buckets in the well, and separate their ropes, which had become tangled.

Once it was understood that there would be no more information until the morning, some people began to leave. Scouts and sentries were set. Perad placed himself near the elders hoping to be given a duty, but he wouldn't speak up or push to the front and he was not noticed. He turned and left.

Back at the inn, he sought work to do. None of the usual tasks of running the inn seemed of any value. If the Gralt came, would they destroy his home? It was stone built like most of the buildings around the village circle, and would not burn easily. In the old tales of war and heroes, the enemy would burn to the ground the towns and villages they encountered and conquered, but why should they bother with a deserted village? Wouldn't they simply check for inhabitants, food, supplies, weapons, and pass by? Perhaps if it was night, they would stay in the homes, sleep in beds rather than on the ground. Would a Gralt choose Perad's bed in the attic to sleep on? Would they drink the ale and fall asleep on the inn floor? He would tell his uncle that they should empty away the ale, break open the casks and tip the barrels. But uncle Tavit would know that already. Perad had seen Gralt on the inn floor before, and looked at the places. His eyes were drawn, as they had been many times these past weeks, to the veins of darker colour in the stone floor. Many of the outer buildings, and the great meeting hall were wooden, and would burn. He went to stand at the inn door and look out across the village and the black sky above.

Uncle Tavit found him there some time later. He put both hands on Perad's shoulders and looked at him. "Decisions in the morning," he said. "But first, something to help us sleep. Come on."

They went inside and his uncle put Perad by the counter, then went to the fire and thrust a poker deep into the embers. Perad sat himself on a stool and leaned his elbows on the counter. It had been a few months since he had last sat here, and he must have grown. He fit more comfortably than previously. Uncle Tavit drew two flagons of ale from the cask in the cool dark alcove at the end of the counter. It was the ale they called "top" and was the first and strongest taken from the barrel. He brought the poker, now glowing dull red, from the fire and held it in one of the flagons. The ale hissed and spat, and after a few moments, began to boil. He leaned the poker in the corner and pushed the hot ale in front of Perad. His own ale, he left cold.

"We may as well have it," he said. "We are not leaving it for the enemy." He appeared in good spirits. He described the arrangements for the watching of the village, for no other reason than to speak, it seemed. When Perad stood to leave, his uncle said, "We will see what tomorrow brings. Things are not as bleak as you think. The enemy are not here yet. Sleep well."

He stood also, downed his ale and went not to bed but back outside. Perad went to stand by the fire. He could see no reason to stack it to burn for the night. He could see no use for it in the morning. He did, though, prepare the kitchen fire so that whatever breakfast was, it could be hot.

In bed, eyes closed, or open and staring at the rafters, he could see horses with their hooves tearing up the turf as they galloped. He mind followed them when the turned and he was aware that out of the focus of his vision, and on the edge of his view, there were bodies on the ground.

He did eventually sleep, and he must have slept well for he recalled no dreams when he awoke, and it was late enough for there to be light already in the sky. Looking out of the shutter, he saw it was even later than he had first guessed. The wind had dropped and the cloud was breaking.

His uncle had been up and was already out. There was a saucepan of hot oats and milk on the hearth in the kitchen, and a pot of honey on the table. He ate slowly, stopping twice to walk through the inn and look out, expecting furious activity throughout the village, but it was merely busy. Henata, wife of Walvin, saw him and crossed to speak. Some of the men, she told him, had gone to take the news to the homesteadings and fetch whoever would come, to a meeting at lunchtime. A soldier had ridden in early to say that the captain would arrive during the morning. His uncle, she believed, had gone to meet the captain.

Before she left, she expressed concern for her husband. "This is difficult for him. He is an old man now, too old for this. If you find an opportunity, suggest a tonic for him," she said.

Perad returned to his breakfast, now set thick and barely warm. He used a large helping of honey to thin it, and finished it quickly.

He spread out his possessions on the bed, considering what he should take, and how he could carry it.

He had two packs, and found a way to attach the smaller one to the large one, with his three rolls of pouches containing his powders, strapped together between them. He rolled a blanket inside his groundsheet and fastened that to the top. He swung the whole of it onto his back and it fit well, although the packs were almost empty at the moment. He fetched a mortar and pestle, and his grandmother's book and packed those. With winter near, he would need his warmest clothing. After that, he would have little room for other belongings. He had not finished deciding when his uncle called him.

The captain had arrived with news and there was to be another meeting. Once again, the gathering was in the village circle. This time, the elders were grouped by the well, the captain with them. Uncle Tavit placed himself at the back, Dran joined him. Perad found a space in the crowd.

Walvin spoke. He mounted the step at the base of the well. The village, already quiet, fell silent.

"We are now clearer about the situation. The Gralt continue their march this way along both sides of the Fardfas river. We do not know why." He was accustomed to making announcements, and his voice carried well. A few folk, particularly homesteaders had been leaning on the walls of surrounding buildings. They moved closer and there was some shuffling to make room for them. "They will be here in less than three days if they continue. Their force is getting smaller as they leave encampments along their route, but if they reach the village, there will still be too many. No amount of courage will save us. We have no choice but to leave. Some of you may wish to take to the woods and hide there. Low Dresswell is better situated and its people have chosen to remain. They have many more men, and the steep valley sides are better suited to defence. You will be welcome and accommodated there, should you chose to go.

"I shall lead those who wish to follow me to the Dry Ravines beyond the Trough of Horan. We believe we will be safe there, hidden. No one should remain here." Perad saw him wipe his eyes. He had more to say, but looked unsteady and his wife took his arm and sat him on the step. Tardeb took his place on the step.

"What are these Ravines?" Dran asked Perad, amongst the rising murmur of voices.

125

"They are a day and a half to the east, across the river at the beginnings of the mountains. Our village and folk from Nerbridge used them as winter quarters long ago. The flux is said to be strong there. I have never been, though I have been to the edge of the Trough and looked over to them. The Trough of Horan is an offshoot of the desert at the head of our valley." He was puzzled, and his voice showed it. "I thought we would hide in the woods."

"And these Ravines, are they a good place to hide?"

But Perad did not have the time to answer. Walvin had regained some strength and stood again. All heads turned back. Quiet returned. "We believe that we can hide there in safety until matters improve. The captain is confident that it will be only weeks not months when our army is ready to force the enemy away."

The captain motioned to him and Walvin leaned to hear whispered words, before continuing. "The captain has asked that any men who feel they can contribute, to consider joining the army until the enemy can be defeated."

Perad looked towards his uncle, who had turned towards him. When their eyes met, his uncle gave a slight nod.

Walvin continued. "The enemy are being carefully watched. They are expected to reach Riversmeet sometime tomorrow. If they move into our valley we will leave the following morning. If they turn back, or away, we may be able to stay."

There were more whispers amongst the elders before Walvin spoke again. "The morning after tomorrow we must be fully prepared to abandon our village. Make plans for the first part of winter in the Ravines. Consider what you will need to take and consider what you can contribute to our survival. Leave nothing for the Gralt. What you do not take, bury in the woods. We may have to turn livestock loose. If the Gralt find nothing here, they may turn back."

And finally Walvin was empty. He sat heavily on the step and no one took his place.

Perad turned to go back to the inn. Dran worked his way to him. "I shall not be trading knives for a while," he said. "They will be a burden. Can you find somewhere for me to bury them?"

Perad nodded, but had nothing to say, and Dran stopped him at the inn door with a hand on his arm. "Do not blame your uncle for wanting to soldier. Tarodash needs his courage more than his ale, for a while."

"I do not blame him. Would they take me?"

"They would not. You are at least two years too young. And your folk will have need of its poisoner in the next weeks."

Perad let out a large breath. "Let me find a pick and we will hide your knives. The bank above the stream behind the inn has deep dry earth. They will be safe there. I will bury them for you, if you wish, but you will need to come with me to see the place. If I do not survive, and you do, you will need to find them again."

Dran looked at him. He opened his mouth to speak and closed it again. He put his head on one side and smiled. "What they say about you is true," he said, "but it is not enough." The smile turned to a grin. "I will fetch my knives and wait for you behind the inn."

Some fifty paces up the slope, the stream which trickled down through the woods splashed between boulders and found a route underground. It was believed that this was the source of the water in the well. It was here that the water for the ale and for the inn was taken, and Perad had carried countless buckets of it down the steps which had been fashioned into the slope. A little to the west was a low outcrop of sandy rock amidst a tangle of redberry bramble. There they took turns with the pick to make two trenches, thigh deep in the pale, soft soil. The flux was up in the valley, strong in some places, but here it could hardly be felt, and the loose soil was difficult to shape. Dran placed his rolls of knives in the smaller trench and kicked soil over until they could not be seen. They dropped to their knees and pushed the soil with hands and arms until the hole was filled. They stamped the ground down, then kicked at the surface to break it up and hide signs of disturbance. Dran dragged long shoots of bramble from the surrounding bushes to cover the place. Scratches and tears appeared on his hands, to which he took no notice.

When he had finished, they stood back and looked. "Here is a task being done all around the Woodall," he said. "If all the treasures of the village are as well hidden, the Gralt will discover nothing."

Blood was drying on his hands and on the way back, he crouched by the stream and pushed up his sleeves, then stood again. "I should not spoil the water in case it goes to the well. I shall wash at the inn," he said. He had one more look at the place where his knives had been buried, and turned away.

Uncle Tavit was piling utensils on the kitchen table. "They shall have nothing," he said. "What cannot be hidden shall be destroyed."

Perad told him of the second trench he had dug. "Good. There is also space for some items under the flagstones in the pantry. They will not be discovered there. What will not fit there, we will wrap in waterproof sheeting and bury in your hole."

"Should I save some yeast?" asked Perad.

"Now that is a good plan. It would take weeks to grow a new batch otherwise. And months to find one as good."

Perad was pleased to have a task to fit his skills and went immediately to work. The yeast for a new brew was taken from each barrel once the ale was almost ready, simply by scooping the froth from the top with a little of the live ale and adding a mugful of honey to feed it. It was then mixed with the new grain and warm water in the next barrel. They had only lost the yeast once in Perad's memory, during one hot summer, when a whole barrel had gone off in the heat while they were away at the sports at Marben. Uncle Tavit had grown new yeasts by spreading old grain and honey on half loaves and using them to brew buckets of ale until he found one to his taste. They had had to walk to High Dresswell with a leather water carrier to bring back some live ale to keep the inn going until his was ready.

Perad would dry some yeast and store it for when they returned. He cleaned a large scrap of soft leather with boiling water, and rubbed in a mix from his powders, which he knew to cure skin infections. Then he washed the leather again with boiling water. He spread the cleaned leather on the counter above the barrels of ale. There were four of them. The newest was working well, bubbles rising quickly, but not yet foaming. The oldest one was ready for sugar for the second ferment and he decided not to take from there. The other two had good foam on them and he scooped handfuls of it and smeared them onto the leather. Using a wooden spatula from the kitchen he pressed the foam into the leather and repeated the process. There was already a good smearing of pale brown yeast covering the scrap. Picking it up by the corners he carried his handiwork to the wall of the yard behind the inn where all his sun drying was done. The sun was pale behind thin cloud, but it would dry the yeast to a powder by the end of the afternoon. He would scrape it up and put it in two pouches he decided, one to store with the possessions of the inn, and one to keep in his vest.

It was a strange day. While no one appeared to be hurrying, everyone was occupied. It made him think of the first day of good weather after winter when the snow had melted and the sun had its first real heat of the year, and homes were emptied and cleaned of half a year's grime and clutter.

Late in the afternoon, Uncle Tavit came in with Dran, and a loaf and piece of cold mutton, which they ate at a table in the inn, rather than the kitchen, with the inn door wide open and the activity in the village visible.

"We shall tip the barrels, and I shall take the sacks of grain to those with fowl," he said. "Many of the animals will be slaughtered and salted for provisions. The hogs and goats will be pushed into the woods. They will survive, although collecting them when we return will not be easy. All that can be done with the remaining hens and ducks is to spread grain around the sheds and hope some are alive when we return. Lanad's ponies will not go the Ravines. They will take some folk and their possessions to Low Dresswell.

"What of Nerbridge and High Dresswell?" asked Perad.

"They are still deciding what would be best. Neither village could defend itself, but if the Gralt went that way in numbers, they would be seen in plenty of time. Those villages could be emptied easily and quickly.

"Some men have chosen to become foot soldiers. We are to carry lances, and swords. We have been told that lances have had some success when facing the enemy." There was nothing in his voice, other than the telling of some news. But there was a sparkle in his eyes.

That evening, Uncle Tavit opened the inn. Many of the men came in for a short while. The ale was free, but no one drank much, or stayed long. Some were going to look for war. Some were taking their families to hide from war. Each choice was respected. A few were leaving the decision until the next day.

Perad spent the evening preparing powders and mixes which could be used as preservatives, then went to bed early. His craft would be needed in the morning.

Chapter 15

Mid afternoon of the following day brought the news Perad was certain would come. He was crossing the village circle, distributing mixes for curing meats when one of the captain's soldiers rode in. Faren, woodcarver and maker of chairs, who had helped overcome the Gralt in the inn, and had been scouting near the plain, was mounted behind him. Faren was clearly uncomfortable on a horse, and as it stopped he slid to the floor and lost his balance. He was sitting in the dust holding the horse's rear leg when he looked up and found himself surrounded. "They are coming. They have passed Riversmeet and are still marching. We must be gone tomorrow. Early tomorrow."

Most wished to hear the news directly and the circle was filling again, when two more soldiers arrived. They remained mounted, and one spoke, his height from horseback allowing his voice to reach all ears.

"Our captain sends his apologies. He cannot come himself. I am told you know what is to be done. All in the village must be out of harm's way when the enemy arrive. We have been dispatched to help. We believe some of you are to go north to the town of Low Dresswell. Our task is to provide an escort. We shall leave at first light tomorrow. It is too late to leave for today. It is unsafe to travel in the dark. How many will make the journey?"

"Sixty, perhaps eighty," said Tardeb. "Some have left already. The greater part of the village will make for the mountains. We shall leave soon after you."

"No one is to remain in the village," said the soldier.

"No one will remain," said Tardeb.

The soldiers dropped from their horses. "Put us to use where you can," said one.

Tea was to be taken communally on the grass banking by the games field. A great deal had been achieved in a short time and there was some sense of satisfaction, and a feeling that a shared meal had been earned.

Besides, they had visitors, the soldiers, who were endangering their own lives to help them. It was important to show that the village, even in direst peril, would not fail in its duty of hospitality.

A few of the lads went for their bows and set up a competition, with talk of wagers, but their aim seemed poor, and their technique clumsy in front of the soldiers, and after the first round, they collected the arrows and leaned the bows on the targets, and went to sit down.

Perad had placed himself within hearing of the soldiers, and when one of them began to speak of the war, he moved a few paces nearer. The soldier was considering a question from a village man about the Gralt tactics. "I have seen one of their encampments," he said. He had been eating roasted duck, and had a platter of bones on his knee. He was toying with them, pushing them around the platter, looking down at them for somewhere to put his gaze. Many of the surrounding eyes watched their continual rearrangement as if the nature and purpose of the Gralt encampment was described therein.

"We had been scouting on horseback on the south east corner of the Rindars and coming out of a patch of forest we spied smoke from over a ridge to the west." There was a quiet intensity to his voice which stilled his listeners. "My captain and I left our comrades, two of them, Gathar and Warn, in the cover of the trees with the horses, while we made our way up a gully with the purpose of looking over the ridge. The gully ran out near the top, but there were enough trees and broken ground on the slope to keep us hidden and we had a good sighting of the skyline and could see no guards. Still, we went on our bellies at the end. It is well that we did for they also were watching the skyline. I have not been a soldier for long, and I had still to learn fully the first lesson of soldiering, which is to never underestimate the enemy. The Gralt encampment was on a low hill in a wide valley and we could see that they had set their lookouts well. They had a wide inner circle of men set some half a thousand paces around the encampment, and another circle of men on higher ground further out. Each watchman would be in signalling view of some of the others. We had to watch for a long time to spot them all, and we saw how fortunate we had been in gaining our vantage position. There was a guard on our ridge who could not have understood the shape of the land, and must have missed the gully. It may be that he had seen the horses in the trees, but we did not know that at the time. There were two riders walking their horses between the rings of lookouts. They circled in opposite directions and would meet twice in each loop, and stop briefly to exchange comments. The outer watchers signalled by arm movements which we could not decipher.

"They were camped in rows of circular tents of grey material, and had larger tents where it seemed, the business of an army must be organised, for there was much coming and going. The tents pleased us. It may be that their weakness is to be found in poor weather, if they need so much shelter in our autumn. They are from southern lands and may find Tarodash winters uncomfortable.

"They had women in their camp and we were amazed at that, and they had cattle roped on the hillside. Whether they were beasts of burden, or food, and whether they had driven them all the way from their own lands or stolen them from ours, we do not know.

"There was some fight training, although it was difficult to see from that distance, and it was all man on man. They worked hard. We saw one go down, and not rise. We did not see them practising group manouvres, and that may be another weakness. They were working with shields, which is new information to us. We have not had them face us with shields, yet. In their practice, they appeared to use the shield as an attacking weapon, thrusting it forward, and following with a blow from the sword. Their sword work is all about heavy blows, which we have faced. We can count it a success if we have forced them to change their tactics.

"They use their voices a great deal in combat. We heard them in practice, as we have heard them in battle. Perhaps they are correct. They understand warfare more than we do.

"Communication appears to be central to their organisation. Riders were constantly entering and leaving the encampment, with reports, we supposed. And that may be a further weakness. If we can disrupt their lines of contact, they may not operate quite so well.

"While we spied, two groups of five riders galloped out, flanking the ridge we were on and we were forced to leave. We crawled down the slope and into the gully. Half the way down we heard hooves and the voices of horses and the cries of men, and saw Gralt. It was perhaps two hundred paces to the trees. We saw no sign of our comrades. There was a little water running in the gully and a patch of reeds where the ground flattened out. We waited a long time in those reeds, until the afternoon was dark enough to creep along the stream, and run for the forest. We waited in the forest through the night.

"The captain's horse, a fine mare by the name of Blackwing, must have scented us, for she came to us at dawn.

We thought it was the Gralt and prepared to fight, and so greeted her with drawn swords. She had taken a bad gash down one flank and had a broken hoof, but she carried the both of us back to garrison, and endured many detours as we searched for our comrades. We did not find them, or the three horses, and they have not returned since."

No one else spoke. The soldier's fingers were greasy from his meal, and he took out a square of cloth to wipe them, a dignified gesture which pleased Perad. If his uncle was to go off to fight, Perad wished him to still be his uncle when he returned.

And then it was the final preparations. A little before dawn, those who had chosen would journey with the horsemen to Low Dresswell. With them would go the men who were to become soldiers, for a new garrison had been established on the plain north of the Dresswell river. Soon after, the remainder of the village would assemble in the circle for their trek to the Dry Ravines.

Chapter 16

And so they left, in a long straggling line, in no particular order, north first, then east just below the ridge separating Woodall valley from Dresswell. Of the three hundred and twenty who set off that morning, sixty seven were men and older boys, only a few armed with swords, and those were old weapons none of which had been used for generations. The others carried stout sticks, chest high, or staffs as tall as themselves, newly cut from the rock oak on the edge of the village. Most of the bows and arrows were stored on the sleds, it having been decided that they would have no defensive value on the trek. The younger boys and the women carried no weapons, their hands being full of the necessities of living. Many carried a pack about their shoulders, or dragged a two poled triangular sled loaded high, or both. Garrett, the old homesteader who lived in a hut on the slopes above the village and hunted rabbits, patrolled the ridge to the rear, a supreme woodsman keeping watch, almost unseen even by those who knew he was there, a shadow flitting from tree to tree amongst the dappled shade. Some of the homesteaders, those individuals and families who lived in the valley but away from the village, had chosen to join the trek, some had not. Perad, with Dran, walked well down the slope keeping the river in view between the trees. They shared with the dragging of sleds. Perad could not see who was at the front. There was little talk and little noise.

The late autumn weather had remained fine, and the walking was easy for these folk of the woods, and by midday they had reached far enough eastwards to be at a place where the paths were beginning to run out. Only the hunters and the collectors regularly came this far. The valley was narrower here and the group, by now an untidy line stretching out of sight into the trees, dropped down off the slope and stopped to eat, closer to the river.

Little by little the trees gave way to bushes and untidy scrubland. Towards the head of the valley, most of a day's walk away, the river curved away to the north and would have to be crossed. It was just before the crossing where the woods thickened again that they stopped to camp for the night. They allowed no fires and ate a cold dry supper and slept poorly. It was chill in the night now, with winter near. The air of solid resolve the village had set out with that morning had turned to grim determination.

At daybreak they set a ring of guards armed with bows, and lit fires to heat oats for breakfast, while two trees were felled to bridge the river. There were remnants of many crossings from earlier times but none recent enough to be trusted. The river was narrow here, and fast, and rattled and splashed between sharp rocks beneath them as they crossed. It did not look like the same Woodall river which flowed gently by their village. Even with the packs and the sleds to be carried, and babies and children, there were no slips, for these were folk of the woodlands and could walk along logs with ease, and the crossing had been well made.

It was decided to keep the crossing in place, disguising it to hide their route. The last men over split the cut ends of the trunks and piled up dirt to cover the axe marks and make it look like a fall of trees.

Beyond the river was a wide swathe of woodland climbing steeply, which ended abruptly as the trees gave way to a great curved ridge of falling ground, with little vegetation and littered with broken rock, and then a jumble of low gorges, before a flat circular plain. Across this desert plain and rising into the foothills of the mountains was the dark green of another narrow band of woodland, but here at the end of the lands of the Valleys, it was bleak. The mountains were little more than a day closer than seen from their own village, but viewed through the thinning woodland they dominated the land. It seemed to Perad scanning the line of those mountains piled ever higher to the east that they were approaching the rim of the world.

The row of ravines beyond the desert plain, seen from here as no more than shadowed cracks in a ridge of hills and cliffs, was the place chosen to hide the village.

The first of the travellers had stopped to allow the entire group to collect before moving down the slope. Without announcement, lunch had been decided, each group of arrivals finding amongst the small boulders places to sit, with the sun on their backs and facing their new home to the east.

"This circle of desert is the Trough of Horan, then," said Dran to Perad, "and those will be the Dry Ravines. Here is another corner of Tarodash unknown to me until now, and unknown to most, I should think. This looks a sound place to wait in safety."

Walvin was leaning on his staff on the edge of the slope, regaining his breath. He lifted his voice, not only replying to Dran, but to speak to all who were close. "The flux is strong here, or so it is said, and the southern valley people once came here in the deep part of winter when there was nothing to tend in their valley homes. They would work their craft in the strong flux and return before spring with products of outstanding quality. But that was long ago. I have not heard of anyone crossing the Trough to the Ravines since I was a child. And except for the foothills, and we only have tales and a few ancient maps of those, the mountains are unknown to us."

"Yes, even though they touch our borders," said Dran.

"The council of Tarodash should finance an expedition one day. Perhaps I should suggest it. Perhaps I could go on it."

"It will not happen," said Perad quietly, but he felt the wanderlust rise in him, as it always did when far places arose in talk.

"Do not be so downcast, Perad," said Dran. "The Gralt will be gone in time and we can reclaim our lives. And when their threat is over, Tarodash will take more interest in its borders.

"Anyhow, this is my limit for the present, I have much to report, and I have neglected my work. I shall head back to the plains."

And he stood up and shouldered his pack. Perad was astounded. "You are leaving?" he said. "You are not staying? When did you decide this? Why did you not tell me?"

"There was really no decision to make. I have my work to do. I mentioned it to your village elders. I did not tell you because I did not know how this journey would work out."

Perad had stood to face him. "Can I…?" he began, but then dropped his eyes and stopped speaking.

"No. You have a part here. Do it well."

He placed a hand firmly on Perad's shoulder. "Thank you for your companionship, Perad. We shall renew it when the land is safer." Then he turned and strode back along the valley angling towards the ridge. Most heads turned to watch him leave, and most heads then turned back to look at Perad. Dran stopped to speak briefly to Garrett sitting on a low crag watching the tree line, then he was in the trees and then he was gone. Perad realized he had not wished him a good journey. He also realized he looked foolish standing there. He sat to resume his meal, but his appetite was gone and his mouth was dry.

After scouting the ridge and arranging guards at the rear, Garrett, with Tardeb, led the trek across the bowl. They did

139

not take a direct line, there being dust and sand which would leave tracks, but kept to the southern edge which was rocky and difficult. Perad realised that he was not helping with the sleds and looked around in shame. The girl Dresana, who had comforted him in the village, was nearby and was watching him. She was hauling at a family sled and struggling to keep pace. She caught his eye and inclined her head and Perad moved to take a shoulder strap. "Thank you," she said. Perad said nothing, but adjusted his grip to shorten the strap and take the bulk of the burden.

It was not far and still early afternoon when they found themselves at the Ravines. Perad could see immediately why this place had been chosen. The near vertical wall of rock facing west was covered with fissures and fractures and there were enormous boulders and great mounds of broken stone heaped at the bottom so that the entrances to the narrow valleys and gorges were hidden, or seemed, unless very close, no more than cracks in the mountainside. Provided they were careful with footprints and avoided any smoke, they should not be discovered here. In front was an untidy line of scrubland, low bushes and stunted trees, which further concealed the ravines.

They chose the third ravine from the south. The first two were short and ended at a wall of rock. They looked unfriendly and felt like traps. The one they chose had a narrow entrance, protected by a tangle of trees and scrub among a tumble of rockfall where the cliff had partly collapsed. Inside, it had many caves and wide crevasses in the steep stepped sides. In length and width it made Perad think of the wide streets he had seen in Darkhope, a lifetime away from here. At the far eastern end it narrowed again to only a few paces wide before sloping steeply upwards over broken ground, and opening to where a ribbon of forest was backed by the looming mountains.

There was some excitement at moving in. The south side had an irregular row of small caves which were taken by families. There were shelves, recesses, alcoves and platforms in these; worked long ago by those who had used them as winter quarters. Other caves were found above, accessed by rough hewn steps.

The north side of the valley had a few larger caves and two very large ones which were quickly selected for communal use. The first one was to be a living space. A protruding shoulder of rock hid its dark entrance from the valley opening and could mask a substantial fire. Those without families claimed berths here. Perad dropped his pack and camping roll under a ledge well into the shadows. The other large cave was allocated for storage.

The elders gathered and walked to the ravine entrance to discuss watchers and patrols. The families busied themselves creating homes and the children explored their new playing ground. Perad was left alone with nothing to do.

He went to the eastern end of the ravine to make an examination. The cold air rolling down from the mountains pushed through the gap, even narrower than it had looked from the centre of the ravine. At one point, he reached out and touched both sides and stood there at the very end of the known world. He stepped through into the place beyond.

At this end the ridge of rock which formed the ravines was less steep than the western side, falling to a rough strip of plain, perhaps two thousand paces across before the mountains began. There was mixed woodland here, more pine of the northern forest than the common valley trees. Perad had made trips to the head of the valleys north of here at times, and seen patches of this, but here it was poor woodland, sparse and ragged. It would provide little to sustain a village.

A light clatter of footsteps behind made Perad turn. It was

Dresana. She held out a deep wooden mug. "Mother sent you a drink of hot milk. It will be the last milk we have until we go home. And then we will have to find our goats in the woods. They may have roamed far by the time we return."

"Thank you, and thank your mother." He caught her eyes with his for a brief moment, then looked down. Her father had gone to fight, and Perad wanted to comfort her, but did not know what to say. He held the mug to his chest and turned to face the forest. Dresana moved to stand beside him, so close that their shoulders touched. They were silent for a while.

The early evening sun was hidden below the cliffs behind them, but its rays touched the top of the tall pines, darkening the shadows beneath. Above, the mountain peaks were pink, with deep blue in the folds. Perad wanted to comment on the scene, but again, he could not find the words.

He sipped the drink. It was flavoured with bittersweet tarok nut and was delicious. He held the mug to Dresana. She hesitated before taking a sip, and kept the mug at her mouth for a while, perhaps breathing in the aroma, before handing it back. "I should go and help," she said. "There is still much to do."

"Thank you, again," said Perad, and turned to look her in the face, but she had gone, running down the slope, with nimble steps and graceful strides, over the broken ground and out of sight through the gap.

He moved into the trees. There were types here he recognized and others which were new to him. He wondered if his grandmother would have been able to tell him, and then thought that his grandmother would not have made the journey here. He walked around without purpose or thought for a while.

He found a larranberry bush, always by a western facing rock face in the Valleys, but here simply standing on a small

142

ridge protected from the wind by a fallen tree. There were berries on it, dull and dusty brown, beneath the leaves and amongst the thorns, rare and valuable for their rich taste and ability to keep for many months. He used soft dry pine needles from the floor to dry and clean the mug. By the time he had stripped the bush, the mug was almost full and his hands scratched and bloody. He would take them to Dresana's mother. They had no usefulness to a poisoner beyond being good food.

Within a few strides of the ravine, he felt the thrill of the flux, strong and clear. There had been none when they had arrived. It rarely rose this quickly in the Valleys.

There were fires lit now, each one shielded from the west by a boulder or spur of rock. Some folk were already at work, making and crafting. The flux was not to be wasted. He passed Lerap, an old craftsman who made straps with buckles, from goat leather and from copper brought from Ledarun in the north. They were used for the fastenings of bags and packs in the Valleys, but a great many of them were sold to the cities. Perad stood for a while to watch him by firelight, crouched by a rounded rock, his hands forming and cutting and tapping, as skilful as any hands in the Valleys, which meant as skilful as any hands in the world.

And watching, he began to feel more hopeful. He belonged to a resourceful folk. Long ago, his ancestors had chosen to winter here. And his people now would do well here, and when spring came and the Gralt had been driven away, they would return to Woodall and continue their lives.

He was called to supper. Stew and bread had been prepared for those without families and was being served around a fire by the entrance to the communal cave. He took the mug of berries to the cave on the other side where Dresana and her family had settled. He could see by the light of candles that they were inside and he would not go in, and he did not call to them. He left the mug with other utensils outside and went for his bowl and spoon from his pack.

His good mood lasted while he ate his food in the company and conversation of good folk. It was black beyond the small circle lit by the glow from the fire, but for the stars, and the faint glow of lamps and candles in the caves opposite. Perad felt protected by the isolation, by the walls of rock and by the wide tracts of land they had crossed.

Before he slept, his back to the wall deep into the cave, wrapped in his blanket and groundsheet, and with his pack for a pillow, he allowed himself to map the world in his head. He saw the whole of Tarodash drawn out, circled by the ocean, the forest, the mountains and the desert. He moved his mind to the east, to the Valleys, and placed himself close to the mountains. He wondered where he could put his uncle on the map, and where he could place the Gralt, crawling their way around Tarodash like insects on a parchment.

Chapter 17

"Leatherfern leaves," said Perad. "Boiled with woodash and pine resin. That is the mix. I need leatherfern leaves. They are found near running water on southern slopes. Steep slopes. They grow in shadow." Hadrath, the goatherd, an outsider from the edge of the plain, had frostbite. He had been scouting in the mountains and had hunted down a snowdeer. He had trapped it in a gully and wrestled it to the floor before cutting its throat. The chase had exhausted him and he had slept on the mountainside. It was a good piece of meat and was not to be left behind. He woke to find that his fingers had blackened. He did not seem to care, talking only of the goats he had left to roam the woods back home in the west, but Perad worried that he would lose some fingers.

"I can take you to a place, north, across the river," said Trall. "I was there two days ago. The hillside there drops all the way to the river. It is nothing but a jump to cross the water." Trall, older than Perad, strong and tall, had joined the village with his family of homesteaders. He had said little, carried much, and done all asked of him.

"I shall come, also," said Trana, his sister. She was twin to Trall, and accompanied him everywhere.

The clear sky which had brought the hard frost in the night had filled with cloud during the late morning and was dark and angry now, with the promise of a storm. Perad took his hat, wide brimmed and lined with rabbit fur, and cape from his large pack and secured them in his small pack. He examined the sky, turning a full circle, and took off his tunic to check the flaps on the pouches on his poisoner's vest.

Trana went off to collect her pack. Trall was already cloaked, a leather garment tied at the throat, belted, and reaching below his knees. His hat was tucked in his belt. He did not take a pack. His family were conveyers with a small string of ponies, and travel was his life.

Perad had never seen frostbite, only learned of a useful mixture, and had no advice for Hadrath.

The river, when they reached it, was dark with mud, and fast flowing. Trall was correct; it could be crossed in a stride. The hill at the other side was almost a cliff, steep and unbroken, and not the place for leatherfern. Trall thought to go west where the hillside was more splintered. The sky darkened further and the first heavy drops of rain began to fall.

They followed the cliff until it fell away to an untidy plain covered in coarse ragthorn bushes, and contained in a loop of the river. They kept to the river bank. Trall was sure they would meet the hills again a little further on. The rain began to fall steadily and they stopped to put on hats and refasten clothing. Perad pulled on his elbow length cape and wished he had a full cloak. Trall was untroubled by the rain.

After the river straightened again Perad was pleased to find that Trall had guessed well. The cliffs began again, close to the river, and were backed, Perad could just see in the gloom, by a towering mountain. The river here was not named, but would flow east then south then east again to become the Woodall river, and Perad was pleased to think that in a day or so, the very water into which he trailed his fingers would flow by their own village.

He found leatherfern plants in the crevasses near to the water edge, smaller leaved and darker than the plants in the Valleys. They would catch a small period of sunlight in the middle part of the day and spend the rest of their time in shadow and dark. He saw other plants he had never seen

146

before and wished for more time, or better circumstances, to examine them. The leatherfern leaves would not break at the base and he needed his knife to collect them.

The rain came down heavier and made the rocks by the river dangerous. They decided to return in the lee of the hills across the small plain and cutting out the loop of river. The rain, intense now, was still no more than an inconvenience. It was a part of their lives. But the ever darkening sky and cliffs of black rock, overlooked by mountains shrouded in cloud and sombre mist, disheartened them. They walked solidly, in line and without conversation, Trall, Perad and, some way behind, Trana. Half of the distance around the loop, the cliffs were relieved by ravines, shadowed and ominous.

There were remnants of the old forest here, dense islands of tall dark pines amongst the more familiar trees of the Valleys, and the carpet of pine needles, already sodden from the rain, softened their footsteps and made silent their passage. They walked carefully now. This distant part of the world seemed to demand respect. The hillside descended in a series of gigantic rocky steps, some of them the height of the trees, to the edge of the plain, and it was here where they found the enemy.

"Gralt!" said Trall, in an urgent whisper, grabbing Perad's arm and almost costing him his balance. Trall dropped to his knees, pulling Perad down beside him. Thorny shrubs and large angular boulders gave them some cover. The man was standing well above them on a rocky outcrop, among the trees. The form was familiar to Perad, as was the dread which brought a gasp and a sudden tightness in the stomach. It was without a doubt a Gralt guard. Perad looked back. Trana must have seen and understood and had sunk behind a rock. Perad could see her boot protruding. The guard was very still, carefully examining the area in one direction, before turning slowly to scrutinize the next quarter.

The other four Gralt were shockingly close, perhaps two dozen strides away. They were crouched under an overhang, sheltering from the rain which was now falling in swirling sheets. To Perad's left in a cleft of a giant boulder was a small fire with a black cooking pot hanging from three sticks pushed in the ground. One of the Gralt had been skinning a squirrel and chose this moment to bring it to the pot. He stood stiffly and uttered a word, or a sound, harsh and short. His face was grey and lined, clearly seen as he approached. Perad was frozen, running was impossible. The Gralt dropped the handful of bloodied raw meat in the pot. There was another harsh word, a curse perhaps. Perad felt some of what it must be to be an invader in a far country.

The Gralt warrior went back to his companions. A gust of wind and an increase in the intensity of the rain caused the four to retreat further under the overhang. Perad let out a long slow breath. The guard on the cliff moved further north, the edge covering all but his head, which was aimed away to the north and west. The rain fell harder, louder, enough to cover a whisper. Trall's hand took Perad by the back of his neck and pulled him close, the brims of their hats pushing downwards obscuring the view. "Quick, poisoner, something to hurt them. I shall put it in their pot."

Perad shook his head. "We must go." He took off his hat to see better. The rain was now almost thundering.

"No. Not until I have tried. Make me a poison, poisoner. Quickly."

"No," began Perad, still shaking his head, but these were the people who had butchered old blind Kerim. His hands were already reaching for the pouches at his chest. He leaned further forward to protect them from the rain.

"Quickly!" The urgency steadied Perad's hands. Greycaps were small toadstools found under loose bark of fallen woodoaks. Dried, and in tiny amounts would be used as a purgative, but too much should cause terrible stomach cramps and worse. Perad emptied the pouch into the palm of his left hand. A large pinch of reedginger to accelerate the poison and a good sprinkling of carrowgrass seed to sensitise the stomach. The rain wet the mixture and Perad rolled and squeezed and formed it into a ball. A mixture this potent he would not normally touch with his hands.

He dropped the ball, the size and appearance of a redbeech nut, into Trall's hand and before he could say a word of warning, Trall was crawling on his belly under the bushes. In spite of the rain, as dark as smoke near the ground, Trall could not fail to be seen should the Gralt turn this way. Perad went from his knees into a crouch ready to run. A glance back showed him that Trana had also moved; the brim of her rain hat was now showing from behind the boulder.

Then Trall was there.

Perad saw him reach to the pot and roll behind the overhang out of view of the Gralt. He would crawl further to the right to stay out of view. Keeping him in sight, Perad backed towards the thicker bushes. He bumped into Trana who was waiting for him. They shuffled away into the trees. Trall joined them. He was covered in mud, leaves and blood from scratches on his face and knuckles.

"Should we stay to see what happens?" asked Perad. He reached for Trall's hands to turn them and examine the palms. They were muddied and wet, but showed no broken skin.

"Too dangerous," said Trall. He was breathing too hard for more words and set off quickly, half crouched, into the woods, heading for the thickest of the trees. Perad and Trana hurried to catch him. Once away from the overhang, they stood straighter and slowed to a fast walk.

"What will that do to them?" asked Trall.

"They will vomit themselves to death," said Perad. Trall wiped his palms on the sides of his cloak.

"Will it taste?" asked Trana. Her voice held curiosity rather than concern.

"It should not," said Perad. "If they were making a broth with oats or dried beans or something, it would not be noticed. I do not know what they eat. Surely even they do not eat squirrel boiled in water."

"Whatever happens, we must give warning that Gralt are about," said Trall. "Let us hurry."

Chapter 18

They worked upstream for a while to give them distance from the Gralt and it was hard. The rain thundered, eased for a while, then hit them in waves when the wind turned into a howling gale. It felt icy, then it looked icy as sleet mixed with the rain, and to seek shelter would have been the best advice in most circumstances. But to get away, cross the river and make their way back to camp was uppermost in their minds and desperation clouded their thinking. The river which they had taken at a stride on the way out, and could have done so at many places, was a savage rumbling torrent. They searched up and down and the best of places was half again a good leap and they could not cross.

Up in the hills it should be narrower, but the terrain was more difficult; down towards the west it would be wider and less violent, but there may be Gralt down there. By the time the little light in the sky began to fade they were in desperate trouble.

Three folk of the wooded valleys of Tarodash, one a working traveller, should not be caught like this. To have sought shelter in a cave or overhang, or to manufacture a refuge from the woodland, to have lit a fire, warmed and dried themselves, was child's play, and they had got it wrong. And now they were shivering and mute. They stood, unable to make a decision. They had tinder, and a knife handle and a rock were all that were needed to make sparks and start a blaze, but finding wood dry enough to build a fire would take too long.

"We must risk the river," said Trana. She suddenly seemed

151

stronger than the boys. "Enough handholds and we can wade. We cannot be any wetter. And once across, a little hard walking will warm us up. We shall try up there." She moved purposefully up the hillside, climbing from boulder to boulder.

Fifty paces higher in the hills, the water fell in a series of steps. An enormous longwillow tree leaned over the river from behind a rocky platform above a mess of white water and jagged rocks, the beginning of what was now a waterfall the height of three men, falling into a swirling pool. This was where Trana had stopped. There may be handholds and places for the feet, thought Perad, but surely the force of the water would be too much to resist. And a slip and all would be over, he thought, his eyes following the path of the water down the hillside. Then he was beyond thought, and only doing was left. He moved to the edge.

"If we link ourselves together," Trall began, then stopped and shook his head. The water, where it punched between the boulders, seemed solid. But there was no choice; he found a place for his foot and leaned into the force of the water to seek purchase for his hands. Perad held a handful of cloak and pulled tight to make them into one body. The water immediately rose to thigh height as it backed up against a new obstruction, and they were less than two steps into the swollen river. The spray, the cold and the desperation made him reckless. He reached back for Trana and she was there, taking hold of his arm and shoulder. But she was pulling him back and shouting. Above the din, he heard her scream, something about the flux. He roared in Trall's ear. "Back." But Trall had not even yet found his next foothold, and there was no need for urgency. Trall allowed himself to be dragged back onto the rocky platform. They sought what little shelter they could beneath the tree.

"The flux. The flux is up." Trana's voice was quiet, the

energy gone out of it now, but the determination was there.

The flux was up, already high, and still rising rapidly, and Perad felt the thrill of it, though he could see no value in it. Even the flux could not help them build a shelter in this place.

But Trana was taking control. "I have some skill in ropemaking," she said, and turned to the great longwillow tree and caught a handful of the thin trailing branches which were whipping back and forth over the surface of the water and rock. "If I pull these branches together, add to them, make them longer above the water, it will support us as we cross; we will be roped to the tree. Look, they already reach the far side." Trall had seen it and was leaning out to catch the ends of branches further out over the river. His cloak billowed, his hat spun away and was lost in the spray. Perad took his arm and Trana took Perad's tunic and then they were leaning back, Trall with a handful of the stringlike strands. "Now I need more pieces to add to these," Trana said, nodding towards the branches over the ledge away from the water.

"I will get them," Trall said, thrusting the handful at Perad and taking out his knife. Perad took them and the whipping and swaying of the tree threatened to drag him into the river. He leaned back to keep them secure.

Trana muttered something and Perad turned to hear. Some of the certainty had left her and her head was down and her shoulders slumped. "My hands," she said, "my hands are too cold to work."

"My neck," said Perad. "The back of my neck." And he dropped to his knees, loosened his cape and let his head fall. Trana pushed her hands down the back of his tunic. Surely flesh should never be that cold, he thought. Trana held her hands palm down and then tucked her fingers under. The movement let in the wind and rain. Perad was shivering uncontrollably. He forced the ends of the branches he was clinging to under his knees to stop them escaping. Then Trall was by them. He had cut lengths of about his own height and laid them over Perad's back.

"Shorter and thinner," she said. "I can weave with short pieces, but not thick ones."

Trall halved what he had, laying the thin strands back over Perad and discarding the other ends, and went off for more.

And so they progressed. Trall catching and trimming the whipping strands, each about a stride in length, Trana knotting and weaving, first above Perad, then, as the rope progressed, by his face, then below him as the rope of strands grew longer, and Perad still kneeling, dropping his head for her to warm her hands whenever the terrible cold made her clumsy. Each time she returned to Perad, she thrust her hands deeper seeking the heat which seemed to retreat further down his back. And all the time the flux rose and with it hope, and perhaps there was a warmth in the flux which he had never felt before. His shivering slowed, and some strength returned.

Once the rope was within his vision, he could watch her hands adding to the tree a plaited strand, the thickness of his thumb, like the additions to the hair worn by little girls. Flux driven, the rope was inspired. It would hold.

Then it was ready. Trall would hold the rope, he had the strongest grip and the greatest weight. Perad on his right, leading, Trana on his left, they pulled together arms around his waist, and faces to the torrent, they entered the water. It was barely waist deep at its worst, but it hauled viciously at their legs. They pushed and scrabbled and at times were almost suspended, but the rope held and Trall's grip held and they were on the far bank among rocks and bushes as comforting as anything they had ever known.

Trall let go of the rope with a nod and a grim smile, and it swung away, back over the river to be lost among the whipping branches, the spray, and the rain.

And then it was walking, as weary as he had ever felt.

Perad led the way, down to more even ground, east first, before turning south towards the camp. Glancing behind showed him Trall leading Trana, and at times Trall at the back. He staggered and fell at one point and the girl caught up with him and passed him as he struggled to his feet. To break step was to lose valuable progress.

But in the end, it was only the cold and the anxiety which had exhausted them. The distances had not been great and the grazes and bruises were a small burden to them. The walking kept away the worst of the cold, and the distance eased some of the apprehension. There was still some grey light in the sky to the west when they reached familiar ground.

Still, they were near staggering when they met Jattog, the young cheesemaker, on a scouting watch duty near the northern edge of the bowl. He had heard them coming and hid in the shadows of the bushes. He began to reprimand them for their racket until Trana spoke. "We have seen Gralt, over the river, but still not too far away. We had to wade the river."

Jattog looked frightened and scanned the trees and rocks for sign of the enemy. "I was sent to watch for you and return with you if you were encountered. You were expected back before dark. "Now I should stay here, or perhaps scout further out." he said. There was a tremble in his voice, but he stood taller and took a firmer grip of his staff.

"The ones we saw will not be here tonight," said Perad. "Even if they wished, they could not cross the river. There may be others, though. You should keep your watch. We shall tell what we have seen and suggest extra watchers. You should not be alone."

"I could stay with him until another is sent," said Trana, but she was shivering and her voice was faint.

"Thank you," said Jattog. "But I shall be safe. I shall hide in the undergrowth until someone arrives."

When Perad looked back, Jattog had placed himself between two dense sowtongue bushes, well hidden from the north by their large dark leathery leaves. He was standing straight and still, watching for the enemy.

The short stop had disturbed the rhythm of their walking, and they could not find it again. And slowing down they began to feel the cold again, a hard, dangerous cold. It was fortunate they had not far to go.

Chapter 19

Even in the rain, they would not take the easier walking on the edge of the Trough, and stayed in the trees. The broken ground and the exhaustion caused them to stumble often, even Trall, the eldest and strongest. There was another guard on watch at the northern end of the ravines sheltering beneath a rockash tree. He had spread a groundsheet across the branches to keep off the worst of the rain, although it had almost stopped by then. They were out of the wind here, and almost back and they found the last of their energy and lifted up their step. Perad saw the guard was Ganat, brother of Dresana, and there was Dresana with cloak and hood, sitting in the rain on the lowest branch with her legs dangling. Perad reached for her ankle to steady himself, and she laughed, until he looked up and she saw his face, white and strained and streaked with mud.

"We saw Gralt, across the river in the woods to the north east," said Trall. "We need more watchers. We saw Jattog. He needs relieving, or help. We shall send them from the camp. You had better come with us," he added, looking up at Dresana.

"We watch in pairs," she said. She twisted and swung down from the branch landing to face Perad. "I shall stay here."

She was tall and graceful and not a child, Perad realized.

Trall would not argue with her, but her brother Ganat would. "Go back with them. We need roving sentries here. You can return to help me with my duty when you have sent help." She took her order well and took Perad by the arm to lead him, let go, and held him again. He thought to remove her hand, but stumbled, and she reached around his waist and supported him. Trall went off to report to the elders, and to suggest extra guards and patrols.

Dresana helped him to the fire in the entrance of the large cave around the shoulder of rock which was shielded from the valley opening. He knelt and laid his hat and cloak between himself and the red embers. They began to steam almost immediately. "I can tend Hadrath now," he said.

But he found his efforts of the day had been mostly unnecessary, for when Hadrath was sent for, Perad saw that the goatherd's injuries were less than he had thought. In his determination to be the healer for the village, he had overestimated the severity of the frostbite. He found little more than blisters and blackened skin which would have healed itself in time. Still, he would make the poultice and apply it since he had the leatherfern. There were only the weak remnants of a waning flux now, but it did not matter. Hadrath was content to sit in the warmth for a while. Someone asked for an account of the encounter with the Gralt, and Trana began the tale.

Dresana brought him hot water in a bowl and helped him tear up the leaves and lay them in the water. His own hands were cold and clumsy. Working on his knees, he added powdered pine resin, and selected fine white woodash from beneath still burning logs. He placed the bowl on the ground to wait for the infusion to develop. Dresana made him sit then and she unlaced his boots and unwound his wrappings and placed them to dry close to the fire. She went to get dry grass from the tinder supply to stuff the boots so they would not lose shape when drying. When Perad almost spilt the mixture in the bowl trying to stir it, she took his hands in hers and held them and squeezed them to bring heat into them. He decanted the water from the bowl to leave a sludge which he spread over the damaged fingers of Hadrath. He then wrapped more leatherfern leaves around the fingers to hold the poultice in place. "These need tying," he said, and Dresana fetched from somewhere narrow strips of cloth to complete the treatment. Others around the fire, mostly women, watched the whole operation and listened to Trana's account of the afternoon with little comment. Hadrath had endured the activity as if the hand did not belong to him, nodding his thanks to Perad as Dresana finished. Trana had reached the end of her tale, and went off.

"Well done," said Hadrath, as he stood to leave. The few men there also stood, and left with him. Conversation between the women began again around the fire. Dresana picked up the bowl with the remains of the mixture. "Will this work on scatches?" she asked, taking his right hand and turning it to examine the back. Both his hands had been damaged by thorns, and were beginning to sting now that they were warm.

"It will do more good than harm," he said.

"Then we shall not waste it," she said, and began to gently smear it along the scratches.

It felt good, and with the warmth, Perad eased back and rested his head on his pack, and closed his eyes.

Something woke him later. The fire was a heap of deep red embers without flame. Dresana had gone, as had the other women. Someone had covered Perad in a blanket and wrapped his feet. His boots were still near to the fire, but had been turned. A man was curled asleep with his back to the fire. He was well wrapped, but for his boots, which were near to Perad's face and shining red with wetness. Perad thought he saw flies dancing in the glow of the fire and looked up and one touched his face, cold and wet. They were snowflakes, the first of the winter. He sat up to see better and to contemplate their importance. Something moved beyond the cave entrance. It was Kadat, who had been playing cards in the inn on the night that the Gralt came, who had, the stories told, although he would not speak of it himself, put his knife into the throat of the last Gralt warrior to enter. He was looking towards the valley opening. He had one hand at his waist holding a club which rested on the floor. He leaned it against the wall and came to squat opposite Perad and held the backs of his hands to the heat. The glow from the fire reflected in his wet face, as it did in the walls of the cave. He seemed made of stone. His movement had brought eddies of snowflakes into the cave entrance to hiss on the reddened logs, and to settle on Perad.

He nodded at Perad and at the snow. "This could benefit us. I doubt the Gralt can read the woods as we can. A light fall will show their movements. We can hide ours. A heavy fall would trap us here, but I do not think there will be a great deal. The cloud is breaking."

"Were we right to come here?" asked Perad. "Should we have gone to Parden?"

"Two, perhaps three days on the plain to Parden. A meeting with Gralt horsemen would have destroyed us. I could not risk my family. I voted for here."

He stood and walked out to look down the valley for a while, then came back. "There are no easy answers to this. We cannot fight the Gralt if we meet them in numbers, but if we are to hide, we will hide best in our own lands."

Perad could see stars between ragged clouds over Kadat's shoulder. The snow had stopped. "I have not yet had a watch duty. Who is assigning them?"

"All of us will take our share of tasks. Do not worry, Perad, you will have plenty to do, whatever happens." He stood again. "Take your sleep while you can. I shall walk the length of the ravine."

But Perad could not sleep. He refastened his bindings and emptied his boots of hay and put them on. He would use his waking time. He found small flat rocks and pushed them into the fire with a stick, then clawed them out again and tested them with his hand. Working on his knees, he unfastened his pack and took out the remaining leatherfern leaves and laid them on the rocks to dry them, careful not to burn them. He repeated the process, heating the stones and turning the leaves, until the leaves were brittle. He would have preferred to have sun dried them and wait for the flux, but felt that his frostbite cure would be needed again, and would not to wait. He had brought one dish and pestle with him and he took this from his pack to grind the leaves. Kadat had returned and stood watching him. Perad went to get his small pack and took from it one of the two rolls of leather pouches and unrolled it. The pouches were sewn in rows, each with a flap and drawstring. Perad knew the contents of each one, and the time of collecting and making, and the level of flux. He tipped the leatherfern powder into one, precise and careful, spilling not one grain.

"Can you make me a mix to warm my toes?" asked Kadat.

"Would you prefer a potion to drink, or something to put in your boots to act quickly?" Perad was already reaching for his packs, considering the options.

"Sorry, lad, I was jesting. My watch is finished soon. I can warm my feet at the fire."

The small task had brought on sleep and Perad took off his still damp boots and replaced the hay, and found his own blanket and wrapped himself in it with his groundsheet over the top and went back to his place by the fire and slept.

Chapter 20

The snowflakes had been replaced by raindrops, and those only in light flurries, by the time he woke. The sky was already lightening and the cave was filled with the sounds of morning activity. He rolled away from the fire to avoid being stepped on as pots of water were brought to heat on the flat stones resting in the red embers at the edge of the fire. His boots had been placed by his head and the hay had been removed. They were dry. He sat up to wrap his feet and put on the boots, and looked at the fire. It had been built for the morning's cooking, and for drying clothing, ranged on frames of sticks and poles at the far side. Making a fire with only a little smoke was in the nature of life in the Valleys. Perad wanted no smoke. He had a task for the morning. He folded his blanket and rolled his groundsheet and went to find one of the council. He found himself watching out for Dresana as he went about.

Barfan, stoneworker and elder of the council, was leaning on a short stick, under an overhang, arranging duties.

"Am I needed for watch duty?" Perad asked.

"They are all arranged until supper. You did well, yesterday, Perad. We are sure the river cannot be crossed now. It is full and fast and should remain so for a day or two, even without more rain. There will be no threat from north of the river. Even so, we have a patrol along there. Fatab had hoped to cross and spy the group of Gralt which you encountered but it was not possible."

"I am worried by the fire," said Perad.

"Yes, I am. It is well hidden, but a quickly clearing sky and a drop in the wind could give us away. And it would be difficult to do without it. What can you do? You have a skill with fire and fumes, do you not?"

"The needles of stonepine will burn fiercely, and the small branches they are on char slowly, and the combination will burn away any smoke. Or so I have been taught. I have never known it necessary until now. They should be laid in layers each time the fire is refreshed."

"If that is what you have been taught, then that is what is needed. And where are these stonepine trees?"

"They grow on dry windy slopes, and there should be some between the ravines and the mountains. I have not been far into the forest there, so I shall ask Hadrath, who has scouted there."

"Take care. Tread gently. Do not go alone."

But there was no one to ask to go with him. All the lads seemed busy and he could not force himself to disturb one of the older men. So he was both anxious and pleased when he saw Dresana coming towards him.

She was crossing the ravine with a pot of water and changed direction and stopped before him. She looked briefly into his eyes and he saw her face, always earnest, even when she smiled, and thought how lovely it was. She did not speak. She placed the pot on the ground and reached for his hands. He almost pulled them away in surprise. She held them up to examine the backs of them and traced the scratches there with strokes of her thumbs. "They have healed well, Perad the Poisoner, you have good craft."

"And you have a healer's touch." He had to work hard for the right words. He did not want wrong ones.

"Have you seen Hadrath this morning?" she asked. She kept her hold of his hands.

"No. I have only just wakened."

"He is looking for you to congratulate you. His fingers are healed already."

"In truth, they were not badly damaged."

"Still, he is pleased. He is skinning a deer and did not expect to be doing so this quickly." She let his hands drop. "I must heat this water for my mother. Have you had breakfast yet?"

"I will find some," said Perad, although he was too late for the main cooking. He was happy to prepare oats for himself, but did not want to get in the way of the womenfolk around the fire.

"And have you a task for the day?" she seemed to know his mind.

"I am going into the forest between the ravines and the mountains to collect firewood. We need a particular firewood to prevent smoke."

"No one is to leave the ravine alone. Who are you going with?"

"I have found no one who is not busy, yet."

"When this water is heated, I shall not be busy. Shall I come with you?"

Perad, excited at the opportunity of her company, was unsure if she should leave the ravine. He did not dare to say to her that it was a task for men. Again she seemed to read his mind. She tilted her head to one side to look at him and challenge any objection.

She left to take care of her tasks and Perad went off to find an axe. Such equipment was deep in the large cave attended to by Fadava, a homesteader from a farm on the road to High Dresswell. "A felling axe or a stripping axe?" she asked, at his request, turning to where tools and stores were piled in the shadows against the cave wall. Perad explained his mission.

"This should fit the purpose," she said, returning from the dark with a small axe. "You will need some assistance. Take Vedan." She called into the blackness, "Vedan come here!" He was a large lad, slow and deliberate in his movements, and about

164

Perad's age, although he had not gone on the same Passing walk to the ocean. Perad had never spoken to him before.

Perad wondered how Dresana would react to the extra company, but she was simply happy at the expedition. She had brought twine to tie the bundles, and had packed bread and cheese. "We do not know if we will return in time for lunch," she said.

Vedan's father and brother had gone to train as soldiers, leaving Vedan to share with his mother the care of three younger children. They had undertaken intense discussions before leaving, as to whether the family should go to Low Dresswell or join Woodall in the mountains. "I wished at first to go to fight in the war, but they would not have me because of my age. But now I am pleased to be here. If I have to fight I shall fight defending my mother and my sisters," he said.

They were out of the eastern end of the ravine, clambering over small gullies and clefts before the ground became more even where the forest began.

Perad had stood here a number of times since the first day. He was fascinated by this mingling of the great forest of the north with the woodland trees and bushes of the Valleys. There was something impressive about their survival in the dry, shadowy place where a chill air rolled down from the mountains on even the calmest days.

They went further in. This was the very tail of the strip of the northern forest, and soon ran out southwards towards the desert. Nor was it wide here. A few hundred paces in, they could already see the lightness which suggested the eastern border and the first real slopes of the mountains. Perad did not know if it had always been so, but there did not seem enough forest here to support the ancient settlements of the Dry Ravines. "I suppose the ancients who lived here would explore the mountains, or the beginnings of them. There can have been little to hunt or eat or collect."

"Little is not nothing," said Vedan. "Hadrath hunted a deer, and we have collected nuts and berries. We have brought plenty, as the ancients must have. We shall get by."

A clearing, backed by increasingly sparse forest, gave them the best view yet of the mountains. They stood in awe. Perad could see now how much steeper and higher they were than he had ever believed. And these were only the beginning. Glimpsed between the peaks were further peaks, higher and more severe, with still more beyond.

Vedan may have had they same thoughts as Perad. "Yet if a mountain range rises at one side, it surely falls at the other. They cannot go on to the end of the world," he said aloud.

Dresana brought their attention back to the task. "Where will we find what we are looking for?"

"North," said Perad. The growth is thicker there, with more pines. A little less distant from the river would give better conditions."

He found the place he wanted, almost two thousand paces to the north, by following what appeared to be a dry stream bed through cracked cloudstone and down towards a darker patch of the forest. The trees, rounded pines with branches almost to the floor were close enough together to eliminate the sky. They went no further than the edge of the thicket.

"This is stonepine. Or a close relative. There is a little in our valley. I have seen much more on the slopes above Nerbridge, and I have been told that there are endless distances of it in the forest north of Porenden."

They worked well together. Vedan took off the lower branches with the axe and Perad trimmed the scar with his knife to reduce the damage to the tree. Dresana arranged the wood into three piles and fastened them with twine. It did not take long. They would each have a dense waist high stack to drag. Dresana had fashioned a handhold for each load from a thicker branch.

"Let us make some of the distance back before we stop for food," she said. The loads dragged like sleds over the carpet of fallen leaves and pine needles while ever they stayed where the trees were thinner towards the mountains. It became more difficult once they drew level with their ravine and had to turn west through the more dense woodland.

"Time for lunch," said Dresana.

"I shall carry on," said Vedan. "I am hoping to join a hunting party before dusk."

"Then take your food as you walk." She had a bag at each side, crossed over her shoulders, and delved into both. She broke a half loaf and pressed a large piece of cheese into the middle. It fit comfortably in Vedan's large hand. He was chewing solidly as he left, hauling his heap of firewood between the trees, and he raised his meal above his head as a sign of appreciation.

"I should like to walk in those mountains, one day," said Perad. "When the Gralt have gone. In the spring when it is not so cold but there will still be snow on the peaks." They were sitting on top of their piles of branches, eating lunch, facing east.

"I should like to go with you." When Perad did not respond, she carried on. "We could leave food in the caves, so as not to carry too much in the mountains. We could explore for a day and return to our supplies in the evening. We would draw maps and set up new bases for further exploration. It is hard to believe that we will not return here now we have lived for a little while in the ravines."

Perad's thoughts ranged further. "If anyone had found the far side, we would know. If there were people on the far side, would they not have crossed themselves?"

"The mountains themselves should be mystery enough to begin with. We can worry about the world afar, later." She had turned to face him, and was laughing at him.

Perhaps the most enjoyed activity in the southern valleys was to leave aside the task at hand and talk. It sometimes seemed that only the flux could put an end to conversation, and for some folk, not even then. Perad was enjoying having Dresana to himself. She spoke of family, life in the valley, work in the orchard, and journeys, and was happy to fill the spaces left by Perad, who found much less to say. Her face could turn from smile to frown and back to a smile again in a moment, but was a delight to watch in whatever mood. She reached over with a handful of dried fruit, to follow the cheese and bread. They ate slowly, and continued talking long after they had finished eating.

Perad had seen behind Dresana banks of dark cloud moving this way. The wind swirled and tiny pellets of hail stung his face. They stood then, and took up their loads. Perad led, and spoke over his shoulder. "This wood will last no more than two days. We will need to return soon for another supply." She replied, but the wind took away her words and Perad thought it sensible not to stop.

Vedan was there to meet them close to the valley. "I thought a storm was on its way. I came to help you back. Have a rest for a few strides." He took a bundle in each hand and leaned forward and pulled, leaving Perad and Dresana to follow behind. "Fires have been seen, and they are not ours. We are being even more careful. They were to the south of the Trough. Garin and Derim have gone to take a look. They will not get caught or seen if it is the enemy. They are good woodsmen."

"There is little woodland cover there," said Perad. "It is close to the desert."

"Still, do not worry. They will be too good for the Gralt."

At the entrance to the valley where the ground began to

168

rise Perad took one of the sleds. They had to walk backwards to get their burdens over the rough ground and through the gap. Once in the ravine they dragged their loads to the main cave. Dresana ran off to her family cave, but not before she had taken hold of Perad's hand and squeezed it.

Chapter 21

To last out the winter here in the shadow of the mountains was no great hardship. It was cold, though. The white on the peaks of the mountains had spread to cover all but the very lowest slopes, and the freezing air rolled down the west side and through the ribbon of forest to funnel into their narrow refuge. The snow that fell came mostly in grains rather than flakes and soon blew into cracks and corners where, out of the sun, it would now remain until spring.

Many wore gloves now, of goatskin, with the fur on the inside. This was unusual for the southern valleys, as were the fur trimmed hoods being sewn onto tunics. There were gloves made without fingers for those who worked crafts.

Those craftsmen and women who had been able to transport their tools and materials, continued as much as possible. The flux was strong and steady when it rose, more so than in the Valleys proper. And it appeared slightly altered. Brighter, some said; a different flavour commented others. A great deal of discussion developed on the matter, and the origin, patterns and behaviour of the flux were considered and argued. No new conclusions were reached.

Those whose work and livelihoods had been left behind occupied themselves with the sound running of the displaced village. There was cooking and cleaning, and the endless task of carrying water from the springs in the forest.

Although Perad occasionally assisted midwife Nadira in her duties as adopted healer, his craft was not greatly required. Always uncomfortable without occupation, he had asked repeatedly for duties, and eventually his persistence paid.

While considered too young for the patrols, he distinguished himself on watch, and brought smiles from the older men, for his ability to remain still and alert for long periods. He was particularly valued for the duties outside the eastern end of the ravine, essential, but where the likelihood of seeing anything but trees and mountains was remote, a watch unpopular with others.

The patrols, undertaken with great care, revealed little. Occasional distant fires were spotted, and indefinite tracks were seen, but three weeks went by without a sighting of the enemy.

The cold dry conditions in the Ravines did bring one interesting test for a poisoner's craft. Many parents had taken to wrapping the faces of their children with strips of cloth to protect them from the icy air. The children had enjoyed having all but their eyes covered, and made play out of it. But, as children would, they constantly removed the wrappings to speak. The repeated freezing of moist breath trapped within the wrapping had left a number of children with sore lips, and had produced a task for Perad.

Most of Perad's powders and mixes were made effective with the addition of water, as washes, infusions, poultices, vapours and soaks. Here he needed a salve which would resist water. He would normally use the oil from the carara leaves, found by rivers through all of Tarodash. It was so plentiful Perad did not keep a stock, and in fact, it was not easy to do so. Carara leaves gave up their oil easily, but it could not reduce to a powder, and the poisoners of the Valleys stored only powders.

With expeditions to the river in both directions now forbidden, and no carara leaves to be found on this dry high land, Perad would have to seek alternatives in the forest between the ravines and the mountains.

"I shall come with you, if I may," said Walvin. "I have not been allowed watcher or scout duty, and would be grateful for some activity." He stood stiffly.

In the time they had been in the Ravines, but for the one storm, there had been little rain, and the stream beds were dry. Fortunately there were a number of springs around which water plants would grow. The nearest of these, from which they collected their drinking and cleaning water, bubbled from a crack, pooled in a shallow dish of rock, and overflowed to vanish underground. The plants around had been flattened by the constant kneeling, but Perad wished to examine them to see what varieties there were, and what could be expected at other undisturbed springs.

Dresana was amongst the small group collecting water by the spring. Perad told her of his mission and they exchanged comments on promising locations for surface water.

Walvin had stood back and watched the conversation. When Dresana rested her hand on Perad's arm, as was her habit when speaking with him, Walvin stepped forward. "If you wish, I can take back your water, and collect more if required, and you can accompany Perad in his search."

"Thank you, but I have other tasks, mostly involving caring for my younger sisters, and I do not think you would enjoy replacing me in that activity," she said with a laugh.

Walvin laughed with her. "Yes, you are correct. I was brought up with younger sisters. They can be a burden."

There were no carara leaves, but at a spring a little further into the forest Perad found other plants, new to him, producing an oily sap when he cut the leaves. One pleased him. "I feel confident of this. Still, it may have other qualities. I shall make tests before I use it." He showed Walvin how to angle the cut at the base of the leaf, and roll the leaves to trap the sap.

Returning from an afternoon watch duty, and seeking warmth before his supper, Perad saw a good fire in the supply cave and made for it. He turned to leave when he saw the fire encircled by a meeting of adults. The five men of the elders were there, and Faren, youngest of those who had fought the Gralt in the inn. Kadat, another who had fought in the inn, was also an elder. The two women elders were not there. Garrett, the hunter and tracker, sat on a ledge of rock away from the fire.

Walvin caught the eye of Perad and motioned him to the fire. He was speaking. The flickering yellow light from the fire caught in his eyes and gave them a spirit which his voice did not have.

"Whatever our courage, no matter how resolute we are, if we meet even a small force of the Gralt we will lose. They will destroy enough of our defenders to reach our families." He stirred at the fire with a stick and his shadow wavered behind him.

"They are trained warriors and we are not. If we meet them, we will fight them and we will delay them. But we will not stop them." He looked for someone to tell him that he was wrong, that determination to protect their families would give the men the power to resist forever. No one spoke.

"We have been correct in our actions. We can only hide and wait for the soldiers of Tarodash to prevail. That is why we are here. Our decisions are about the best way to hide. We must not make a mistake. The Gralt should not be here in this far corner of the world, but they are. They must not discover us."

"Perad. Let us hear your thoughts. We wrap ourselves in these discussions daily. We repeat our thoughts with the words almost unchanged. We cannot stop ourselves. Come. You have seen them from close up. You have seen them more than once. Give us a different view. Release us from this spell."

Perad took a while to arrange his words. "I believe they are exploring in order to make plans for an invasion. The small groups we have encountered will be sent out from a main force, to report back. That main force will be the business of our soldiers." His mouth was dry and he stopped. These men, whose duties as elders were to arrange for the maintenance of bridges, letters of introduction, the seating at a festival, had had the very survival of their village thrust upon them. "Our actions have been correct. Our concern is to avoid their patrols. I doubt they are seeking us. I believe they are exploring the limits of our land." His voice trailed to a whisper and his head fell. "They are not woodmen, and they do not like being here. They will go away. We must hide until they are persuaded to do so."

"Faren, you also have seen them."

"Perad is correct. They do not belong here. They are from southern lands and will not easily endure our winter. And the resistance of Tarodash may have surprised them. Perhaps they do wish to avenge the killing of the four in the inn, though I doubt it. I doubt they even know of it. I suspect their motive is plain. They are exploring as part of an intended invasion. Their purpose does not affect us. We must remain well hidden, but be prepared to fight if the time comes."

There was a long silence, before Walvin spoke again. "Forgive us, Perad, Faren. It is our duty to worry. We hide and know nothing of events around us. A careless footprint can destroy us. We must not make a mistake."

A child cried briefly in a nearby cave, and was scolded and silenced by a mother's voice.

"There is one matter we have resolved," continued Walvin to Perad. "And you shall be the first to hear it. I am no longer senior elder of Woodall. That burden goes to Tardeb. There are decisions to be made requiring a younger and healthier mind and body than mine. Do not look shocked. It is an

174

obvious course, and one I am completely comfortable with. Tardeb shall be senior elder, Kadat shall make judgments concerning warfare, and Garrett those concerning travel."

He pushed himself to his knees and began to reshape the dwindling fire.

"You have been kept too long from your supper, Perad. Off you go."

Chapter 22

It was a morning of brilliant blue sky and hard shadows. The sun had cleared the mountain tops and its rays angled along the ravine. The flux was high and folk were at work. Perad had a watch duty high on the southern shoulder at the ravine entrance, with a view across the Trough and the approach from the north. He sat in the shade between two boulders, a good position, unseen from the west. It could be cold, though.

It had rarely been windy in these parts, but in the mornings the cold air rolled down the mountains, now fully snow covered, and pushed along the ravine. It eased through the gap between the boulders and made the watcher shiver. Not Perad at this moment, though, for Dresana had a short time ago made the tricky climb to the lookout post to bring him a pair of mittens she had made for him. She had sewn them from goatskin, double layered with fur on the inside and outside. She had hurried away to her tasks and he turned to watch her as she crossed the ravine below. His hands were warm now, as were his shoulders from the brief hug she had given him before she left.

Stanal, older brother of his friend Danat, had duty on the opposite side of the ravine entrance. His perch was higher and more precarious, reached by severe climb involving holds rather than steps, and the ledge chosen as a lookout point was so narrow that the watcher had to twist himself into a vertical crevice to be secure. Here it was possible to crouch, kneel or stand, but not sit. At least, thought Perad, that position would be warmed by the sun this morning.

Stanal had changed stance often during his watch, as Perad himself had done when on duty at that post. It was an uncomfortable, but important lookout, affording a view across the southern part of the Trough all the way to its edge, and to the woodland towards the river crossing.

Perad watched Stanal struggle to his feet once more and lean forward for a better view. This time, though, there was an urgency in his movements which could not have been brought on solely by discomfort. Perad stood also. His view to the south west was hidden. He watched Stanal. "What is it? What do you see?" he asked. It was a soft call, but louder than he had intended, and heads below turned to look up.

Stanal did not answer, but leaned further forward, one hand thrust in a crack for purchase. He shielded his eyes with his other hand and kept his head steady. There was something claiming his attention, and low in Perad's stomach, a heavy feeling grew.

On the plains and in the cities, Perad had been told, were people who believed that the course of their lives was already determined, drawn out as roads on a map; that events were to happen to them and encounters were to be had which could not be avoided, or that to attempt to avoid would bring destruction onto the poor soul who could not accept his fate. But in the Valleys where the world was guided by the seasons and the weather, and the growth and change of the woodland, and where the actions of the people were inconsequential to the cycles of nature's life, these were foolish notions. You woke each day to face that which the day provided.

But Perad had no doubt that he was to face the Gralt again one day, and he now knew that it was to be this day. The Gralt were coming.

With a careful check to the north to ensure there was no danger there, he turned to clamber down the rough hewn steps to the floor of the ravine.

He reached the ground and ran towards the clutter of rockfall at the ravine entrance. Others had sensed the urgency and were hurrying there. Calls and arrangements were being made. Stanal was also climbing down. Perad watched him jump the last part, a little too far, which left him sprawling in the dust. He scrambled up and crossed to Perad. There was blood on his hands and chin. "Come and look," he said. "Careful. Do not be seen."

They hurried up the heap of slabs to peer over the jagged edge. Others had arrived and were climbing to find viewpoints. "What is it?" asked Kadat, reaching a position beside Stanal.

Stanal rested his elbows on the top of a boulder and held his head to steady his vision. He was breathing hard. "I cannot see them from here. But they are there. In the Trough. Seven figures from the direction of the river crossing. I saw two at first, and thought it to be Fadrab and Herth who have the patrol out there, and then I saw them wait for others who followed. There were five others. They joined and came on together. But then I spied what must have been Fadrab and Herth hurrying towards us in the scrub to the south. They will be here soon."

They were not soon, and it was an anxious wait. Fadrab was first. He came slithering between rocks and was white with worry and fatigue. "Gralt, seven of them, they bridged the river at our crossing yesterday evening. They set out at daybreak and are in the Trough coming this way." There were questions, many at once, in a confused rush. Fadrab did no more than shake his head. "We passed Derim and Garin on watch duty. They kept to their position." He pointed to the south.

Herth arrived, an old man, too old for this. He could barely stand. Perad took his arm and placed it around his neck to support him. The rise and fall of his chest frightened Perad.

But he found his strength and controlled his breathing.

178

"We watched them from the woods. The found our felled trees and crossed. Last evening. One of them slipped and went in, but the river is low and he was pulled out. We could hear them curse. They lit a fire to dry his clothes, otherwise they may have come this way last night. We watched them through the night. They camped separately, two and five. Once we knew their direction, we hurried back. We have tracked them from the edge of the Trough staying on the edge out of sight in the trees and rocks, but it is a long way round. They will be here soon.

"We were not seen. They do not know we are here. I am certain of this. This is a chance encounter."

"But if they come this way they will find us." Kadat had kept a high position to watch the Trough. His voice held sadness and resignation, as if he felt something of what Perad had felt. But there was a solidity to it, also. "There cannot be time to run. We cannot gather what we need to survive. The time has come to face them." He climbed down to join the gathering crowd of villagers, turning amongst them to make his point.

"We will fight them. It is only a scouting group. There are only seven of them, and there are many more of us. It will be costly, but we shall beat them. They will take back no report of us." He looked towards Tardeb, but the elder had no reply for him.

Trekana, mother of Nidal and wife of Herth, spoke up. "We can run. I will not lose my men when there is no need." Her son stared at the ground. Her husband pushed himself away from Perad's support, and stood straight. Neither spoke.

Kadat shook his head. "If they come this way they will pass our camp and they will see our camp and if we have run they will follow us. It would seem we have to fight them sometime. Better to face them here where we can take advantage of a defensive position."

Tardeb found words at last. "Even if we surprise them, we would suffer many losses, and we cannot hide a battle; if others are nearby, it could give away our position. We would still have to run."

Stanal had continued watching the plain. He had climbed part way up the cliff for a better sighting. Bloodied handprints marked his way. He spoke from his perch. "I see them. They will soon be here. Though not so soon. Their heading is a little to the south. They will meet the cliff face and travel north along it, I think. A thousand paces, perhaps a thousand and a half. We do have a little time."

But the decision was difficult, and the time was passing.

"We have men out on patrol," said Fadrab. "We passed Derim in the woods, and I suggested he stay there. If we run we will be abandoning them. We should fight for them." No one would offer an argument.

"Then we shall fight," said Tardeb. "Though I fear the consequences." His hand shook, but he took out his knife and stepped forward.

"Wait, wait," said Perad. He had been staring along the ravine at the dark shadows and the low, blinding winter sun and turned to examine the ground. "We are not so visible, our marks are not great. And we can become less visible. We can hide. Hide the village. We can do it." He unbuckled his tunic and took it off, holding it by the collar, trailing on the floor. He began to sweep, spreading stones and sand, removing footprints. The dust lifted and settled. There was no shape or pattern to the markings. "Look, it can work. They may not see us. They need not know we are here. Quick. Hide what can be hidden. Cover what cannot be moved. We have the flux. Use the flux."

"We can," said Tardeb, staring into the harsh light, and down to the ground. "Yes, it is worth the attempt." He caught the eyes of Kadat, who gave one firm nod. "Spread the message. Cover or hide everything."

Stanal kept his position, calling. "Five hundred paces. They are at the cliff face and cannot see the entrance. Hide the footprints. They are coming this way."

"All the children into the supply cave," called Tardeb. "If things go wrong, we fall back to there."

"Four hundred and fifty." Stanal was easing himself lower.

Perad dashed further out, ducking to remain hidden. It was mostly bare rock and there were few markings except in dust and sand in the lee of the largest boulders. He kicked, swirled, scraped. The flux helped; his movements were sure and precise; the signs of their activity vanished. Another was at the same task at the northern shoulder a few strides away. He did not see who it was.

"Four hundred paces. Stay well back." Stanal's voice was quiet now, urgent, controlled.

Perad retreated, clearing the marks of his own boots. He stood to scan for signs that would give them away. When he looked up he saw that it was Trall who was working with him. Their shoulders touched and they stood to look into the ravine. Here near the entrance, harsh sunlight, hard shadows, no colour. The tracks chosen as best paths had been strew with stones and looked no more than chance markings, creations of the wind and weather.

Further along, there were folk everywhere, crossing the ravine, carrying bundles, dragging children, all in silence.

Then, quickly, magically, it began to clear. "Three hundred paces," came the call, whispered now. Someone further down relayed it.

What could not be moved easily had blankets thrown over them, and handfuls of dust, sticks, pebbles. Perad saw a loom covered and become a low, untidy heap of stone in a few heartbeats, a skin stretched on a wooden frame changed to a slab of fallen rock.

"Two hundred paces. Hide now!"

And suddenly the ravine was deserted.

The men of the village came then, hurrying along the cliff walls, silent, grim and with knives drawn, to take places crouched behind rocks and boulders and in the shadows in fissures and crevasses.

Stanal had slithered from his perch and was pressed into a crack in the cliff face. His face was white and stood out. He was unsure what to do.

A gash, deeper than nearby ones, looked sound, and Perad pointed to it. Stanal pushed himself into it. The strong sun reflecting from the rock face deepened the shadows, and Stanal disappeared.

More men moved past, phantom like, to melt into the rocks nearer the entrance, some crouched, some standing, all with knives held low, and became still. Perad had time to wonder, then, how these men who had lived their entire lives without violent conflict could suddenly become deadly warriors. He saw Kadat take a forward position, down on one knee, a knife in each hand.

Perad backed into a fold in the cliff face.

Fear and effort had made him breathe hard, loud and ragged. He controlled it and quelled the panic, leaving the fear to keep him prepared for what he had to face. He fumbled for his knife, failed to grasp it and realised he still had mittens on. He shook them off and they dropped behind him.

Then he heard the voices and froze. He did not have his knife in his hand, but he could not move.

His head was pressed into the rock and he could not see the ravine entrance. By swivelling his eyes he looked back into the ravine. It was empty, hostile, uninviting, a crack of wasteland in a deserted corner of the world.

Across the way men waited, poised. A single command would bring them to battle. Above one, red brown smears of still wet blood from Stanal's hands, caught the light, and Perad's attention.

The Gralt were passing the opening. Perad could hear the creak of leather and the dull tone of metal in contact with something hard. He thought of their heavy swords. He heard a short bust of speech, a pause, a single word, another in response. Curses surely, thought Perad.

He could not see and he could not move to make a view. He should not move.

And then they were past. More speech, moving away. Another word, and another, fainter, or perhaps the wind. Then nothing. No one moved. Perad waited, and still no one moved. He had been holding his breath and his vision blurred from the effort. One of the men opposite made a signal and crept forward. Another man, almost within touching distance of Perad, came out of a crack and slid by. Perad had not known he was there. A long time passed. Then a voice, a soft voice, a valley voice, and words of his own speech, saying that they were gone, that we were safe.

Perad eased away from the rock face. He had his hand on the hilt of his knife, utterly without memory of reaching for it. He had not drawn it from its sheath, and he let go and bent for his mittens and moved out into the open. Other folk were moving out with no obvious purpose. Perad felt the cold wind and remembered he had thrown his tunic in a fissure somewhere. He found it with some others and shook the dust from it and put it on and checked the pouches sewn inside.

There were faces further along the ravine peering out as the news was spread. Perad joined the men gathering at the ravine entrance. They were discussing patrols and watchers.

"We have four men to the north. I can only hope they are alert," said Tardeb.

"Those Gralt make a great deal of noise," said Garrett.

"Our men will hear them coming. They will be safe. I shall follow the enemy, see where they head. This was hunters' work, and Garrett took charge. "Fadrab, are you well enough to come with me?"

Fadrab was tightening his tunic. He nodded and moved into the shadows amongst the scrub and rocks, trailing the enemy.

Chapter 23

"Stanal, bring your good eyes here." It was Tardeb on the ledge recently occupied by Stanal, peering to the south west. There was puzzlement in the voice, but no distress. Still, it brought new concern to those below.

Perad had examined Stanal's hands which were torn, without being a real worry. He would clean them later, with warm water and a mix, when there was less urgency. Meanwhile, someone had handed Stanal a pair of old mittens. He took them to stuff in a pouch on his tunic, and climbed to the watch post, wincing at each hold. Tardeb reached for him and hauled him onto the platform and they stood holding on to each other to keep balance, staring into the distance.

Tardeb pointed and directed Stanal, who looked hard before making a report for those below, his head still and his voice soft and clear. "It is not the Gralt. There are three of them, following the line of the Trough, staying in the trees. They are moving cautiously, and will be out of sight of anyone low down. They must know of the Gralt and have seen their passing. I believe it is Derim and Garin. The third one is between them and is cloaked, and may be a prisoner."

The initial easing of the tension amongst those on the ground, gave way to an excitement at the possibility of a prisoner. More information was called for.

Stanal shifted his feet, perhaps relieving tightness in his muscles. Tardeb spoke to him, unheard below, and Stanal looped an arm around his waist. "They have withdrawn further into the rough ground. It may be that they are in line of sight from the north and are making sure that the enemy do not see them."

Some time passed. Stanal rubbed his eyes, stretched his neck, and reset his concentration. "Ah, I have them again and it is Derim and Fatab for certain. And the third is no Gralt."

"I see them well now," said Tardeb. "And I can follow their course. Take a rest. You have done well." There was a good deal of shuffling as they arranged themselves in a position where Stanal could begin to climb down, made more complicated by the elder's determination to keep his target in sight. He stopped on a wider ledge and examined his hands. Even from a distance, Perad could see fresh blood.

"And what of the Gralt?" Tardeb called to Jattog on the other lookout. "Is there anything to the north?"

Jattog called his report. "Neither the Gralt, nor our folk are to be seen. The enemy must be well away by now. We shall receive good warning if they return. We are safe for now."

Stanal jumped to the ground once more, and Perad went to examine his hands. He could do little until he had time and water. Stanal was unconcerned.

"I would value someone relieving me here," Tardeb called down. "I am a little large for this place.

"And I believe I know who is to join us. This is interesting. We should have news of events soon."

Trall was already climbing and the two passed on a wide step. "Look along the line of the ravines to beyond the corner of the Trough. They are in the trees. You will find them easily."

"They will be here presently," he said, as he reached the ground. "Unlikely though it is, I believe we have a visitor. Let us see if I am correct."

He smiled and would say no more. The danger had clearly passed and a few of the womenfolk had joined the group at the entrance to the ravine, scattered amongst the rocks, all looking south.

Tardeb strode out to take a position a hundred and fifty paces away, amongst the rockfall by the entrance of the next ravine, to watch the approach. "Here they are," he called through cupped hands, and left his post to meet them. He was out of sight for a while in the shadows of the cliff face and among the rubble. Long moments passed before the group came into sight. They clambered over broken ground, heads down, watching their feet. Once on clear footing, the cloaked one looked up.

"Dran," said Perad softly.

"Good, good, good," said Walvin. "Matters cannot be so grave in the west if Dran has found his way here safely." He took a few steps to meet the approaching party.

Dran's cloak was open and a sword hung from his belt. His face was strained and his eyes dark, but they sought out Perad, and he had a grin for him. He had a scar, newly healed, on his cheek and jaw. "Your entire village safe, I hear. More than I believed possible. We watched the Gralt from the far side of the Trough, and we watched them pass. That was a bad moment. I came on their fire by the river crossing, the soil still warm, and knew they were near. I was fortunate. Had they stayed a little longer, I may have walked into them. I ran, then, and was found by these good men.

"But first, there are other Gralt in this area, thirty, perhaps. They have become separated from their other force, and they have followed the Woodall river, mostly along the northern bank, but some have crossed and come this way, as you have seen. There were no spare patrols of ours to send this far east. We do not know if the Gralt are gathering, and we do not know their intent. Keep good guard. We have passed two of your lookouts, and you will have set watchers and patrols to the north. Take great care." He looked around, assessing the ravine as a stronghold, or hideaway, and nodded.

"What of the war?" asked Walvin. "How are things?"

"Yes, I have news. A good part of it will please you." He found himself a low boulder to sit on. The villagers remained standing. A few more of the womenfolk had joined them.

"In the main, the war is going well." He was eager to reassure, and reinforced his words with nods. "Perhaps not so well in the west, where the main Gralt forces are, but then, not so badly either. It will soon be over.

"Here in the eastern plains and the border of the Valleys, the enemy are on the run. Perhaps not on the run. The Gralt do not run easily. But they have fallen back to the river. It may be that they have spread themselves too thinly. We have a sizeable army of good and determined soldiers, and have had success raiding their smaller forces. We simply avoid their main force. It has been a successful policy. They have chosen not to attack Parden, and so have no real target in the south east. Each of our raids fragments them a little more. We are winning. But for remnants, we may have won in this part of Tarodash."

He stopped as Nadira handed him a water bag. When he had drunk, she lifted his chin and examined the scar which stretched down his neck and below his collar. "It is nothing," he said. "I have discovered I am no warrior. I have survived by the courage of others." Nadira let go, and his head fell and he stared at the ground for a while.

Perad, unable to contain himself, asked, "What of my uncle Tavit?"

Dran looked up and smiled. "When I last saw him, you uncle was fine." He looked around the watching faces. "They have been well spread and I have seen little of them, but truly, I know of no casualties among the men of Woodall, who are distinguishing themselves as soldiers or scouts. The men of the Valleys have proved particularly good at tracking and, somehow, in anticipating the enemy.

"In skirmishes, we have devised a strategy of seeking the

high ground and charging down into the enemy, spears at the front, swords following, and horsemen at the side. The enemy have not yet found an answer. We have knowledge of the land, which they do not, and so long as we avoid their larger forces, we are besting them.

"I suspect they came expecting little resistance, and have been surprised by what they have encountered. They are losing the appetite for this. They will depart."

His head fell again. "I set out with little idea of where I would reach and filled my pack with dried goatmeat. I have eaten little else for three days. I should not complain, but a change of meal would be welcome." Nadira took his arm and pulled him to his feet and led him into the ravine. Some of the group went with them.

Tardeb discussed exchanges of watches and patrols with a number of the men. Perad was not required for a further duty and hurried after Dran. He found him already eating by the fire. Others were there and the news was being shared.

"And you?" Nadira asked when he placed his bowl on the floor. "By what means did you arrive here?"

"I had been providing information of the surrounding land to one of the captains. We had been clearing the enemy from behind our main forces, and I persuaded the captain to allow me to make this journey. I felt the information would be of help to you. If you can remain hidden for a few more days, a week or two, our soldiers will be here. This is almost over.

"You will be pleased to know that your village is intact. I passed through Woodall two days ago. The enemy cannot have failed to have done so, for they were following the river, but I saw no damage.

"Nerbridge is safe, by the way. There was some indication that the enemy would go that way, and the villagers were persuaded to leave for Marben.

"Any Gralt in this area may be seeking a rendezvous with another group, but we do not know of it. They may look to join their main forces on the plain. Now I have seen the shape of the land, I am beginning to worry that they will head south for the desert and their own lands. If so, they will pass this way. It is important to be prepared." He looked towards Walvin. The elder had hobbled back from the ravine entrance to sit near. His wife, as so often now, remained close.

He smiled at Dran. "I am not the one to decide. Younger men, better able than I at the tasks required, are arranging our welfare. But our course now is obvious.

"This morning's events have shown us that we are not as safe as we had hoped. We were fortunate today. We may not be next time. We shall prepare to depart, possibly for the mountains." He had difficulty getting to his feet, and Henata helped him.

"We must live as travellers, prepared to move on at a moment. The drag sleds should be lightly loaded with firewood and we must be able to live out of our packs. If we have to leave, what we cannot take, we can return for when the enemy have gone. I shall go and ready my pack."

Dran stood, and placed his bowl and spoon on the pile of used utensils, and looked around for someone to thank. Most were leaving to attend their tasks. "Perad, Your ravine is open to the east, is it not? Is it safe from the enemy that way? I believe there is forest there, before the mountains. Linked to the northern forest by my home. It would be good to see it, out here in the east. Can you show me?"

Perad stood. "I must be ready to leave, first." He turned towards the cave interior.

Dran followed. "So this has been your home."

Perad's groundsheet and blanket were tucked under the overhang, along with his large pack which he had been using for a pillow. "I shall travel with my large pack and bedroll only.

190

I have a few items I can leave." He shook the contents of his small pack to the floor. Amongst them was grandmother Katada's book.

He held it and weighed it in his hands and in his thoughts. "I shall carry this no further for now. But I shall return for it one day." He sorted through his belongings and filled the small pack and fastened the straps and placed it under the overhang. Still kneeling he drew his cape over his head and put on his hat. After a moment's thought, he took out his spare foot bindings and wrapped them around his neck, tucking the ends into his tunic. "This close to the mountains in winter, it is more sensible to wear clothing than carry it. Wearing your bedding is not unusual."

He rolled his groundsheet and blanket tightly and strapped them to the top of his pack. He pulled the brim of his hat low, and put on his mittens and stood and swung the pack to his left shoulder.

"You look like a wanderer from the ancient tales," said Dran. "Come, we should save the tour for later. Let us see if we can be of use somewhere."

Perad dropped his pack with others just inside the cave entrance. He reached down again and pulled at the shoulder strap to free it and place it so that he could pick it up in one movement. Dran had left his pack near the fire, and he brought it and placed it by Perad's.

But for the collecting of firewood, no one required assistance, and Perad found an empty sled to drag and took Dran to the eastern opening of the ravine. Ganat was on watch there. Jattog had joined him and was describing the morning's events. As he listened, Ganat continually scanned the distance, moving his head in a slow arc from left to right, from northwards along the line of the falling cliffs of the rear of the ravines, through the line of forest, to the south where the line of the mountains met the hills bordering the desert.

There would be another watcher, Perad knew, five hundred paces to the north, hidden amongst the rocks. The view to the south was clear enough to require no extra guard.

They loaded the sled with firewood, mostly fallen branches of leaf fall trees. The branches of the pines would give a good blaze, and they added some, but they would burn quickly and were not as useful. Dran pointed out trees he recognised from the northern forest. Some were known to Perad, though by other names, some were not.

They left the sled and moved further into the trees, to where the mountains could be seen more clearly. The peaks were lost in haze, and even as they watched, the mist thickened and rolled down and hid the flanks, so that only the nearest cliffs were visible, a gigantic wall baulking all from the west.

"They do not invite us to them," said Dran.

"Yet they are not so bad," said Perad. "We have explored the beginnings of the mountains, and found ways into them. See the cracks there. And once inside, they are surprising. There are pathways to be found, which have been followed for some distance. It is believed there could be routes to the north and south which would provide an escape, from the Gralt, and from the mountains."

"But these escape routes have not been followed all the way, yet?"

"There has not been the opportunity."

"Then the mountains could be a trap?"

"Yes. Though the enemy would be unwise to follow. Those narrow ways can be well defended."

"The enemy do not need to follow. All they would require is to wait until your food runs out."

Dran bent to pick a small branch and tested it as a staff. It was too short, and bent when he put weight on it, and he threw it to the ground. "Still, why should they do that? They surely wish to go home, now. I believe you have made the correct decisions. Hide until our soldiers arrive. And if we have to hide in the mountains, so be it."

His eyes followed a line from the mountains to the Ravines. "I wonder why there is no river here. A good deal of rain and snow must fall up there."

Perad looked with him. "The slope is to the south. Perhaps the water finds its way to the Fardas river. The springs suggest it goes underground."

"This is an intriguing place, a meeting of the desert, the forest and the mountains, with a little of the Valleys," said Dran.

"We have found the flux here," Perad told him. "It is weaker than in the Ravines, though, and has a different feel. Some have suggested it is deep underground, also.

"When the Gralt have gone, I expect we shall return to explore more easily. There are no surviving maps from our ancestors."

"I shall seek an invitation from your elders to join any expedition," said Dran.

Chapter 24

Dorot is the seed covering of a plant grown on the wetter parts of the plains, often at the base of a slope, where water collects before seeping off to find its way to a stream or river. The thumb sized pods are covered by a fragile husk which, when split by the heat of the summer sun, burst to reveal in a ball the size of a fist, a dense tangle of fine white fibres surrounding the small black seeds. These fibres can be rolled, twisted and spun to produce a strong thread which is traditionally woven into cloth on a small loom placed across the knee. This is a fine cloth, which takes a dye well, used for fine clothing. There were weavers in the Valleys who produced garments of exceptional quality, sought after by the very wealthy.

Lower quality dorot, still containing its seeds, is beaten and flattened into sheets until it forms a mat, and sold in broad rolls. It is an excellent material for trapping heat. It is light in weight, soft and easy to work. Some of the finest coats and tunics, particularly for winter wear, were padded with dorot, the material sewn between the outer skin of leather or oiled cloth, and an inner lining of fabric. Its other quality, an ability to hold moisture when damp, makes it useful as a swab in healing, but also presents a problem with clothing. Should a coat receive a good soaking, the dorot filling needs to be separately dried, the stitching of the lining unpicked and the dorot removed. It is a straightforward task, requiring little skill and performed by many. Perad, always anxious for the condition of the pouches worn inside his tunic, had done it many times, even after little more than a heavy shower.

The day after the hiding of the village, and the arrival of Dran, saw the weather change. It began with a wind from the north west bringing long lines of ragged clouds which piled above the mountain peaks, then onto the peaks, then down the flanks of the mountains. There would be snow in enormous amounts up there, but here on the edge, it fell in sweeps of tiny grains which were picked up by the eddies of wind, moved like ripples on the surface of water, and piled in the corners. The wind shifted steadily to come more from the north, and gained in strength through the day, until by dark, the sky roared with its fury. The shapes within the gorges caused complex flows to the cold air, so that there was no hiding from it, even far into the caves.

Dran's news that the end was in sight had been outweighed by the near disaster of their discovery, and had not lifted the spirits. That night was a difficult one for most. The noise of the gale, and the chill and discomfort it brought, added to the worry. Morning brought no relief.

The tricky and vicious wind, swirling and buffeting within the caves, found a piece of beaten dorot, the lining of a man's tunic, stretched over a boulder to dry, and held in place by four stones. The gusts and tugs of the wind constantly rippled the material, worrying at it, until an edge lifted sufficiently for the whole piece to billow, causing one of the stones to roll to the floor. The corner now released, bent back by the next rush of wind, pulled at an adjacent corner and dislodged another stone. The now violently flapping sheet of material attracted the attention of its owner who hurried to capture it. But not quickly enough. Yet another violent blast pulled it loose of the stones and snatched it to the cave entrance. There, it twisted itself into a ball and fell and rolled, before the wind found its way inside, and it spread and soared and swirled into the sky, a brilliant and unnatural white against the dark clouds. It caught the eyes of those about their tasks in the ravine, and those sitting in the entrances to caves, of which Perad was one, so that many eyes were following its course as yet another gust took it along the ravine to the rocks near the eastern opening, where it caught for a beat on a jagged edge. The man on watch there, seeing its possible course, leaped for it, missing by an arm's length, before the gale took it fully and lifted it away out of the ravines and above the rocks and bushes and stunted trees towards the Trough.

Derim was scouting a little beyond the northernmost end of the ridge of cliffs which formed the ravines, hiding in the undergrowth on the margin of the band of woodland, looking west. He was watching a group of five Gralt among the boulders on the ridge edging the Trough. They were staggering in the gale, looking out across the sandy plain, shielding their eyes from the grains blowing up the slope. Derim was confident of avoiding this group of the enemy, but needed to know their intentions, and had been tracking them since they first appeared from the north. He had left Garin two hundred paces into the trees; a second group of Gralt in the trees would be a serious danger to himself and the village.

Derim favoured a hooded tunic, and he had the hood up now, held tight to his face. There was nothing to hear above the howling wind, and the buffeting had disturbed his concentration until he covered his ears. With his view restricted, he would have missed the sign, if he had not seen one of the Gralt, who was facing south, take the shoulder of the nearest of his companions and spin him and point to the sky. It was then he saw the piece of fabric, which he took to be a baby's shawl, high above the ravines and backed by a dark sky. Dropping his eyes, he watched the Gralt point upwards, and then down, to the dark vertical break in the cliff which was the entrance to the hiding place of his folk.

There was discussion amongst the Gralt, and more

pointing, until they turned and headed north. They were hurrying.

Garin, among the trees, had puzzled at the white thing in the sky, glimpsed through the whipping bare branches, and seen danger in it. He took it for a warning sign of some sort, released on purpose by those in the ravine. He was standing waiting, his worry increasing, when Derim came back to him, moving not like faint smoke through the trees as he could, but running and leaping.

"We have been seen?" asked Dran above the roar of the wind. He was the first of those advancing towards the two scouts as they approached the entrance to the ravine. Many had collected there, to watch the track of the cloth, to see what harm it would bring.

Derim was breathing hard. "They saw it. They saw where it came from. They will come."

"Are you certain of this?" said Tardeb.

"They saw. I watched them mark the place. They will come for us."

"But they cannot know who we are, only that someone is here. We could be an army, or a race of mountain dwellers."

"I do not know what they will think. But I do know they will come. With what I saw, I would come. And not knowing what they face, I would come in force. They will come."

"Then we can no longer hide. The choice now is to run or fight." Tardeb looked towards Kadat.

Kadat was still for a while, weighing his thoughts. "Remember, they have to be cautious. They do not know what they will encounter." He moved to crouch in the lee of a boulder where the wind was less severe. The others closed around him. "The numbers will decide. If they come in force we will run. A few and we shall fight. But we must know their numbers." He could see their plan, now, and his voice became

197

more certain. "A chain of watchers, our fastest, to keep us informed. But not too great a distance. We must not spread far. And they are to fall back before the enemy. We shall leave no one in danger. But they must remain in hiding. We shall not give up our position easily. Or the opportunity to surprise them. If we choose to defend this place, we will begin with arrows. We can remove some before we get to swords and knives, and we shall have a better chance.

"Tardeb, set the watchers, cover the area north of the ravines. I shall position bowmen."

Tardeb was looking around to see who could be used. "The present danger is in the north. We must recall those who are patrolling in the direction of the river to the south." Perad caught his eye. Tardeb nodded, and looked for another. He would not wish to send out his fighters. Vedan stepped beside Perad.

"Go quickly," Tardeb told them. "Be careful. Leave the near watchers until you return, find the other two. Arrive here together. Take your packs. Take care on your return. If the Gralt are here, look for us towards the mountains, or work your way carefully back to the Valleys. The situation will decide for you. I doubt the enemy will arrive so quickly, but if they do, you may encounter a fight. Remain hidden until you see the outcome."

"The outcome may not be obvious," said Derim. "Even if we overcome a small group, the others will know. They will keep coming."

"And if they keep coming in small groups, we shall stop them." Kadat was scanning the cliffs, the fallen rocks, the scrub.

He looked along the ravine. There were children wearing backpacks, old folk sitting amongst their possessions, women carrying babies. "Still, the greatest likelihood is that we shall run for the mountains."

"We can leave at a word," said Fatava. "We are ready." She was one of a number of the women who had gathered.

"Begin to gather by the eastern escape. But keep it clear."

There was further discussion, which Perad did not hear, for he ran for his pack, and set out on his errand, Vedan beside him.

The first two scouts were quickly reached. Perad silently watched the plain while Vedan shared the news. The lookout position there was on a slope amongst trees, and was a good one, with wide views. They went on around the curve of the Trough and found the other two on patrol half the distance to the river.

It was midday when they arrived back. There was nothing to be seen outside the ravine, and Perad crawled through the last of the scrub dragging his pack until a hidden watcher called to say that all was clear. Perad stood and waved the others from their hiding amongst the rocks.

Inside the ravine food was being taken. Folk ate with packs by their sides, or on their backs. It was very quiet. The wind was easing, still gusting, but with brief periods of calm. Perad was given a strip of dried meat, and took it to sit amongst the rocks outside the ravine.

It was Derim again who brought the news they knew would come. They watched him approach at speed, ducking and scurrying between bushes. Behind him, others were following.

"They are coming. They have left the woodland and are coming this way."

"Then I can see them," said Kadat, shielding his eyes. There were black specks on the edge of the Trough.

"I counted thirty. There may be more. Too many to fight. We must find a new hiding place for our families."

Faren, who had returned from the southern watch with Perad, had his sword out. "There are good positions here." He was looking at the shelves and ledges and vantage points high on the walls of the ravine. "Bowmen up there. Fighters with swords hidden amongst the rocks. We could surprise them."

Tardeb placed his hand on Faren's sword arm. "We have considered that. But our safety is in running and hiding, not fighting. They are all soldiers, we are not."

"Then should some of us remain and fight, while the rest of the village hides? We would fight to the end and not run. There would be few of them left to harm our folk."

"And we have considered that. And we have had many offers. But they do not have us yet. We will continue hiding. It has served us so far. The time to fight may still come."

They watched, ducking further into the shadows until the specks became figures seen through the gaps between rocks. They were dark and cloaked, and there was little doubt of their direction.

"We must go," said Tardeb. "Remove any marks. There is a small hope they will pass by."

He waved the lookouts from their perches and signalled along the ravine for the flight to begin.

Faren was the last to turn away. He cursed and struck at the air with his sword.

Those at the back, Perad amongst them, used their feet to scuff away the tracks which crossed the ravine. By the time they reached the eastern gap a good part of the village was through and into the forest.

The plan was no more than to cross the forest strip and enter the mountains. There were openings all along the range, the nearest one directly east. The first parts of it had been explored, and there were many places to hide and, Hadrath believed, routes within through which they could escape.

They would not slow themselves dragging sleds, other than two of firewood, and much equipment had been left, pushed to the back of the caves. Food, clothing and blankets, carried on backs, or in the arms was all they dare take.

There was no gain in waiting. The first of the villagers set off through the trees at a run.

Chapter 25

There was no attempt to hide the tracks of over three hundred folk crossing the forest floor. They would hasten through the trees and enter the mountains. Should the opportunity to deceive followers arise, the steep rocky slopes, bare of snow, within the mountains could be crossed with little trace.

Two men with bows were at the rear, facing backwards mostly, watching the gap, urging the stragglers, Perad still among them. He had stayed almost to the last at the gap, braced against the rock with his arm out to help folk over the rough ground, until one of the men pushed him on, almost lifting him from his feet, ordering him to run.

Someone dropped a pack and looked back as they ran, not daring to stop and return the few steps to retrieve it. Perad saw her face as she turned. It was Hamana whose child Perad had healed of an infected leg on Harvestend. That had been in the middle of autumn, but seemed so long ago. Perad bent for the pack as he passed and took a strap and dragged it with him. It was heavy, heavier than it should be for a young mother with a small child to carry. She could not afford to lose it and he swung it up to take both straps and a better grip. Hamana had looked again and saw him and mouthed something, but he did not know what.

It was a little over two thousand paces across the strip of forest, farther than many could run. Perad remained with those near the back, more and more the older folk. Amongst them were Walvin and Henata. Walvin had wished to be the last, his duty, he had said, but had conceded when others had insisted he lead the escape. Even so, with anything more than a fast walk beyond him, he was quickly overtaken. His wife would not leave his side, and indeed, could not, her speed being no more than his.

Still, they crossed the forest with no sign of pursuit.

The mountains began abruptly here. Out of the trees, a last few grasses and bushes among stony ground, a low ridge of broken slate, and then near vertical walls.

The opening for their escape had already been chosen, a cleft around a fold in the rock face. Unavoidably, the disturbed ground led directly to it. If the Gralt crossed the forest, they would find it.

The earlier explorations within had revealed a surprising structure. The towering flanks of the mountain sides appeared to grow from a flat rock floor, quite smooth, a gigantic version of the ravines, so that in many places it appeared that there were roads and tracks and pathways between walls and corners of cliffs. When Perad had first been on one of the surveys, he soon felt himself closed in, like an insect, he described to others, in the cracks of a broken pavement. Now, with the fear of pursuit and with low cloud closing them in, it felt worse, more like moving along tunnels and caves.

Once through the initial gap they had entered a gully where vertical sides crowded in on them. Through this, the way forward widened, sloping upwards towards a flattened ridge between perpendicular sides, before narrowing and dropping steeply directly to the east. But this way had been investigated and dismissed. It was littered with rockfalls and snow drifts, and led to a series of forks all believed, eventually, to be impassable.

There was, though, another exit, around a cliff wall towards the south, through which the last of the main group of villagers were now clambering. It looked to be no more than fissure, near invisible from the west, and was not an obvious escape, but had been well explored, and offered a number of routes.

The swirling breeze had pushed the grainy snow into corners leaving large areas of bare rock which showed no tracks. Once they reached divisions in the paths, they would be almost impossible to follow, if they could remain far enough ahead to not be seen.

He was looking back and saw it happen. Henata simply went down, crumbling in a heap, pulling Walvin on top of her. Perad heard her gasp, and stopped. She rolled from her husband and sat immediately. Walvin was on his knees watching her. "My leg," she said. "Broken." She was breathing fast and hard, but showed no distress.

"I heard it break," said Walvin.

"Yes. There is no doubt. That is an end to my running. I believe I am relieved." Her cheeks were red and she looked at Perad and managed a smile.

"Up," said one of the men, a homesteader whom Perad could not name, "I shall put you over my shoulder." He reached out an arm.

She pushed it away. "You shall not. It would slow you down and risk discovery. And for no benefit. I am finished with this. I shall stay here."

The man crouched to take her under the arms, but she lay back to prevent it.

"No. I am done with this." She struggled, and sat again, pain across her face, but the smile came back. "I have become a burden and a risk. I shall not endanger my folk. I had thought to have one more summer, but it is not to be. And it is only one less than many. Leave me and go. Go Walvin. Plant a twig for me."

Walvin's voice was soft, and his face glowed. "I shall not go. You are right, we shall run no more. This will be our end. Your last summer was always to be my last summer. I shall stay with you. And you have lived most of a lifetime with my stubbornness, so you know it is pointless to argue." He had fought his way to his feet as he spoke, and he pressed his hand to her cheek.

The man was looking from Henata to the opening where Faren was watching the forest. "This is madness. The Gralt will slaughter you. I can take you out of here."

"To what end? I have decided. You are not to risk a village for the sake of one whose time is over."

"They come. They are through the ravine," called Faren.

Henata looked to where the last of the villagers were clambering out of sight, then nodded to the east where the ground rose, a road cresting a pass in the hills. "There. Why have we not chosen that way? Quickly now, tell me." The enclosing walls of rock added an echo to her voice, and an authority.

"We have explored a little and believe it to leads nowhere but a tangle of hopeless paths. You cannot hide there."

"I do not mean to hide." She was almost angry for a moment, before returning the smile. "See, that looks to be the way we would go. If you place me there, the enemy will believe that is where we went. They will continue in that direction. There is a diversion which could delay them for a good time."

"They are in the trees," called Faren.

"We will not leave you."

"You will. You will not alter my mind."

The man knelt to lift Henata. "No," she said. "My village is not to be risked."

"They have our course," called Faren. "They are coming this way."

Henata reached for the man's hand and caught it and held it. "Under my arms now. You will not hurt me. I feel nothing in my leg. Pull me up there. Those Gralt will spent a good deal of time looking for you the wrong way."

In the end he had no choice but to do as he was told. She cried out once, softly, and apologised when the man paused. He stopped at the highest point and released her. Walvin had hobbled alongside and stood over her. Perad had followed in an agony of indecision. They should lift her and run with her, and let her protest.

Henata waved the man away with a flick of her hand.

"However it happens, the end will come quickly. I am prepared for it. Indeed the end has already come. I have no fear. Unless it is for my people. Leave us. Quickly. If they see you, our diversion will not work. Let us finish this knowing our people are safe."

She shuffled to turn to the east, dragging her useless leg. "I shall pretend to watch my people. It will aid in the deception. I shall not look at the enemy."

The man bent to kiss the top of her head. He squeezed Walvin on the shoulder, and ran for the gap. Perad followed.

"No more time," said Faren, and ran also.

From lower ground, Perad looked up. Walvin was on his knees collecting stones. When he topped the rockfall leading to the escape route, he looked again. Walvin was sitting besides Henata, his arm around her shoulders. There was a small pile of stones by his side. He had taken out his knife and held it across his lap. Perad began to raise his hand to wave, but they had eyes only for each other and would not have seen. He raised his hand in salute, anyway, and was round the corner of rock, and they were out of sight.

And then it was running.

A succession of corners, turns and narrow spaces to scramble through was made more difficult by the tears in his eyes. At each twist or fork in the way, there was someone to call them through or point the direction.

There was much climbing of rockfall, which slowed them, and they gained height steadily. The pace slowed to a walk, and the cold increased. Perad could only wonder how the old and the children and those burdened with babies could keep going. And eventually they could not.

"Is that everyone?" asked Tardeb. "Is anyone missing?"

Perad could only shake his head.

"There is no one to follow," said Faren, who had remained at the back.

"A short rest here. We have folk who can run no more. If the enemy come, we can face them here. Here is a position we can defend forever."

"Not forever," said Faren. "But it matters not. They will not come. They will not follow us further into this place. They cannot track us. They do not know where we have gone. And they have a diversion."

"One more march, then we rest," called Tardeb, later in the afternoon, when they stopped to collect again. "Hadrath has scouted ahead and found us a way to the south which he has hopes of. We dare not stop here, though. I fear the snow may slide on these steep slopes. We shall halt for the night at the next sound place."

It was almost dark when they did stop, in a roughly circular space the size of the village circle, enclosed by mountainsides which curved out of sight above them. There were folds and breaks which offered protection from the wind, and overhangs where the snow had not collected. They had entered through a break in a wall of black rock, after a short steep climb. They mostly stood, waiting, too exhausted to speak, until the last man arrived and announced that there was no sign whatsoever of pursuit.

Chapter 26

They crammed themselves under the overhangs and into crevasses, where the air was still and the warmth of their bodies would not be so easily lost. There were places where ridges of deep snow had collected around the base of the slopes, and these they avoided, fearful of snow and ice sliding from above.

They were surrounded by mountain peaks and hidden from the west and the north. There could be no risk to a fire here, and a hot meal would benefit all. Perad passed branches from a sled and estimated three days worth of wood. He did not know how long the food would last.

There were discussions, and calls for the account of Walvin and Henata, which Perad would not join.

He walked the perimeter of their refuge, and looked for a further venture. He chose a slope to the east, not too severe, and climbed for a good while, high enough to be rewarded with a glimpse of the tops of the trees of his world no further than two days of striding away, and the plains beyond, and the lowering sun turning red beneath the layer of cloud. It was almost black in the depths below him but for a short while the snow caps above him blushed, and the colour of the mountain rock around warmed, and the view amazed Perad. When it was over and the last peak darkened, he slithered his way back into the shadows below.

A meeting of elders and others was ending and folk were climbing stiffly to their feet.

Tardeb placed himself centrally to make an announcement. "We believe we are safe here for a while.

There is little likelihood that the enemy have followed us, and the way into here can be defended. Also, we have the beginning of a south easterly route away from here, though Hadrath requires more time to explore. And we are in need of a rest. We shall stay in this place for one more day and night. That will leave us firewood for one more night after that. If we can find a route out of here, we will be no more than two days from the woods. And we are hopeful. We know that Maradan Pass is in that direction. We are not so far from our world. Some of you have been to Maradan Pass. And from there we can soon reach the head of our valley. We are not such a great distance from home. If we can avoid the enemy, and with good fortune, we will reach our woods and be safe." He let his head fall and paused for a while. Without being aware, he had taken on Walvin's manner of speaking.

"This is not so bad a place. Rest and stay warm. We shall take all of tomorrow to explore. If we cannot find a route through, we shall return the way we came. Our hope then will be that the enemy cannot suffer the cold and will have retreated. We do not expect that to be necessary. I am convinced we will find a route out of the mountains, even if it is to the desert."

Night had fallen completely. The circle of folk around the fire was solid, and very little light escaped and Perad had to feel his way to his pack. He wrapped himself well and curled to sleep. He tried to clear his thoughts. He could not rid himself of his last sight of Walvin and Henata, and he could not stop his mind from playing out the endings of that story. There were no outcomes which did not make him squeeze his fists until they hurt, or squirm and turn until his blanket became loose and the cold reached him and worked its way deep inside.

Exhaustion finally overtook him, and he slept deeply until

close to dawn. He woke with numb fingers and toes and carried his boots to the fire to warm himself.

The snow had fallen heavily while he had slept, ankle deep and powdery away from the fire, knee deep in drifts by some of the vertical walls. There was a half circle of folk by the fire, bundles of sleeping children before them. The other side had an arc of steaming pots of oats, broth and water. Perad took a mug from the stack and dipped it in the broth and sat in the circle with his knees up and his hands cupped around his breakfast. His breath caught the glow of the fire and he watched as each cloud of reddened vapour rose and dispersed. He had not been asked to explore or watch, and there was no call for his skill, and it would be a long day, with a long night to follow.

The hushed talk around him was hopeful. The watchers had worked their way back along their escape a good distance, and seen and heard nothing. There was little expectation of being followed. Groups were poised to set off at first light to examine possible ways out to the south and south west.

Perad was restless. He drank the hot liquid from the top of the mug and looked around for a spoon. Not seeing one, he stood and tipped the mug and used his fingers to push the solids from the bottom into his mouth. He sought around again for somewhere to wash the mug and found nothing. No one spoke. He sat again and rewrapped his feet and put on his boots, tying them with great care. He left the mug on the floor and went to his pack to find his mittens before walking towards the opening on the western side where they had entered this space. It was dark and there was nothing to be seen, though he knew men were there watching for the enemy. He could not keep still. He wished he had been chosen for the scouting tasks.

When he turned, he saw Faren, sitting on a rock, staring into the darkness. Even in the poor light, Perad saw in his face that he had shared the same nightmares.

He went back and when he passed the main group of sleepers, the soft sounds of breathing rose to greet him. He went on towards the east. Away from the others, he could hear the snow creaking under his boots. There was no wind at all and the snow in the mountains around him also creaked. He climbed the slope he had climbed the evening before. It was steep enough to not hold a great depth of the dry snow. It was dark at first and he went on hands and knees until he was out of the shadows. There was a little light in the sky now and the peaks glowed blue above him.

It was colder with the height, and he held his mittens between his knees while he pulled his hat hard down on his head and refastened his tunic and tightened his belt. His fingers were numb by the time he replaced his mittens.

The slope he was on was the flank of a mountain whose peak was lost behind the swell of the rock face. The view to the west was hidden in mist and cloud. He found with his eyes a course which curved steeply upwards to his left and around, along a fracture which suggested footholds. He would follow it to its limit, and explore to the east. The light was better now, and day had begun. The clouds were heavy and deep and there would be snow in them, but he did not believe it would fall for a while.

A series of ledges, always climbing, took him further around the flank. When he could no longer see the camp, and all of the west was hidden, he stopped. The scale of the place was beyond his understanding. There were ridges and peaks, and more peaks, and the nearest of them could be days away, and were small in comparison to the ones beyond.

A steep drop to a narrow valley faced him, northwards of east, and across the end of it was a ridge, like a wall, hung between two peaks.

He felt that the remains of the world were on the far side

of that ridge. If he could climb to look over there, he would be satisfied to end his venture.

He should not have left without informing someone. But it was to be a long day of inactivity, and it was early in the day with many of the folk still asleep. He would not go back yet.

He made his way downward into the valley. It was difficult, and at times he had to turn and face the rock and use his hands. At the bottom, he saw that it was more a trench than a valley, the claw mark of some fabled giant idly scratching at the surface of the world in its making.

The snow, knee deep when it gave way, mostly held his weight if he stepped carefully.

The wall which closed the end of the valley was not as it had first seemed. There were breaks and folds in it, and from below, the line of the top was ragged with pinnacles and clefts. The shattered nature of the surface left places for feet and grips for hands, and he worked his way up to find a place where he could look over.

It was not what he had hoped. There was another ravine, steeper sided than the one he had already crossed, also closed with a wall of rock at the far end.

The descent was shallower than the climb he had just made, and snow covered. He would continue his exploration one stage further. He made his way to the bottom walking sideways and upright, stamping on the snow to form steps.

Once on the ravine floor, he kicked away the snow to test its depth, knee deep near the slopes, less away from them. He began the walk the length of the ravine.

The snow was different in this space, some function, perhaps, of the more easterly alignment, or the steepness of the sides. This was far enough and high enough into the mountains for snow to have been here for weeks at least, and looked solid enough to walk on. He did not know the state of the ground beneath, or yet trust the firmness of the snow, and went slowly, testing each step. It continued to hold his weight, and he increased his speed.

When he reached the end, the rock wall facing him was sheer and without visible hand holds. He went to his left to where the rock face met the mountain flank which formed the side of the ravine.

Some strange nature of the wind had piled snow into the corner, and testing it, he found that it would hold. A wedge shaped lightness above told him there was a limit to the climb, and not too far. He would make the attempt.

He had never climbed snow before. He straightened his fingers and stabbed at the surface to create grips, and kicked with the toes of his boot to make footholds. The snow held, and step by step now, he moved slowly up. Nearer to the top, the snow depth was less and his hands found sharp projections of rock beneath and his progress was easier.

When he reached the top, the wonder of what he saw took his breath away.

Enclosed in a ring of mist shrouded slopes was a plain, a lake of snow, startlingly white against the mountains and clouds, the surface of the snow punctured over the whole width and breadth of the plain by countless needle rocks, narrow arrow head shapes, pointing at the sky. They were black and smooth, with many flat surfaces like whittled sticks, and of all sizes. They looked as if they had been placed there, an army of silent and eternal watchmen guarding the way to the east.

And winding through the middle of all this, twisting and turning between the points, was a crack, a fissure, a break in the evenness of the snow, like a crooked footpath coaxing him across the plain.

The slope down was a little less than the one he had just climbed, and covered in deeper snow. It would need to be firm enough to support his return; there would be no other way out.

It was climbing, not walking, and he set off backwards, using his hands, and found that once again he could kick toe holds in the snow which held. After a while, the slope became less and his hands were not needed. He twisted slowly and faced forward, making progress by shaping small ledges with his heels. They would crumble at times and he would slither a little until the snow compacted enough to hold. Twice he had to lean back and sit to avoid toppling forward.

At the bottom, he looked back. He had formed a stair which would take him back up.

But not yet.

He took a few steps towards the nearest of the needle rocks. The largest of them were twice his height, haphazardly spaced, with others of different sizes between. There were points which just broke the surface of the snow, and when he moved the snow aside, there were smaller ones below.

Their flat surfaces reflected like polished metal.

Fifty paces from the cliff he met the beginning of the fissure. It appeared as a crack in the world, filled with snow. It was impossible to tell its depth.

To go further, he would need to tread this path; there would be no walking amongst the rocks.

The impulse to go on was overwhelming.

He tested a first step. The snow was packed solid. He began to walk, carefully at first, then with increasing confidence.

A good way across he stopped to look around.

He should not be here. This was a place not of his world, not meant for folk. He knew with absolute certainty that no one had ever been here before.

Perhaps it was the thrill of that which caused him to continue.

Back, he could see his trail of shadowed footprints. He felt a flicker of guilt at bruising this landscape.

Snow began to fall, large dry grains that rustled and whispered as they landed and shifted and rolled. The marks of his boots would soon fill.

The plain was not flat, as he had first thought, viewed from above. Approaching the centre, he saw that it was a shallow dish in shape. From here was an upward slope, gentle at first, then increasingly steep, to a rim with nothing but sky behind it. He would not turn back without looking over there. It could only be mid morning. He had not been gone long.

Once across the plain of needles, the fissure ended, and he was climbing through soft snow. Gaining height, he began to see mountain peaks over the edge.

The last few steps were difficult. The slope steepened further and the rock beneath the snow was broken, with edges like blades. He placed his feet with great care.

The snow had become wet and was treacherous. This should not be, he thought. This was as cold as anything he had ever experienced. All water here should be frozen.

He reached the top of the rise with his head down watching his footing. Then suddenly the climb ended and the ground flattened and he lifted his gaze.

The shock made him reel and he sat heavily in the wet snow. He may have shouted out. The echoes of a silent scream filled his head.

Below him was a vast circular plain edged with towering mountains, startlingly white against the grey sky, with deep blue shadows and black rock where snow could not rest on the steepest slopes. Within this circle of mountains was a plain, many times the size of the Trough, and there was a structure in the centre of it.

It was as if a mountain had grown there, and the mountain had been twisted away leaving the base and roots. Or a tree, Perad thought, untidily hacked or broken off low down to leave the lower trunk, with roots like great fingers and knuckles crawling out in all directions. But a tree trunk made of the rock of the world, and the size of mountains.

And there was something else beyond the vastness and the shape of the thing. There was a tingle and a power and a heat like the air from a cauldron, pushing against his face.

And he knew what it was. There was no shape to his thoughts, no consideration. He simply knew.

It was the flux. This was where the flux began.

One of the great roots of the thing, a ridge of steep and rounded hills, climbed towards him, up and then down to plunge into the ground at the foot of the slope below him. It would reach and spread underground to the west, towards the Valleys. He could imagine it, see the nature of it, growing out and up, to surface in the Valleys. There was another to the south west which would reach under the desert; three more to the east and north, and other smaller ones crawling like vines between the main structures.

He wondered why he was here. He wondered if this thing had brought him.

He scrambled down the slope, slithering, striding, almost running at times, losing control. It was a long way, much further than it had seemed, his perception tricked by the incomprehensible scale of the place.

He fell once, near the bottom, tripped by some hidden obstacle. A pointed rock, shin high, and clear of snow loomed instantly towards his face. He relaxed his knees and twisted, a wrestler's move, and took the fall on his shoulder, and came to rest with his throat touching the side of the needle of rock. He reached up to press his finger to the point, and felt its sharpness through his mitten.

When he stood, he was so close that he could no longer see the structure in its entirety, his view obscured by a hill of rock rearing above him, growing out of, or in to, the floor of the plain.

He went to it, and reached out to its surface.

It was dark and smooth, and shone with wetness. There was snow falling now, melting as it touched, though it was as cold as any other rock when he pulled off his glove and reached out to press first his fingertips and then his palm to it. Tiny rivulets of water ran down to gather between his fingers.

The power in the rock was the flux. It flowed into him, filled him.

But it did not thrill him as the flux of his home would do. Something was strange about it. It was a distorted flux, different, disturbing. There would be no making here, no enhancement of craft. This was not his flux. Here at its origin, the flux was changed. He felt sick.

He pulled away his hand and wiped it on his tunic. He leaned close to see better. It was the same rock, dark grey and flecked, which he had found in the desert, the same rock which outcropped all through the Valleys.

He must leave at once. He turned his back to it, and began to walk.

When he topped the slope, he believed he could detect the sun behind the layer of cloud and estimated it to be early afternoon, though he no longer trusted his judgment. He must be back with his folk before dark or he would die in this place. He looked back, the only time he had done so on this climb. The snow was falling heavily now and the distance was shrouded in it. Only the nearest part of the root like protrusion was visible. He imagined he could see water running down it, and steam rising from its surface, though surely he could not do so from so far away.

He came close to panic part way across the plain of needles. The snow fell steadily, and straight down. The grains had turned into flakes, small and silent and so numerous that he could see no more than a few paces.

Taking care with his direction and placing his feet, he had slowed down, and the cold began to penetrate his clothing. He dare not hurry. If he lost the line of the fissure, he would not find his way out and he would not survive.

The distance was more than he felt it should be, or his progress less that he expected; he should have crossed the plain by now. He could only keep walking. And when he did reach the boundary, it was a wall of rock which faced him, not the snow filled crack he had worked down. Try to the right, he told himself, and he had said it out loud. He may have been talking to himself for a while, and turning to see his bootprints behind him, filling quickly, he fell silent. This dreadful place did not want him there, or his marks, or his sound.

But neither should it wish to keep him. He moved right and found the near vertical crack in the rock filled with a slope of snow and with the steps he had made on his journey down, rounded now and disappearing quickly.

The climb was easier than the descent. With only a few steps he knew he would return safely.

From the top of the ridge, he looked back. There was nothing to be seen but heavily falling snow, backed by mist. He turned away from it, and headed for his folk.

Chapter 27

It was late in the afternoon and almost dark when he got back to the camp. There would be watchers all around, but he saw no one and no one spoke to him. He found his pack and sat by it with his back to the rock wall. He was shivering and drew up his legs and covered himself in his groundsheet. No longer walking, he was even colder and he unrolled his blanket and spread that. Snow was falling and he saw that he had put the blanket on the outside of the waterproof sheet. He was struggling to rearrange them when Dresana came to him. He could not stop the shivering. She sat close by him and arranged the blanket and sheet to cover them both. "You have been gone a long time. I asked, and you were not one of the scouts or the watchers. You are a restless one, Perad." There was warmth in her voice, and warmth in her breath on his cheek.

"I wished to see further in to the mountains to the east, and found a route I could follow for a while."

"Was it not dangerous, alone?"

"I was careful. But it was foolish to leave the camp. Had we been attacked and had to escape, I would have been separated." His voice sunk below a whisper.

"You would have found your way to us."

She leaned on him and placed her arms around his neck and her head on his shoulder. He warmed then and became still. He closed his eyes and fell asleep.

The first time he woke, Dresana was still there, sleeping softly, but when he awoke deep into the night, she had gone.

He got to his feet and walked to the fire, his blanket over his shoulders. There were oat cakes, now cold, on a flat stone and he stood there to eat one. A log fell in the fire, and sparks leapt. He watched them float and fade. There may have been moisture or fungus in the wood, for a smoke rose, also. Pushed by the soft wind, it coiled between his legs and rose around his body. There was a smell within which he could not identify.

He ate another oat cake and returned to his place and wrapped himself tightly. He slept deeply again.

By morning, the cold was intense. The fire was gone and the snow was steadily deepening.

Perad was still waking when Hadrath stood to speak. A few others stood with him, though most remained seated and wrapped.

"Good news, which most have heard by now. We have found a route to Maradan Pass. It is not far, less than a day, though it is difficult. Garrett had sight of the Pass before returning. A day beyond that is the river, them home. We need only to avoid the enemy and we shall be safe.

"We shall leave with the good light. Prepare well. We shall encounter difficult ground, and the snow will add to the difficulties."

The first of the snow was a nuisance, large wet flakes which became ice on the cold rocks underfoot, and made the walking treacherous and progress slow.

Before long, the snow was falling heavily and was no longer wet. The wind lifted these new loose flakes and grains, and swirled and stirred them, so that they were walking, it seemed, on a smoking white blanket. The new snow filled the depressions and smoothed the surface, and hid the unevenness beneath. Each step required evaluation.

Those at the front slowed, and the group bunched, and they proceeded for a good while with their heads down, treading the steps of the ones in front.

There were periods of standing while a particular obstacle

was negotiated, and without the movement to work the muscles, the cold was shocking.

By midday, many were exhausted and a complete halt was needed.

They found a cleft, a cave almost, and crammed the whole of the village there. Those with the most strength stood at the entrance and packed themselves to keep out the wind.

The short rest was enough. The snow eased and the sky cleared and Hadrath encouraged them on. "There," he said, pointing to a gap between two peaks, "Garrett tells us that is the final obstacle before we descend to the Pass."

The ground fell for a distance, and they made good progress. And lower down the wind eased and the cold was less penetrating. They collected again at the lowest point.

Garrett pointed out a break in the line of the ridge before them. "That is the way I scouted yesterday. Above there is a small frozen lake, and another climb. From the top of that we look down on Maradan Pass. But the climb to the lake is demanding. And the summit is exposed. We must not be caught there at nightfall."

"Nor should we remain here until tomorrow," said Hadrath. "We do not have sufficient food or firewood."

"And if we delay, this snow will make the climb even more treacherous."

"A good rest, then one mighty effort," said Hadrath. Once over there, even if we do not reach the Pass, we can at least find shelter for the night on the descent.

"But a good rest first. I want those who are suffering most to regain some energy. We shall confront the climb together."

Garrett pointed to the south where the ridge ahead of them fell before meeting the side of a mountain. "The shapes there suggest a possible gap and, perhaps, a less arduous route. I did not have the opportunity to examine it, yesterday. It may be worth exploration during the rest time."

Dran spoke immediately. "There is nothing to be lost by taking a look. I shall do that."

"Good," said Garrett. "I can use the time to choose the safest route up here. Do not go alone, though."

"I shall go with Dran," said Perad.

"We dare not wait too long," said Hadrath. "If you have not returned by the time we are sufficiently rested, and Garrett declares an acceptable route, we shall be forced to leave."

"Leave when you are ready. We shall follow," said Dran.

And at first, the southerly route looked promising. The footing was sound and they made height quickly. But approaching the summit, the wind, seeking its way around the mountainside, increased and became filled with ice and snow lifted from the surface, a blinding, suffocating white fog. The villagers below were lost to sight, as was any view to the east, then any sight at all beyond a few paces.

Every few steps brought an increase in the wind, until it was difficult even to stand. Dran sought a fracture in the rock face and crammed himself into it, and pulled Perad to him. He had to cup his hands around Perad's ears to make himself heard. "This is not possible," he said.

Nor for a while was it possible to leave the safety of their tiny refuge. The wind increased further to a deafening roar and the snow came so thickly that the world diminished to two edges of dark rock by their cheeks.

The worst was over in a few moments. The wind eased, and the world returned, and the snow fell as it should, and they could see again and speak again.

"We shall not attempt this way," said Dran. "If those gusts come again while the whole of the village is here, there would be folk lost down the mountainside."

"The summit is there," said Perad. "We have not been about this for long. Before we return, let us at least look over and see the shape of the land."

222

It was only a few paces of climbing. A low wall of snow filled a breach in the ridge and they climbed to it and leaned their arms along the top of it to survey the landscape.

The mountains had deceived them. There was no way through. A steep drop led to a chain of peaks which stretched forever to the south, blocking any access to the west.

They stared in silence for a while at the impossible vastness of these mountains, then turned together to make their way back. As they did so, the movement disturbed the structure on which they had been resting, and the entire ridge of snow collapsed and slid away, taking Perad and Dran with it.

Perad fell face down. To curl and roll was his natural reaction, but he fought against it and spread his arms and legs hoping to catch some protrusion beneath the snow, or reduce the speed of the slide. He speared his arm deep into the soft snow and the action spun him and threw him onto his back. His slide continued and increased in speed and he thrashed his feet to find purchase in the snow, until his pack caught on something and he spun again, high this time, turning in the air, and he shaped his body into a dive with his arms in front. He ducked his head and hit the surface with his forearms and buried himself in the soft snow.

It was sufficient. The slide had stopped. He fought his way to the air and sat waist deep and cleared his eyes and looked around.

Dran was a few paces away, on his knees, his arms buried to the elbows in the snow. He climbed with some difficulty to his feet, and tottered backwards and sat heavily, facing Perad.

Neither could find the breath to speak.

The slope down which they had fallen levelled and rose slightly before reaching an edge and plunging to some unseen depth.

They sat looking at each other, in a white world of snow and sky, and absolute stillness.

And into the stillness, a sound, faint, distant, almost below hearing, a long slow drumming, becoming louder and stronger, approaching. It filled the air around them, above them. And crossing the sky was another white, a darker shadowed white against the white of the sky, a shape, indistinct at first, then taking form, a bird, an enormous bird, its great wings beating the air with a slow rhythm. It was so close, Perad felt the draught on his face, and saw the individual feathers on its tail, each one edged with yellow.

It passed and disappeared into the cloud.

Another came, and another. They heard a fourth pass, perhaps below them, for they did not see it.

The sound faded as it had come, to leave silence.

They stood, then, and shook and stamped the snow from their clothing, and began to make their way back up the track defined by their slide.

Fatab was climbing to meet them as they came down the final part of the ridge. "We are preparing to leave," he called from a distance. "Has this way anything for us?"

They shook their heads.

Fatab turned to hurry back. "I shall inform Hadrath to begin the climb."

It was difficult and exhausting, taking them to a limit and beyond. They kept tightly together, pulling and pushing, supporting and assisting; the village of Woodall slowly crawling its way up a mountainside. It was a dry stream course which they were climbing, and there were rocks which rolled underfoot, and ice beneath those, and there were many slips and near falls, but the close packing and the determination won, and together they reached the summit.

This was no place to halt. Between the two peaks was a plain, desolate and exposed, filled with a frozen lake. The wind was steady and from the north east, and brought a coldness Perad scarcely believed possible. They split into two groups to skirt the frozen lake on either side. There was little room before the rocky sides began, and they had to go single file, and the wind and the cold were terrible.

It was not far, though, and the final climb was a ridge no higher than a building, and once over there they were shielded from the north, and protected from the wind. They huddled together to rest and ease muscles and comfort the young.

Behind them the sky was dark, and the distance lost in heavy snow. In front, the cloud was thinner, lighter. As they stood to finish their trek, the air cleared and the wind parted the curtains of snow for a moment, and they looked down on Maradan Pass, and their way home.

Chapter 28

As they lost height, the snow eased and then stopped. The sky cleared a little and the clouds could be seen, rolling from the west, bringing wetness from the ocean, to meet the cold air above the mountains. There was clearance behind the banks of cloud, and a break let the late afternoon sun through to redden the peaks and slopes behind and around them.

In front, the ground fell more gently and became more even, and the walking became easier, more of the track like structure they had found throughout the mountains, leading directly westwards down to a wooded glade a few hundred paces east of Maradan Pass.

This was a strange part of the world. The furthest east of all the explored parts of Tarodash. There were folk here who had been to the Pass and to this place a little beyond it, though Perad had not. Half a day from the desert, well into the mountains, and yet an offshoot of the woodland of the Valleys.

Perad looked around in wonder as they entered a space where the height of the cliffs lessened and the distance between them widened, before narrowing again at the Pass. There was a mixture of leaf fall trees and pines, a fair amount of undergrowth and even a few late flowering plants amongst rough grass where the trees had not taken hold. It was a day to the west before they would meet again woodland as dense as this.

The way they were following held a straight course between the trees.

"Perhaps soil has collected here, washed down from the

mountains, or blown by the wind." said Perad, checking the variety of plants. "And perhaps there is warmth trapped here at times, though it does not feel it now."

It was strange to drop their packs amongst trees, and to sit on the drifts of fallen leaves, and some did not, preferring to rest themselves by the rocky walls and amongst the fallen slabs and boulders. This misplaced woodland made many uneasy.

The clouds pushed together and the last light of the setting sun was lost behind them, and dark came quickly, allowing Perad only a short examination of Maradan Pass.

It was perhaps fifty paces wide, though felt narrower because the edges were littered with rock fall, and two hundred paces long. The sides were towering vertical walls of rock, pocked with cracks and crevices, ledges and overhangs. There were jagged edges and viciously sharp projections. It was along that rock face that Maradan had earned his place in valley folk lore. The gentle flow of cold air rolling down from the higher ground increased a little as it pushed through the Pass, and Perad felt it on his back. It may have been the same flow of air which was keeping the Pass clear of snow. This had not been so in the legend.

The story of Maradan Pass was told throughout the Valleys, and known in detail in the southern valleys. Dran claimed that he had never heard the tale in full in the north; a ruse, perhaps, to encourage one of Woodall's storytellers.

With supper handed out, and a fire blazing, Fadava was happy to give the telling, and a good gathering sat close by.

From Woodall village, Maradan Pass was a significant walk, requiring two nights of camping, the second camp, clear of the woodland, was regarded as the furthest part of their own valley, and the south easterly limit of the land of Tarodash. It was considered a point of honour amongst descendants of Maradan to make the journey to the Pass at least once, the more hardy in winter, but mostly during one of the summer celebration holidays.

Maradan, as an old man, many generations ago had taken his family and others above the Pass to hide from the king's forces during the civil war, the last real conflict in Tarodash for over three hundred years. Trapped above the Pass, starving and freezing, and with the snow inside it twice the depth of a man and still falling, the old man had set out to follow an impossible looking ledge halfway up the near vertical cliff, high above the snow line on the southern wall. With the weather worsening, there was no option but for the fifteen others to follow, clinging to the cliff face, the snow rapidly filling the traces of footsteps and handholds he had marked. Maradan did uncover a route out, but the effort was too much for him, and his frozen body was found bridging a deep fissure in the ledge near the lower end of the Pass. All others survived, each one having to step on the old man's stiffened body to cross the final hazard. They returned to the Valleys to find the king overthrown and the prince apologetic to the whole land for his father's follies.

It had been a good account. Fadava named and described separately each member of the group, as was customary with this tale. She omitted none of the background, explaining the origins of the war, and Maradan's reasons for running. Throughout, she fixed her eyes solely on Dran sitting opposite her across the flames, so that all others felt themselves secret listeners to a private telling.

Garin, who had become ceaseless in his vigilance since the escape from the ravine, had gone further into the Pass than the watchers, and returned as the story finished. There was a purpose to his walk, and concern in his face, exaggerated by the shadows in his features as he approached the light of the flames. "I have see fires in the distance, to the west," he said. "Or smaller flames nearer. It is difficult to tell. I would be more comfortable if this blaze was out." He took out his knife. "Armed men a little further into the Pass would be sensible. It may be nothing. I shall take a second look and would like other opinions, if someone will accompany me."

Two men were already on their feet. They moved down into the darkness. There was a little of the light from the moon through the cloud, and it caught on the metal of their weapons before they were lost from sight. Then everyone was standing. The mood had changed in moments. The fire was stamped out. Swords and knives were drawn. There was much staring into the darkness in the east. Perad looked away from the last embers towards the blackness of the cliffs to wait for his eyes to improve. When he looked back down the Pass, he could still see no more than vague shapes.

The chill of the night steadily increased as they waited.

Kadat came out of the darkness.

"Garin is correct. There are fires beyond the Pass and not too far away. I saw shadows pass between them. There is someone there. They must know we are here."

"Could it be our people?" a voice asked. "Could it be soldiers or folk of Tarodash? The enemy surely cannot have tracked us here."

"We shall see in the morning," answered Kadat. We can only set guards and remain unseen and unheard. And hope. It could be our folk, and the end of our ordeal.

"Take what rest you can. Be assured that if it is the enemy, they will not pass our watchers unannounced."

"Should we move further up the slope?"

"Remaining amongst the trees would seem best. There is no need to disturb those already asleep. We shall keep good watch."

Perad took a few paces forward to offer himself, but Kadat

spoke to all who were near. "If we require a change of watchers, you will be woken. Take your rest."

Perad wished to see the fires and determine for himself the message they told, and make his own evaluation of the danger, but would not risk disturbing the attention of the watchers.

He found his pack and took it to place himself with a view along the Pass into the darkness in the west, and he wrapped himself and sat far into the night.

At times the glow from the moon showed him the outline of the cliffs, and at times he believed he saw shapes moved somewhere below him, and at those times he put his hand on his knife.

Sometime after midnight, the moon fell behind the cliffs, or the cloud thickened to obscure it, and the darkness increased. He lay on his back then, and stared into the blackness above and attempted to judge the passage of the night, and the remaining distance to the morning.

Chapter 29

Perad must have dozed, for when he opened his eyes he saw, through breaks in the cloud, the pattern of stars which told him that dawn was near. It would be daylight by now in summer and he would be about and busy, he thought, and even in winter he would have a blaze going in the kitchen grate and would be reading. Here, near the end of the year and the end of the world, waking seemed more difficult.

He rolled to his side and lifted himself on his elbow to look down the Pass. He stayed in that position for a while, but there were only vague shapes which may have been the walls of the Pass with blackness between. Even as he watched, clouds filled the gaps in the sky and the stars were obscured and the darkness increased. He flexed his back to ease some small pains there.

He had slept in his boots, and he sat to remove them, and the bindings, and he stretched his toes. He wrapped his feet and replaced his boots and fastened them well, all by touch. There was no fire. He sensed movement around him, and caught whispered voices, and as his eyes adjusted, or the darkness lessened, he could see from the shapes backed by a different black that many folk were sitting and many were huddled in groups.

Presently, he rolled his ground sheet and blanket and strapped them to his pack. There was a tone to the whispers around which he did not like, and he stared hard to see faces and read expressions, but it was still too dark.

Dresana appeared before him and knelt and reached out, and took his hand. "I saw you had awakened," she said, and he did not know how she could have seen. He blinked largely in an attempt to clear his eyes.

"Breakfast," she said, softly, and placed something in his hands. "It is dried fruit rolled in a slice of ham. Do not let the fruit fall out. It is almost the last of the food. We need to be in the woods within two days."

"What is known?" asked Perad.

"I believe there is some news, but I have not been told it. Someone is camping west of the Pass. We do not know who. I must go. There are preparations to be made."

He shuffled until his back was to the rock wall and sat and chewed.

It was two and a half days to Woodall, a little more with the young children. If the food ran out before that, they could live off the woodland as they travelled through it, even in winter. And the woodland of their valley was within a day's walk. They needed only to escape this place. And avoid the enemy.

The sky was becoming paler and he could see the shape of the day's weather. It would be a grey morning. The cloud was still from the west, piling above the peaks, and would be dropping snow in huge amounts. It would snow here, too, before midday. The air which rolled down the mountain flanks and through the Pass was becoming colder. They could not stay in this place.

He finished eating and wiped his hands in the dust. More folk were moving, and the whispers were more intent. He stood and took his pack in one hand, and went the few paces towards the group furthest down the slope. A woman from another group stood and went with him.

Heads turned and even in the dark he saw in their faces what the news would be.

Someone spoke. "We believe it is the Gralt." Close up, Perad could see knives had been drawn, and there were swords across knees and on the ground. "They can only be waiting for us. Our fire last night was unfortunate. They must have seen it. They know someone is here. If they attack now, we are lost."

Kadat replied. "If they did not creep up on us in the dark, they will not attack now. They will be waiting for full light. They will want to know our strength. They cannot be certain we are the group which ran from them in the Ravines. This is not their land. They cannot know who inhabits this area. We shall remain vigilant and see what daylight brings." He fell silent, and no one added to his words.

The woman turned away to share the news.

Daylight came soon and brought nothing but ill tidings. They could see cloaks and helmets. It was the Gralt and they held the exit to the Pass. They were perhaps three hundred paces away, where the Pass widened and the cliffs fell away. Perad could see now that this was the end of the mountains. In the distance was the broken land which bordered the desert.

The Gralt stood in twos and threes, and came no nearer. A few were on the cliff sides. They were watching the Pass.

With the strengthening light, Garrett climbed the southern wall. He climbed well, choosing a course up and across, and leaned out from a vantage point to examine the Gralt encampment. "There are thirty to forty," he said when he returned. "My guess is that it is the group who ran us from the Ravines. The shape of the land hides some of their camp, but I am convinced there are no more than forty."

Tardeb stood to face him. "Is there any escape for us up there? Anywhere we can go?"

"The best climber amongst us would be forced to return before long. There is nowhere we can take our families. There is no route out of here."

"Maradan's route, there is no sign of that? Can we search for it?" But his voice held no hope.

"It has never been found, and it cannot be now found. The tales say it was on the southern wall. And even if it could be discovered, it would bring us down on the Gralt in a single file, to be picked off with ease. We are trapped." He looked back, up the rocky slope and through the patch of woodland to the mountains, and some heads turned to look with him. Snow was falling there, and all but the nearest slopes were hidden by weather. There was no way back.

Faren sprung to his feet and strode to his pack leaning against a rock. He had a scabbard fastened across the top, and he drew the sword and strode back. It was an ancient weapon, perhaps a family relic, but it looked flux made and the edge he had put on it glinted dangerously. He was breathing deeply and quickly, and his face had no more colour than the clouds.

"Enough. We have hidden for too long, and we have run when we should have fought. No more. Now I shall fight. I shall take whoever will come with me and we will run at these mad dogs and…"

"Then you will die," said Tardeb.

"Then I will die. But I will die going at the enemy, rather than hiding from them or running from them. And some of the enemy will meet their deaths."

"And so will your family, soon after. Wait. Wait." Tardeb stepped forward, close to the point of the sword. "You are correct in that we have no option. Yes, we shall fight. We must fight. But consider, first. Let us investigate a controlled charge, an attack with some thought. We at least equal them in number. We must make an advantage of that. If we could but take one each, we save our folk. We have the slope. And we have more to fight for. They have the position, but if a charge were to take us through them, the situation would change."

Tardeb place his hands on Faren's shoulders. Some of the desperation had gone out of the younger man. He had lowered his sword. Tardeb dropped his voice, and only those near could hear. "To charge thirty of the Gralt army in a defensive position is a desperate undertaking. Few of us can expect to survive. But do it bravely, and do it well, and our families go home.

Tardeb lifted his voice. "Men, here. To me." Some men had been with their families, and came striding. Those near crowded closer. "This is it, men. This is the end of our time in the mountains. And it has come upon us quickly. We have no choice. We must attack the enemy. And we shall do it soon, before they have time to prepare."

There were nods. Many turned to look at the Gralt positions.

The Gralt appeared unconcerned. They strolled between their camp and the untidy line facing the Pass. Perad could hear them call to the lookouts on the cliff. He hated them for their arrogance, their unreasoned cruelty, and for the pointlessness of what they did. They would kill him, and they would kill Dresana, and they would slaughter his folk. And they would do so without gain to themselves. If Dran was correct, they were leaving Tarodash, being driven out. What made them delay to destroy a few village folk?

He stepped back from the group and looked away, up towards the peaks. The cold air was in his face, and he dropped his gaze to the small patch of woodland, this strange distant corner of his own land out here between mountain walls.

Tardeb was continuing. "Quickly, now, before our resolve goes. We shall attack the enemy. What shall be our tactics?" he looked at Kadat.

Kadat was staring down the slope, measuring, assessing, visualising. He took a stride forward and men moved aside for him. He spoke as if telling a history, moving his hands to shape the story. "Fast. Close together. Lots of noise. Pull them

235

in. Just before we meet their line, break wide to spread their attention. They are confident, they will stand to meet us. Go for individuals. Hit them with the force of the charge. Put them on the ground. Trample them. We shall run onto their blades, but it will be a sacrifice to be proud of. There may be no more than twenty of them ready to face us. We can break that line. Those out wide on the edges may outflank them. Turn and take them from the side. We shall be around them. Then we shall be among them, and it will be man against man. Get inside their blades, use knives, boots, gouge, wrestle."

He let his anger come then, and raised his voice. "We shall go at such speed, we shall not be stopped. As you approach, choose a target. Hate that target. Take that target."

The Gralt did not hear him, or if they did, took no notice.

"Those without swords, a stout stick, used as a lance." He thrust forward, hands gripping an imaginary weapon.

"Soon. Prepare yourselves. A word with your family. We go soon."

He fell silent. Men began to turn. There was no value in delay.

"Hold," said Dran. "Wait." He held up his hand, and did not look around. He had been watching Perad. He kept his gaze on him. "Perad. You have something. "Speak out."

Perad was looking at the trees, muttering to himself. He did not reply.

Dran was more urgent. "Tell us, Perad. What have you seen?"

Perad turned to face the men.

"There may be something here to aid us."

Chapter 30

All eyes were on him.

"There are materials here," said Perad. "There is a mix I could use." He shook his head. "It is near impossible that it could work." He was looking from the woods to the Pass, making judgments.

Kadat pushed men aside to take him by the shoulders. "Anything, Perad, anything. We have our resolve. Have you something you can add to it? Give us your thoughts."

Perad's mouth was dry. It was an effort to speak. He looked at the ground. "It is no more than a hope. Less, even."

Kadat increased his grip. Hard enough to cause pain. "Quick now. What do you have?"

"A smoke, a fire. Here." He spread his hands over an area of ground. "I could make a smoke and the wind would push fumes down the Pass onto them. I can make fumes which would trouble the enemy."

Kadat released his grip and spun to stare at the Gralt. "Then we shall do it. How long will you need?"

"Little more than the time to build a good blaze." He faced the mountains and felt again the cold air on his face. But it is only a fancy. It cannot work," he said.

"Then at the least, it will spur us in our charge. And even smoke in their eyes will assist us. What do you require?"

"A fire." He took a few steps to position himself centrally. "Here. Circular. Three, four paces across, quick burning, made with thin branches and twigs. Windfall, mostly, it will be drier."

"I shall fetch the wood," said Faren, striding back to

the trees. He inclined his head and three men went with him.

"Low and flat. Do not put light to it until I say," said Perad. "Three things, now." He was near mumbling, and forced himself to lift his head and his voice.

"The bark from the blackpine. Strip it, flatten it, place it here by the fire." He went to scratch marks in the dust with his boots. Kadat nodded and more men left. They were running. Some of the women had sensed the urgency and were hurrying to help.

Perad was more sure now. He gave the order himself. "Gargrass, it grows below the rock wall there, I have seen it. It should be pulled from the ground. Don't break it. We need the roots. Leave the soil on. We need lots of it. All of it. Here behind the fire." He scraped more marks.

"See to it," Kadat said to the women. "We must keep most of the men here. If the Gralt see us leave, or preparing some action, they may come at us before we are ready."

Perad ran after the women and pulled at a shawl. "And the moss from the beran trees. There is a little. Collect it all."

Faren was back with firewood. Even though he had not released his sword, he had a mighty collection in his arms.

"Here said Perad. "A good fire, well packed, built for heat, and to burn quickly. Knee high."

Faren was on his knees placing and weaving the wood. He would not let go of his sword, and watched the enemy over his task. More wood was arriving. He selected from it and continued to shape his construction. Satisfied with the progress, Perad leaned over and spoke to him. "I shall go to check on the gargrass." There was no reply.

He ran through the trees to the wall of rock. A line of backs faced him. There were children among the men and women. Gerana, who had trained with his grandmother for a short while, watched him come and handed him a plant. The blades were narrow and hard, the roots thick for a grass. Clumps of soil clung to them. Perad hit it against his knee, and some of the soil fell away. He nodded and held it out. "That is how it should be," he said. Gerana took it from him and went along the line to show it.

He took two handfuls and ran back to the fire.

"Our activity has been noticed," said Faren, pointing with his chin. The circle of firewood was building well, dense and even.

The Gralt had taken some interest and had moved closer. They would not enter the narrow part of the Pass and stayed in a loose group a little less than two hundred paces away. They had not drawn swords. There were calls between those on the ground and the ones on the high ledges. Their tone suggested jests to Perad, and he believed he heard laughter amongst the speech.

Faren stood. "I do not think they will advance on us. Why should they? They only have to wait." He returned his attention to the fire, stepping around it, making adjustments. At some point he had put aside his sword and now picked it up again.

Three piles were building. Folk arrived in near silence, placed what they had brought, and went for more. No one ran now. They were at a task, and would do it well.

The bark was reluctant to give up its curve and two men had crouched to flatten the sheets over their knees. All the bark had been place with the outside uppermost, and Perad considered this and decided it would be most effective this way.

The moss would be sparse and difficult to collect. It arrived in handfuls to make a small heap. It looked like dark green hair, Perad thought.

"There is no more," he was finally told.

Perad saw the last of the gargrass arrive. "Soon," he said, aloud. The instant he spoke, the men nearby stiffened.

He knelt to better appraise the sheets of bark, and stood and raised his hand to stop the work. "We have enough. Light the fire."

Faren took tinder from a pouch on his belt, and his flint from another. He held the flint and tinder in his palm and struck the flint with the hilt of his sword. There were sparks and, moments later, smoke. He tilted his hand and the flint slid out and fell to the floor. One breath brought small flames; another and he held a handful of fire. He placed it at the base of the wood where he had prepared a tangle of small twigs, and pushed it in with his fingers. The flames grew and licked around the thicker wood. He pulled out a small branch, already burning well, and quickly circled the fire, pockets of yellow flame growing behind him.

He bent to retrieve his flint. "A good one, that, I should not wish to lose it." He stepped forward and pushed lightly with his boot at a perceived fault with his work, and stepped back. The circle of flame spread towards the centre, met and grew.

Perad fussed with the materials, arranging them. "I must be able to pick them up easily. Each layer must go on in a short time, but spread well to burn evenly. There will be little room for mistakes." He spoke to himself, and Dran leaned close to hear.

Perad sought around amongst the discarded wood and picked out a small branch and tested its length across the fire. It reached past half way, and he selected another. He looked towards Dran and handed him the stick. "To shape the fire," he said.

So intent on his tasks, he had not been aware of the movement around him and the arrangements which must have been made. All the men were around the fire, and remains of the village gathered some way back. Some men had swords, some had sticks and some had both. Most spare hands held a knife. There would have been arguments as to who would go and who would stay, but Perad had not heard them.

"What is to happen?" asked Faren. He was watching the fire, a near perfect circle of flame.

"I am waiting for the flames to finish and give me red heat. I shall then put on the mix in three layers and as it burns through it will make the smoke. I would like it to happen quickly and concentrate the fumes." He turned to feel the breeze once again. "Then the wind will do its work."

He turned back and looked over the flames and down the Pass. The Gralt appeared to be a little more organised.

The flames were already subsiding. "It will not be long, now," said Perad. He pushed at the fire with his stick, and watched a small part of it crumble, revealing an intense redness. He put down his branch and loosened his tunic to allow him to reach inside to feel the handle of his knife. Taking up the branch again, he moved close to the fire and spread his legs for balance.

Dran took the same position, across the fire. The flames had almost gone.

"Almost ready," said Perad.

"Tell me when and how," said Dran.

"No more thought, men," said Kadat. "Into line." There was no need to lift his voice.

The men of Woodall jostled for position in the front, there being insufficient distance for a single line across the narrow gap of even ground between the walls of the cliffs.

"Behind the fire," said Perad. "Five paces behind the fire."

The men retreated. Perad looked along them, along the rows of faces. They seemed made of stone.

Then the flames were gone leaving a heaped circle of glowing embers. The breeze caught in patches and brought out yellows amongst the reds. "Ankle height, quick," said

Perad and began to rake the embers, moving his stick from side to side. A last ripple of flames, and the ash compacted and the red strengthened.

He worked quickly and surely, head down. He did not want to lose the heat. Dran worked the fire from the other side.

"The bark, now. Cover the whole fire. Overlap the pieces. No more than two thicknesses." The bark was at the other side, and Dran waited, a piece in each hand, until Perad came round and began covering the embers. In opposite directions they circled the fire, laying the bark, obscuring the glow. There were sparks as each piece was dropped in place. The centre had to be covered by throwing. Their aim was sure and the task completed. The bark began to blister and the edges curl. Tiny twists of smoke appeared.

Someone in the line squatted and retched, stood again and spat.

"Now the grass. Spread it evenly." Perad threw and placed and dropped. He had to hurry. Dran copied his every move.

Flames were finding their way around the edges of the bark and into the grass. Perad used the branch to separate a clump and broke the layer of bark in his haste. Yellow tongues shot through.

"Moss," said Perad. "Now. Fast."

Dran dropped his branch and lifted the entire collection to his chest and heaved it to the centre of the fire. It clung together and Perad leaned over to reach with his branch and achieve a better spread and he felt the heat on his face.

As he stood, an eddy of wind in the lee of his body swirled the smoke, and he took a little of it in his next breath. There was a taste of iron to it, and of blood, and a bitterness. Immediately, his sight sharpened. He lifted his face and felt a rhythm, a beat, to the light from the sky. A ragged darkness encroached around the edges of his vision; there was something growing behind him, close, dark, horrible, a bird, a bat, gigantic, black.

His balance went and his knees gave and he stumbled forward and his foot went in the fire. He was jerked backwards by his collar.

"Speak to me," said Dran.

"Soon," said Perad. "It is beginning."

They watched as the heat worked through the bark and the resins boiled and hissed, and flames found their way amongst the grass, and the roots began to smoke. Above the roots, the moss caught the fire, and began to burn, and turned the flames green.

More smoke came from the fire, thick, dark, grey and heavy. The wind from the mountains took it and rolled it. Perad moved his branch back and forth, disturbing the surface of the fire, mixing. Dran followed his lead. The sheets of bark began to split and more flames burst through, low and intense, still edged with green. The smoke thickened and the wind pushed and a column of smoke began to move down the Pass towards the enemy. "More," said Perad, and stirred the fire and the embers more vigorously. Dran copied. A great cloud of the smoke rose and spread. "Back," shouted Perad, but there was no need, for the breeze took it and it joined the rest, an oily grey ribbon, winding down the slope.

Chapter 31

"Ready men," said Kadat. "We shall go soon." He had taken a step forward of the line and leaned there on his sword. There seemed no anger to his voice, which was clear and untroubled. He could have been calling them to a day of fruit picking.

A light snow was falling, the flakes drifting with the breeze. Above the fire they caught the heat and swirled and were drawn down the Pass.

"Wait," said Perad. He was watching the smoke, judging the distance, the spread. The Gralt must have sensed that something was happening, for more of them had joined the untidy line across the Pass.

At the far side of the fire, Dran let fall his stick and withdrew his sword. He looked to Perad for a sign. Perad nodded, a single drop of the chin.

Dran backed from the fire and towards the line. There was not room for him and he remained in front. His dark ankle length coat marked him out as different from the others, a guest amongst the men of Woodall.

"One each," said Kadat. "One each to save your family, your village. Take one and take his throat, and Woodall will live. If you need to, run onto his sword and take his throat. Find your man and down him."

"Wait," said Perad, but it came out as a breath, and no one heard.

The smoke had thinned to invisibility, now. The last flames flickered and died, the ashes dimmed. A small gust of wind lifted the hems of tunics and cloaks. Kadat raised his sword above his head.

There was movement amongst the Gralt. A sentry high on a ledge on the southern wall scrambled to his feet and drew his sword. He spat out words, short, hard words which echoed from rocky walls, and faded to nothing. There was silence for a moment, before the words came again, faster this time and higher pitched, running into one another until the sound became a scream. He raised his head and thrust his sword at the sky and slashed at the air. The scream went on without breath, and he stepped out from the ledge. His cloak wrapped around him as he fell, and he thrashed again at the air with his sword until he hit protruding rock near the base of the cliff, spun and landed out of sight among the boulders. Any sound from the impact was lost among a rising tumult of noise from the Gralt who had broken their line and were shouting and waving and turning.

"Now," said Perad, his voice unheard again, for Kadat had also called, "Now, now, now," and even that was unnecessary, for the men of Woodall were already charging the enemy. Perad saw two go down as their legs tangled, and they were back up in an instant, and running.

"Noise," shouted Kadat amongst the thunder of galloping boots, "Give them some noise," and he screamed and called and yelled, wordless, blood chilling sounds, and curses, and animal noises, and his shouts were taken up by the others, until the Pass was filled with a roar of forty men of the Valleys charging into battle to fight for their people.

And the Gralt were running, with no order or direction. They were dropping from their perches, scrambling, pushing, colliding.

For three beats of his heart, beats which filled his head with thuds surpassing the sounds of the charge, Perad was rigid with fear. But only for three, for in the next beat, he was a man of Woodall, overwhelmed by the passion for battle and charging the enemy.

Already running, he stamped on the end of the branch he had been tending the fire with, and it broke leaving him with a weapon, a cudgel, arm length and jagged.

Even with the jolting of his run, his hand found his knife and he unsheathed it and held it wide.

The slope increased, and his speed increased. His feet pounded. He gained on the men in front. They were already among and through those of the enemy who had run up the slope, and had downed them and trampled them.

Perad reached the first of the fallen, and they were all dark cloaked, and there was blood at their throats and around the slashes in their clothing. He stamped on one face in his run and stumbled and regained his balance, and there was another of the enemy who may have been struggling to his knees, and he took him in the head with the point of his club which was wrenched from his grasp, and he went on without it.

He saw two more dark heaps a few strides apart and he changed direction to kick and slash and stamp, and he ran on, until a change in the sound of the battle slowed him.

The screams and yells were less, and there were words, and names called, and they were in the language of Tarodash. He looked up to find a meaning to it, and caught his feet and fell and rolled, and when he stood, he went on at a stumbling walk. He heard more shouts and words, and there seemed no urgency to them. They were the calls of men about their work.

He lifted his head, and looked further on, and what he saw stopped him. The battle was ending. There were few left standing of the dark cloaks of the Gralt, and around them all, amongst the villagers, were uniforms of greens and blues, soldiers of Tarodash.

In the short time it took him to make sense of what he could see, the slaying was over. He saw the last of the enemy go down, two swords in him. One sword must have caught somehow, for the soldier placed his foot on the chest of the fallen Gralt and pulled with two hands to release it. He leaned on his colleague, and bent his knee to raise his foot, and wiped the blade on his boot.

Others were striding about, checking the enemy, finishing the chore. Confident voices called out.

"There."

"That one moved."

"Behind those rocks."

"Watch your back."

"Be sure to finish that."

As they worked, there was a general movement up the slope, soldiers checking amongst the boulders, the men of Woodall with them, returning to their families.

One strode ahead of the rest, purposeful, determined, ignoring the scattered bodies of the Gralt. He swung his head to survey as he came and when his eyes fell on Perad, he stopped and leaned on his sword, patched with dark red from tip to hilt. There was blood and dirt around his head. His uniform was muddied and torn. One sleeve was ripped open from elbow to wrist, showing an arm strong, thick with muscle, bloodied. Even from a distance, Perad could see his eyes shine with life and sparkle within the dark mask of his face. The face split into a broad smile, then an enormous grin. It was uncle Tavit.

Chapter 32

The womenfolk from Woodall were streaming by, hurrying down to their men. There were passing words and nods for his uncle, and grips to his shoulder. There were replies from his uncle, but the eyes and the grin were for Perad.

Perad moved forward, his legs slow and heavy. He stumbled and fought to regain his balance. His head throbbed enormously from the effort of the charge and from a dark presence which had wedged itself behind his eyes.

His uncle let go his sword which clattered to the rocks, and placed both hands on Perad's shoulders. There were no words. After a long time Perad stepped back and took his uncle's injured arm and lowered it to examine the damage. He rubbed at his eyes to clear his vision. "That needs cleaning and binding. My pack is up there."

"Come then. The fumes, I would guess, were yours. I felt something of it as we approached, a taste. There were shadows of nightmares in it. I would not have liked a breathful.

"We had seen the fire from hiding. We thought it had to be Woodall who had delayed the Gralt. We were considering an attack, deciding between a sneak and a charge. And then Woodall charged. You can show me the place of the fire. I would like to see that." He turned to look back, and Perad looked with him. Across the battlefield, there were greetings and meetings, and welcomes, all in the quiet way of the Valleys. Perad bent to pick up the sword. He held it out for his uncle.

"You are a soldier. Should you not be with the others?"

"The Gralt are finished, and I am done with soldiering. I am an innkeeper once more. Though I shall require a release, I expect.

"Perhaps I shall save the sword." He took it and set off up the slope. "I can keep it behind the counter. I can wave it if the customers annoy me."

"Tavit," came from behind them and Dran limped towards them. "I did not see you as we charged. But then, I saw little. Others from Woodall told me you were here."

Uncle Tavit pointed to his leg. "Have you taken an injury?"

"From the run. I took no hit in the fight. It is nothing."

They stood by the dead fire. Uncle Tavit scuffed the ashes with his foot and the breeze lifted grey dust and moved it down the slope. He walked around the circle and looked down the Pass, at the distances and the shapes, and back at the fire. He turned to examine the woodland, and to feel the breeze on his face. "You did well, Perad," he said. "You did well."

He found a rock to sit on and rolled back the flap of his sleeve. "Tell me what you used," he said. "Tell me the whole tale. It will mean little to me, but I claim the first hearing of it."

Perad fetched a bag of water from the pile of supplies. He picked up a fallen plant as he came.

"This you know as gargrass which grows in corners out of the sun where the soil never dries. Its roots entwine with a fungus which has not been named. Or its name has not been passed on." He held it out for his uncle to see the white string-like threads. "Long ago, the roots and fungus, fresh and damp, were burned over a candle by tellers of fortunes, scriers, tricksters perhaps. It brought dark dreams and visions, but it brought illness and it fell out of fashion. It was considered dangerous. Some of this I have been told by grandmother Katada, and some I have read. This was long ago. I saw the plant as we approached the beginning of the Pass. The blackpine bark was fortunate. It will strengthen the effect of any infusion which is breathed in from hot water. I gambled that it would work with smoke. But it is a rare tree, I know of only three patches in our valley. I would not have expected it here. I have a small pouch of the powdered bark in my pack."

"And the moss?" asked Dran.

"I do not know," said Perad. "I felt it would open the mind to doubt, cause indecision. But I do not know why I thought that. It has many uses, but that is not one I know of. Perhaps it had no effect."

"What you did saved lives, Perad. Even though we have defeated them, the Gralt are brave and fearsome warriors. The battle would have been difficult otherwise."

"The flux helped."

Dran and uncle Tavit looked at each other, then back at Perad. "There was no flux, Perad," said his uncle.

When Perad lifted his pack with his left hand, he gasped with pain and dropped the pack. Holding up his hand, he saw his thumb was swollen at the base and there was a narrow line of deep bruising, front and back, from the knuckle to the wrist. "That looks broken," said Dran. "When did you do that?"

"I do not know," said Perad. He was puzzled and shook his head.

Dran reached for the hand and turned it and tested the swelling with his fingers. "Show me what movement you have," he said.

Now that he was aware of it, there was an ache from his elbow downwards. He made a fist and felt nothing more, but when he opened his hand, pain arrowed the length of his arm.

"Broken, I am sure," said Dran. "But the bone is not

displaced. A simple binding and a sling will take care of it. I would be happy to do that, unless you wish the soldier healer."

Perad was weighing the problems of being without the use of a hand for a while. "Now would be best," he said.

"Sit down then. Rest your arm across your knee. Once your thumb is supported, you can mend your uncle's arm." Dran went for his pack, leaning with others by the wall of the Pass. He took a roll of cloth from a pouch.

"Is that a spare foot wrapping?" asked Perad.

"Perhaps, and a number of other things when required. It will serve the purpose. Do you wish to add one of your mixtures, first?"

"There is no broken skin and nothing which will help," he said.

Dran packed a few folds between the thumb and the palm, and wrapped loops to bind the thumb to the hand. He was precise and careful, taking the binding down onto the wrist and arm. He held the binding in place and reached to his belt. "My knife," he said. "Ah, I know. It is down there." Something passed over his face, which Perad could not read.

"Dran, trader of knives, and cannot cut a strip of cloth. Let my have yours." He slit the binding and tied it. He fashioned a loop to hold the arm and pulled it over Perad's head.

Perad tested his fingers. Though the thumb was secure, he had some movement. "I did not know you had a healer's skill."

"You have just seen me extend the little I had. I shall go look for my knife. It should be where I last put it."

He left Perad with his uncle, and went on down the slope.

Many of the soldiers had walked up the Pass to stand and look at the place of the fire. Perad saw some bend to take a handful of the ashes, or rub their fingers in them, or smell them, and many turned to raise their hand to him.

A few of the soldiers, like his uncle, were men of Woodall, and some had come with their womenfolk and children to gather their possessions. Jevan, the butcher, strode to Perad and gripped his shoulder. He had grown a beard since Perad had last seen him, and seemed larger and more powerful, a warrior from the old tales. But his voice was the same, soft and friendly. "I cannot stay to hear your story. The captain has not yet relieved those of us who wish to be with our families. There may still be enemy about, and we are preparing to march. Woodall shall have a fine escort."

Perad checked the straps on his pack and shouldered it, still sitting. When he attempted to stand, he dropped back to the rock and almost fell sideways to the floor, and his uncle caught him and took him by the wrist and pulled him to his feet, where he stood unsteadily. His head pounded and his sight was blurred. "I may have taken some of the fumes," he said.

His uncle took him firmly by the sleeve below his shoulder. "Let us see if walking can clear your head," he said.

A line of three soldiers was striding to meet them, the centre one the captain. The pale strip on the shoulder of his tunic had ripped, and flapped as he walked. He stopped before Perad. "The young poisoner," he said. "I am beginning to get some sense of what you did." He looked from the mountains to the trees, from the fire to down the Pass. "You did well, Perad. I would have lost men without your actions. Your village will be grateful, and so will other families when their men return alive. Well done. Though I suspect you will soon tire of telling it, I would like to hear your tale directly, if I may, when we stop later." He stepped aside. "On your way, then. There is much for all of us to do, but I have been told I would regret it if I missed seeing the place of the fire." He continued up the hill.

Perad had lost some of his dizziness, and was walking better. Once amongst the cluster of villagers, uncle Tavit released his grip and stepped away. "I shall see if I can be of assistance somewhere," he said.

Preparations for a trek were being made. Packs and burdens were being distributed, cloaks and tunics fastened.

A soft snow was now falling, already making gentle the shapes of the field of battle. It was becoming colder. They should leave this place.

The dead Gralt were not to be buried. There was little depth to the soil here, and no enthusiasm for dragging them elsewhere. "Leave them where they lie. The birds and animals can feed on them," the captain had said.

Once through the Pass, the cliff walls receded and the slope levelled out. Perad stopped to look back. The snow began to fall heavily, covering the dead enemy. The cloud from the west, still pushing against the air from the mountains, was darkening rapidly. Perhaps the snow would fill the Pass as in the time of Maradan.

A few soldiers delayed to take from the bodies some weapons and other items, waiting until the villagers were out of sight.

"Let us make what distance we can before we rest," said Tardeb, turning away.

Chapter 33

The going was slow.

A day's walking west would bring them to the beginnings of the woodland where they had the choice of continuing south of the river close to the desert, or turning north to cross the river at the trees they felled some weeks ago.

There was talk of making the trek to the Ravines to collect possessions left when they escaped, but the captain forbade it. "There may still be a few Gralt in the area, or further north in the east of the Valleys, working their way south. I will not split my forces to accompany a diversion. What you have left behind, let it wait. Spring will be here soon and we shall be able to declare Tarodash free of the enemy. You will be safe to travel then."

Their marches were short, and at each stop the villagers and the soldiers not on watch would gather closely to exchange stories and news.

There was debate amongst the men who had fought them, as to the effect the smoke had on the Gralt. "I do not know what made them run, but they appeared blinded," said one. "They could not see us. We only had to avoid them stumbling into us." Others told of a darkening of their own vision as they had approached the battle.

"I think rather than blindness, they would have seen shapes, visions," Perad said. The dark wavering edge to his own sight, caused him to blink often and shake his head in order to rid himself of it. "They would not have trusted what they saw. A little confusion amongst the enemy is what I had hoped for, to aid our attack."

At another stop, the account of their flight from the Ravines was requested. "You were near to Walvin and Henata at the end, I am told. What happened?" Perad was asked by Gored, council elder and oldest of those villages who had chosen to soldier.

"Even though I have heard all the ancient tales, I have never imagined such bravery," he replied. "When this is all over, I shall go back there and leave a marker." He left the telling of the events to Faren, who stood to recount the tale and stumbled away in tears on its conclusion.

On the next march, Perad found himself among a group containing the captain and elder Tardeb, and heard how the soldiers found themselves at the Pass at the moment of the charge.

Uncle Tavit's group had spied the Gralt a good distance away, from the north, and had followed when they left, believing them to be retreating, aiming for the desert, leaving Tarodash. They had watched and worried, too far away to help, while the Gralt turned aside to explore the Ravines, before continuing south. Their own examination of the Ravines led them to believe that Woodall was hiding in the mountains. After discussion, the belief was that Woodall must be safe, and the decision was to follow the Gralt to the edge of Tarodash. Matched in number, they had been reluctant to engage the enemy, and saw no need. It could only have been misfortune which placed the Gralt at Maradan Pass the previous evening.

"What guarantee is there that the Gralt will not return?" asked Tardeb.

"I would wager that the Gralt will return," said the captain. "They are warriors and they have encountered an enemy within reach and they have been driven away. What brought them here will bring them again. And better prepared. We have been fortunate. More so than we think. We shall watch our borders with care, now. When they return, we shall be ready for them."

"So we shall always be at war, now?"

The captain sighed. "I am sorry. I have allowed out my bleaker thoughts. I have become a soldier, and to my surprise it suits me. I have too quickly become accustomed to seeing the world in terms of conflict.

"Perhaps I should restate my thoughts. I very much believe that the Gralt will return. But I also believe that, with preparation, we can prevent them from entering our lands. When I was last at garrison, I heard talk of the desire of the Brother Princes to negotiate a treaty. A well armed envoy to meet with them. Perhaps a negotiation arranged by the pirates. I would be delighted to be part of that venture. But I ramble. My thoughts are based on no more than a fragment of a rumour. For now, the Gralt are a dangerous and deadly enemy who have murdered and slaughtered our people, and we must be vigilant. And we will be. It is my guess that the southern border will be well patrolled, and as far as the mountains. They have used an easterly route. They may use it again."

Perad had stumbled a number of times, and Dran had placed himself to walk beside him, supporting him, when necessary, by taking his arm. He did so again, as he spoke. "Yes, it is clear that the Valleys, and Woodall in particular, will require some level of protection. At a distance, I hope. It would be a shame if the Valley way of life became too much altered. Still, I would not be surprised if, in the coming months, your village of Woodall saw a lot more visitors, and your uncle's inn were to receive an increase in trade. Extra ale will be needed."

"Fine ale, I have heard," said the captain. "I hope I have the opportunity to sample it. It may be worth requesting an assignment out here for that very purpose."

Perad could not clear his vision of its wavering edges, or the heaviness in his head, and was as grateful as anyone when they called an end to the march in what may have been an ancient quarry carved into a cliff face. He shared with the collecting of firewood, difficult for the trees were sparse, and it was near dark. He could barely lift his feet, and continually scuffed his boots as he carried his load of sticks to drop on the pile.

He found a place to rest by the wall and sat and realised his pack was still strapped to his back. He struggled to his feet to remove it, and Dresana came and took him by the arm and led him to the fire. Hands removed the pack, and someone unrolled his blanket. He was made to stand while his groundsheet was arranged, and he was wrapped in his blanket and sat again. He wished to thank folk, but his words came out in mumbles and he soon ceased. Dresana spooned broth into his mouth. He was surrounded by a sea of faces, which swayed and bobbed, grew and retreated. When he closed his eyes, the faces were replaced by flashes, arrows of dark colour, and brilliant white streaks. He tried to speak of it. A blanket was wrapped around his head, covering all but his nose, and he was lowered to the ground.

Immediately, a darkness grew in his vision and dimmed the lights and he slept.

He woke in the dark, with the fire low. He removed the wrapping around his head and tested his eyes. The flashes had gone, perhaps retreating inside his head, for there were darts of pain there, intense and sickening. He rolled to his side and felt more comfortable and the pain lessened.

His back had become uncovered and he attempted to adjust the blanket. Someone fixed it for him, and wrapped his head again, this time leaving his whole face free. There were huddles of folk all around, and soft conversation. He could see small flames among the embers and the glowing logs, and he stilled himself and watched them and attempted to read the stories told within.

There was a little of dawn in the sky when he woke fully. He had rolled away from his pack, and his neck ached from lack of a pillow.

He knelt and looked around. It was very peaceful.

A soldier was sitting on a rock watching him. He had a cloth over his head and his feet were in his pack. He had out a knife, long and double edged and not a workman's knife, though his voice told that he was of the northern valleys, and was trimming the soles of his boots. "I did not think it to be this cold so near your desert," he said.

"We are in the mountains. It is not so bad in the valleys." Perad's words came out well and he felt a little better.

He sat to wrap his feet and put on his boots. He counted the number of times his boots had been removed for him in the last few weeks, and thought about that for a while. A flash of anger at the Gralt passed behind his eyes and he thought about that, also.

He stood, then, and stamped his feet to test them, and stretched. There were pains everywhere. He accepted them and stretched again. The soldier watched him without comment.

With the light, he circled the camp to seek and examine the plants of this area. He found lichens and tiny flowering plants with shiny leaves, new to him, but little else.

They stopped at mid morning when they reached the first of the trees, and cut branches to make sleds. The soldiers from the plains watched this and requested one to take their packs, and fought playfully for the honour of dragging it.

The end of the afternoon saw them near the river. The captain called for a halt and chose the place to camp. "We lost two men here a week ago. I wish to take time to bury them.

Keep your children close. There is the body of a Gralt somewhere nearby."

It was good to collect the nuts and berries and seeds of their woods, and it was good to have generous fires, and sit around them and eat and talk. The soldiers without a duty joined them.

The talk turned to the Gralt.

"They are terrifying fighters with swords in their hands," said one soldier. "A band of five would defeat fifteen of our men, as we soon discovered. They work close together, attacking in one area, regrouping and attacking elsewhere. We learned rapidly to avoid such confrontations. We met them instead with lances and arrows and charges on horseback, which they seemed not to expect. They also learned quickly, and developed new defensive techniques, and in the end, it was cutting their supply and communication lines which defeated them. They were a long way from home in a strange land. We knew the landscape and they didn't. We would not confront their main forces and only met with scouts and roving bands, and only if we had superior numbers and better positions. Had they not spread themselves so far, they would be crossing Tarodash by now, unstoppable. That is why most believe this was as much an exploration as an invasion."

Later, Tardeb led the whole village to the graves of the two fallen men, graves dug in the earth in the manner of the Plains, to stand with the soldiers, barefooted, and sing the ancient songs, and newly learned songs for those lost in battle.

Afterwards, the captain released from their contract as soldiers those men of the Valleys who wished to return to valley life. Not all took up the offer.

These were short days, near the ending of the year, and the plan had been to rise well before dawn and be off at first light and in Woodall by evening, but it was not to be.

A distant fire had been spotted to the west and scouts reported a sighting of Gralt. Only two it was believed.

They waited for news that the enemy were moving, and set off late, staying on the south of the river, following at a good distance. In this way, they could continue the journey home, and observe the Gralt.

Reports came back that the two had met with another five, and were heading south at a good speed. They were well into the barren land bordering the desert and no longer considered a threat.

The captain wished to view their retreat, as did Perad and many others.

A peak along a ridge to their left promised a good view and Garrett led them to its top to look south.

The desert was topped by flat grey cloud and its distance was lost in mist. They pointed out to each other faint thin lines in the sand which may have been the tracks of the Gralt marching south. Nearer, amongst the rocks were moving dots, the enemy, they thought, leaving Tarodash.

They would not reach Woodall before dark, and stopped late in the afternoon close enough to home for there to be tracks which were familiar to many. Certainly, Perad had been here collecting, and knew the slopes, trees and rocks, and the small streams and the plants.

To find Woodall in the dark was not difficult, and the walk was considered by some. In the end, they chose to remain together and return together. They camped amongst the trees and slept early and rose early.

From a distance, they saw smoke, and worried at that, but not for long. Once in sight of the buildings they saw it was from the homes of those who had sought refuge in Dresswell, now returned.

They came to a halt on the low escarpment above the east bridge, and gathered to look down on their village, softly coloured by the early sun through a gentle mist. A quietness fell on them.

It was the children who broke the spell, pushing through to charge down the slope, yelling and laughing and calling, feet pounding over the wooden bridge, and racing into Woodall and to their homes.

The inn door was open and leaves and dirt had blown in to cover the floor in small swirls and drifts. Perad pressed his broken hand to the place where old blind Kerim had sat, and looked past there along the room to the fire with leaves amongst the old ashes, and to the small stool by the side where folk liked to sit to warm their feet and dry their boots, and where Perad would read by the flames early in the morning.

Chapter 34

The first day of Sun Return was not normally celebrated in the Valleys as it was in the rest of Tarodash. Most years, the wind which brought the first real snow to the Plains was from the north east. The Valleys, in the shadow of the mountains, would escape the snow, and be left with half a month of thick cloud, cold rain and fog. The sun was not to be seen and the folk of the Valleys would catch up with indoor work. The evening of Sun Return was the Valley's celebration, scurrying by candle light between cosy homes for songs and food and drink.

This year was different, though. The wind was northerly, and the cold had come, but not the rain and fog. The twenty days since the battle of Maradan Pass had been a time of clear spectacular weather, with blue skies and bright sunshine.

The folk of Woodall had even held a ceremony of Sun Return, lining along the western edge of the burial ground at dawn and singing the ancient songs of welcome, not heard in the Valleys for years, as the sun climbed above the snow capped mountain peaks and sent long blue shadows pointing the way to the ocean.

Perad had gone to the ceremony, to please his uncle, but had left first, and alone.

There was even some heat in the sun. He was in the inn yard, now, where the warmth, trapped between the building and the yard walls, was surprising, for it was still early in the day. He had been chased out of the kitchen by uncle Tavit, who had returned to find him slumped by the fire, and whose good nature and long temper had been sorely tested by Perad during the past few days.

His eyes had cleared within a week of arriving home, and the pains soon after. Something remained, though, a darkness in his thoughts and a heaviness in his limbs. He appeared distracted, withdrawing himself from conversations, struggling to undertake the simplest of tasks. His skin paled, and he failed to gain the weight lost in the mountains.

Dran had left, promising to return in the spring. He had dug up his knives and stored them in the cellar at the inn.

His intention was to call first at the quarry hamlet of Getar, and Perad had set out with him, only to turn around at the first ridge, with a mumbled goodbye and a half-hearted excuse.

Dran could do nothing but restate his intention to be back soon, and watch him trudge slowly back down the track.

Perad sat on the stone bench, now, and kept the sunlight from his eyes by lowering his head and gazing at his boots.

They told him no story, and he did not seek one. He sighed deeply, and ceased at last his attempts to clear his mind, and he allowed all that was in his head the freedom to roam and grow and shout as loudly as it wished. The uproar there increased, and the words and thoughts and memories and scenes crashed and merged and expanded. The tumult filled his head, and his being, the Valleys, the whole of the world, and further.

And as it spread, it thinned, like smoke, and dispersed. A stillness was left behind.

Some other thing left him, also. It drained from him, flowing from behind his eyes, down through his body, to his boots and into the ground. He felt lighter.

He leaned over to place his head on the arm of the bench, and closed his eyes.

He slept then, for the rest of the morning, through lunchtime and into the afternoon. Uncle Tavit lifted his feet and placed a rolled tunic under his head and covered him with blankets to his shoulders leaving his face to be warmed by the sun. Each time he came out to check on him, the young man's face seemed a little softer, and he would nod and return to his work for a while. Dresana came once, Perad believed, though it could have been a dream, to touch the back of her fingers to his cheek. They were damp with the tears she had wiped from her own cheeks.

He slept again, deeply, and dreamt fully.

In his dream he was on a raft on the river. It was no part of the Woodall river he knew, nevertheless, it was his river. The raft was built of great beams bound together with iron straps, and was immensely strong, and contained all the folk he knew.

He was at the back of the raft watching the ever-retreating past become distant and hidden around bends and behind hills. "The past will help us understand the present, but we cannot dwell there," said a voice at his shoulder, which may have been Dran's. "And the current of the river will not allow us to go back."

And he was at the front of the raft straining to see forward, to anticipate what was to come. Ahead, there would be rapids and jagged rocks and long stretches of wide calm water, and always new things to be seen. "These belong to the river and not to ourselves. We shall face them when we reach them," said the voice.

At times, the raft would lodge against the bank, and folk would spill out and sit there for a while. But the river never stops tugging, and soon the raft would begin to move on, and folk would hustle to board, though not all were successful.

But he was most comfortable at the side of the raft watching the world slide by, immersing himself in the interaction of the flow of the river and the passing of the banks. "There has always been a river of life," he said aloud. "We should rejoice in its flow."

"The current will take us where the current takes us," replied Dran.

And when he awoke, he was mended. He sat up and stretched, catching the blankets before they fell to the floor. The sun had crept behind the building, and he was chilled and stiff, but he was better.

He was still folding the blankets when his uncle appeared with a large bowl of stew. He stayed to watch as Perad ate.

"This is good weather for collecting mosses," Perad said. "I should go up river a way. There is still enough daylight left."

"And the flux is rising," said uncle Tavit.

Perad swung his feet to the floor and felt the power of it. "This feels like a good one. I should hurry. I can spend the evening at my workbench making powders."

"I should take the time to find Dresana, if I were you. She will enjoy helping you collect."

"She may be busy with other tasks."

"She may not be."

His uncle went in and was out again with Perad's pack.

Perad stood and lifted his pack onto the bench and checked it and strapped it. He kept his face down, unwilling to catch his uncle's eyes, or see the broad grin which he knew would be there. He squatted to refasten his boots, and stood again. "She is very interested in my poisons, and listens to all I say about materials and mixes," he said. "I wonder if she wishes to be an apprentice."

He shouldered his pack, and it felt good.

Uncle Tavit followed him to the inn door and watched him walk across the village circle towards the home of Dresana. There were other village folk around who also saw him go, and each one turned towards the inn door and gave a small nod at uncle Tavit.